LOST AND FOUND

THE HEART OF BATH, BOOK 1

Jenny Worstall

ARE YOU SIGNED UP FOR DRAGONBLADE'S BLOG?

You'll get the latest news and information on exclusive giveaways, exclusive excerpts, coming releases, sales, free books, cover reveals and more.

Check out our complete list of authors, too!

No spam, no junk. That's a promise!

Sign Up Here

www.dragonbladepublishing.com

Dearest Reader;

Thank you for your support of a small press. At Dragonblade Publishing, we strive to bring you the highest quality Historical Romance from some of the best authors in the business. Without your support, there is no 'us', so we sincerely hope you adore these stories and find some new favorite authors along the way.

Happy Reading!

CEO, Dragonblade Publishing

CHAPTER ONE
Kitty

"NAKED? YOU WERE *naked*, Henry? I can scarce believe this."

Merciful heavens! Henry, with no clothes on! Kitty's cheeks flamed.

"Well, half naked. And then I felt the fellow's cold pliers pulling at one of my front teeth. Kitty dearest, I cannot tell you any more, lest you faint with the shock."

"Go on! Don't stop, Henry! I am not the fainting sort. What happened next?"

"I lay on the ground exposed to the elements; despite being a summer night, it was cold and relentlessly rainy. All the soldiers around me were exposed in this way – our outer garments missing and undergarments torn and ruined. Not that it made much difference to the others."

"Because they were – dead?" Kitty interrupted.

Henry nodded. "I am afraid so."

How terrible it was to think of Henry suffering in this way. What he must have gone through during his experiences on the Continent! 'Twas almost impossible to bear thinking about.

"The others were indeed dead," Henry said. "I lost many good friends that day at Waterloo. Not to put too fine a point on it, I was surrounded by a pile of the deceased, waiting to be disposed of – which would have meant being buried alive, in my case."

Kitty shuddered. Buried alive! She had read of such a horror in one of her library books – but for it to become reality? For her Henry? No! A million times no. . . .

However, Kitty could not be downcast for long. For Henry had returned – Captain Henry Templeton, the young man she adored – the young man she thought had been lost in battle many months ago.

When Henry had disappeared, the light had drained from Kitty's life as color drains from the face of an invalid. Nothing was enjoyable – all became unrelentingly bleak and hopeless. She had been particularly dreading the arrival of Christmas, her first without him – for how could she celebrate the birth of the Saviour when she was in such a dark and dismal place?

But now, a few weeks before the festivities, here Henry was. Alive!

"Tell me more, dearest Henry," Kitty said. "Spare no detail, for I want to know all. I must know *everything*!"

"Luckily, I came to at that point, when the rascal with the pincers was wrenching my front tooth. How I screamed to feel the fierce metal grip! I was but minutes away from losing my smile."

"I bet you gave him the fright of his life," Kitty said. "How dare he rob the dead?"

"Or the not-so-dead! He had not expected my life force to still be there. I reached towards him with my good arm and swiped him across his jaw – sadly I missed, but it seemed enough to scare him away."

"My brave Henry! Well done! But I am shocked to learn 'tis true they try to take the teeth of fallen soldiers. I have heard it rumored many times but did not want to believe such a vile thing were possible."

"Oh yes! They collect them by the sack load – worth a fortune, I'm told. The fellow trying to rob me had a brimming bucket of pearly whites he had collected – from the fallen of both sides, I presume."

"I can see it would make little difference what nationality the teeth are when they sell them on," Kitty said. "They are hardly likely to continue fighting when made into a set of false teeth, are they?"

"No, certainly," Henry said. "In fact, it is a way for former enemies to live in peace, is it not? To join together to help another person speak and eat."

"I feel a little bad that we are jesting about such a subject," Kitty said. "Stealing teeth from the dead and dying – well, 'tis a shocking trade, carried out by desperate people."

Kitty felt a revulsion sweeping over her. Stealing body parts! Selling them on! Admittedly, she had once contemplated selling her hair to buy books, but she had only been eight and desperate for reading material. Her mama had made sure to furnish her with new books after finding her hacking off a lock of her hair.

Kitty stood as tall as her five-foot one-inch frame allowed. Henry was alive! To be sure, he was unaccountably changed since she had last seen him, thinner in the face and rather sad and tired around the eyes, but he was still her Henry – she knew it. Nothing could ever change her Henry – her close friend, her soul mate, her . . . how she longed for even more!

And what had Captain Henry Templeton done next, after scaring away the would-be tooth thief? How had he managed, only half dressed?

"Did you find your clothes? Your lovely scarlet jacket?"

Henry had looked so very handsome dressed in his military uniform before he left.

"Oh no. They were long gone. They had probably already been sold on several times. My sword and pistol undoubtedly suffered the same fate too, worst luck – for they would have been mighty useful for protection in the months that followed. As for the loss of my clothes, I managed to find a few rags to provide a little more warmth and coverage, but I had precious little energy and was soon forced to lie down again on the battlefield amongst the bodies. I remember the rain, the cold – and the smell. Loneliness and despair. Thereafter, for a time, my memories are but hazy.

"I know much time passed as night turned to day and then to night again, maybe more than once. And I know I eventually ended up trapped in a distant ditch under a pile of branches, half out of my mind with pain, not knowing who or where I was. There is much I could tell you about being dragged to that ditch by an unknown person – and yet more I still do not remember or understand."

Poor Henry was trapped in a ditch? A distant ditch? How did he get there? This is hard to hear . . .

"But Kitty, our time together today is short. A fuller account of my epic adventures will have to wait. No one knows I am returned from abroad save you and my family, plus Carter, of course; I trust that man with my life."

William Carter was Henry's manservant, and despite being at least twenty-five years older and from a different class, he was also Henry's dearest friend and had gotten him out of many scrapes in the past.

But coming back from Waterloo months later after being missing, presumed dead, was a far bigger scrape than anything Henry had previously gotten himself embroiled in.

Out of the corner of her eye, Kitty saw a man on the other side of the alley way. He lifted his head, regarded her with his dark, inscrutable eyes, grinned, and nodded. Carter! Still doing his best to protect her dear Henry.

"Ah," Henry said. "I see you have spotted Carter. He has been by my side for many months now, through all of my troubles. Why, he even rescued me – but no matter. That tale will have to be enjoyed another day."

"But Henry – where have you and Carter *been* all this time? Why has it taken you so long to return?"

"I spent many months abroad, recovering in hiding, then more months in London, also living in hiding. I had much to sort out discreetly with a few of my superiors – trusted senior army officers. They know my story, such as it is, and were fully sympathetic to my plight; they urged great caution, saying I should severely limit the circle of people who knew I had survived – at least for a time. Consequently, none of my friends and fellow officers know I am alive and back in England; they mourn me still. 'Tis too dangerous to spread the news – yet."

How terrible! Henry had been forced to live under cover both abroad and in London. He had been living a lie! But why the need for all the secrecy? Could he not have sent word of his rescue to friends and family? There had been such great and deep abiding sorrow.

"I am mortified to have been the cause of extra suffering to my family and friends," Henry said, "but I simply was not allowed to send news of my survival, for fear it would be intercepted. Carter says there is more at stake than a threat to my life. A bigger plan, involving others, and I did not want to put anyone else in danger. Least of all my family – and you, dear Kitty."

Henry always thought of others! And how lovely he was looking . . . the way his eyes creased to the corners, the way his lips curved . . . ah! His beautiful lips . . .

"And so now Carter and I have been here in Bath for a little while," Henry said. "We've been staying incognito in one of my father's houses on Beechen Cliff for the last stages of my recovery. Carter has made an excellent nurse. And you know the dwelling – the terrace house looking out over the city – for we used to go for walks nearby as children, did we not? Luckily the house stands empty at the moment, as tenants have recently left."

Kitty bit her lip. She had often seen that house from the outside and had entertained fantasies in the past about living there, married to Henry. She'd adored him ever since they had first played together as youngsters. Over the years, the adoration had turned to deep love, at least on her part. She had never been completely sure what Henry thought, for he had gone to war without declaring himself.

When the terrible news had come in the summer that he was missing in action after the battle of Waterloo, she had reluctantly and sorrowfully had to face the fact that she would probably never see him again. And as the months had rolled on and there remained no news of him, despite the fact that his body had not been discovered, the possibility that he was still alive melted away. Until now!

"And your parents know you are alive and well?" Kitty said.

"Oh yes," Henry said. "I went straight home to the Royal Crescent to see the family when I arrived back in Bath a little while ago and, much as Mama and Papa wanted me to stay with them there, after talking with Carter, they thought it more prudent for me to lie low away from the hustle and bustle of the city for a while. They trust their own servants implicitly to be discreet, but were worried about me being seen coming and going too frequently from the Royal Crescent, for it is a busy area. The empty house on Beechen Cliff seemed the perfect solution."

"I cannot think how you are managing without Cook to pamper to your every need," Kitty said.

"Carter knows how to do all that," Henry said, "as do I, for that matter, after my recent experiences. My needs are simpler than they used to be, too. War changes a man."

Henry's dark brows pulled together for an instant, and Kitty's heart turned over. She did hope he had not suffered too greatly during his ordeal.

"Do you always visit your parents in the Crescent, or do they drive out to Beechen Cliff to see you?"

"I go to their house in the Royal Crescent, often under cover of darkness, and always very unobtrusively, wearing my largest hat – for my parents do not want questions about why they might be taking a sudden interest in their house on the Cliff. There is danger around."

"So you keep saying. But what danger? You have returned from the dead, and we should celebrate. I am not sure I understand what is going on. *Why* must news of your return be limited to a tiny circle of people?"

Henry opened his mouth as if to speak, then pulled his cloak round him and winced.

Alarmed, Kitty stretched out her hand and touched his chest. "What is wrong? When you mentioned recovery, I thought you meant recovery from your ordeal. Please tell me you were not injured in battle."

"Merely a slight injury," Henry said. "My shoulder – I was shot – but it is nothing."

"Shot! With a bullet?"

"Yes! A very fast bullet. From a French musket."

"That does not seem like nothing to me," Kitty said. "Such wounds are often fatal – or so I have heard. Thank the Lord 'twas only your shoulder. But how did you manage? Were there doctors on the battlefield?"

"There were some there, but unfortunately I was not treated by one," Henry said. "However, I was well tended after my eventual rescue from the battlefield. Carter made sure of that. He himself administered the best of treatment, for he knows how to clean a wound and keep infection at bay. Nevertheless, there is a slight weakness in the shoulder – which I have been assured will go in time. Sometimes when it's cold, like today, I feel an ache. 'Tis of no consequence."

Kitty let out a sigh. Why were men so determined to make light of their afflictions and injuries? She felt sure Henry's shoulder troubled him a great deal more than he was saying – but she would let it pass, for now at least.

"I still don't understand!" she said. "One minute I was standing outside the library in Milsom Street, and the next, you were pulling me into this alley. You need to tell me more – what *is* this danger you speak of? And how did you find me?"

"Today, I felt bold and strong enough to risk coming into the city to look for you." Henry pulled his hat down over his eyes. "I thought no one would recognize me like this – and I am changed too in appearance from the young man who left for war. I know you often like to go to the library on a Wednesday morning – you are a creature of habit, and always have been – and so I thought it would be worth standing nearby in the alley to waylay you."

Kitty scrutinised Henry – his eyes seemed a deal older than when she had last gazed into them. His hair was different too, longer and curling, and he had lost much weight. But he was more dashing than ever – Lord, he looked for all the world like a soulful poet bursting with sensibility and emotion. The sort of man Kitty ached to embrace – and to love.

Her brain felt as if it would explode. Henry was alive! This was a trifle challenging to process when she had mourned him for many long months. Why, it had been half a year since the battle last summer! And now there was but a short time until Christmas.

"But Henry," Kitty said, "my parents too will be overjoyed to know you have survived. When you were missing after the battle, we feared the worst, and when you did not return with the other survivors, in the end, reluctantly, we surmised you must be dead. Come home with me now and greet my parents; there will be such rejoicing!"

"No, sweet Kitty, not yet. You must understand that although I was lying injured on the battlefield because of a French bullet, there was someone else who wished me dead – someone from my own side, an Englishman. 'Tis no use asking me who he is, because I do not know. His identity is what Carter and I must discover. All I know for certain is that I have a sworn enemy – one who thinks I am dead – which is why I must creep around in this absurd fashion. He must not know of my survival until I manage to unmask him and foil his master plan – whatever that might be. For the moment, I have the advantage."

Henry dipped his head down as a couple walked past. "Do you trust me?"

"Of course."

"Then it is imperative you do as I ask. Tell no one I am alive, not your parents, friends, servants, nor your governess Miss Steele."

"Miss Steele is my companion now, Henry; I am too old for a governess. She still gives me some lessons, but mostly she chaperones me when I go out, as Mama is often not well."

"Ah! I am sorry to hear your mama is in poor health. We have much to talk about – but for now you should go back to the steps of the library to wait for Miss Steele."

Henry

Even as Henry urged Kitty to go back to her companion Miss Steele, the one thing he wanted to do more than anything else in the world was to throw his arms around her, tell her he loved her and that he wanted her to be with him always. Her beauty and perfection quite distracted him, and he was in danger of being overpowered by his senses.

"I will go for now," Kitty said. "You are right, Miss Steele will be looking for me. And I absolutely promise I won't tell anyone I have seen you and that you are alive – I will keep your secret, even though I do not fully understand the reasoning behind it, for I always trust you. But I need to see you again, H. Very soon!"

Henry felt a joyous rush of good spirits as Kitty used his childhood nickname, "H." Was it possible that they would be able to pick up where they had left off before Henry had gone to war? Would it be that straightforward?

Henry and Kitty had been friends from a very early age, for their families had socialized together for years. Kitty was the same age as Henry's sister, Selina, and the two girls had been to school together and were the best of friends. Henry, together with his brother Edmund and sister Selina, would play with Kitty several times a week either in the Templetons' house in the Royal Crescent or the Honeyfields' house in Russell Street.

If he had been asked when he first fell in love with Kitty, Henry would have found it hard to answer. The sentiment grew from the first day he saw her, grew from companionship to friendship, then to an abiding love so subtly that it took him a while to realize how he felt. But he knew now! He adored her, worshipped her – and desired her.

"Kitty!" Henry's voice was hoarse. "If only we had more time! If only I could say to you what I want to say."

Kitty smiled, and Henry had to fight the urge to plant a kiss on her beautiful lips – a fight he nearly lost. But what was he thinking? He must not delay her or put her in danger. She must go back to the library steps to wait for Miss Steele.

Henry wondered whether Kitty realized the seriousness of what was going on – that he had a mortal enemy. According to Carter, if this enemy found out Henry was still alive, he would dedicate himself to finishing off what he had tried to do at Waterloo. And that might mean Kitty would be in danger too. Unthinkable! Henry regarded Kitty tenderly. She was very young. He felt a good ten years older than she was, now he had been to war.

"What is it?" Kitty said. "What is troubling you?"

"I am a different man since I went away. Feel older. I, I've seen things . . . done things. . ."

"You are the same man you always were – and still but a few years older than me," Kitty said. "Now, when will I see you again?"

Sweet Kitty! So practical! So adorable.

"Come to tea this afternoon?" Henry suggested.

"I cannot come to tea! You said you're staying in your parents' house up on Beechen Cliff. 'Tis quite a way, and I can't just decide to set off anywhere on my own. I would have to have permission and be accompanied. How would I explain where I was going?"

"No, I do not mean to the house in Beechen Cliff," Henry said.

As if he would suggest that she should defy her parents and simply slip away from Russell Street to walk two miles across the city and up a steep hill! Henry noticed the dusting of freckles across Kitty's nose and remembered how much she loved being outside. Such a walk across Bath was well within her physical capabilities, no doubt about it, but of course she was not allowed to make the journey on her own.

Henry grinned. "Dear Kitty, I meant you should come round to my parents' house in the Royal Crescent – our family home. I intend to go there now with Carter and am confident there will be minimal risk, for I will go through the servants' quarters at the back."

"I would love to come to tea, but my parents will ask where I am going, and I cannot say I'm going to see you because you don't want me to tell anyone you have returned. And I will not lie to Mama and Papa."

"There is nothing to worry about on that score," Henry said. "Simply say you are going to see Selina, which will be true. She will be there, and you often visit her, so 'tis not an unusual occurrence, is it? You are the best of friends."

"Truly, we are," Kitty said. "She has been my best friend forever, and I am incredibly lucky that she has lived but a short walk from Russell Street all my life."

"Do you remember when we used to play dressing up?" Henry said. "You, me, Selina, and of course my brother Edmund. Both our mothers always had such a good stock of useful old clothes."

Kitty chuckled. "Yes, and once when we ran out of clothes at your house, you and Edmund pulled the curtains down and draped yourselves in them. Very dramatic!"

"Great fun!" Henry said. "Although the governess was not best pleased – nor was Mama. I seem to remember not being offered supper that night."

"Poor H! Although I know for a fact that Selina managed to convey some bread and cheese to your room without detection that evening, so you did not starve."

*I never knew what it was like to feel starving when I was young —
but after the last six months, I do.*

"I'm not altogether sure your brother Edmund enjoyed the
sessions quite as much as we did," Kitty continued.

Henry nodded. "Ah! The occasion when you insisted we
were going to act a scene from *A Midsummer Night's Dream* and
that Edmund should be dressed as a fairy sticks in my mind."

Kitty answered with a giggle, her dark curls bobbing around
her exquisite face and her china blue eyes dancing with mirth.

*She is even more captivating than I remember! I wish I could run
away with my love right now.*

A small cough sounded from Carter, who was standing close
by in the alley.

Henry needed to get a grip on his emotions! He turned and
nodded at Carter, then whispered to Kitty, "See you this
afternoon, then, at about 3 o'clock. I'll let Mama know you are
coming when I get back to the Royal Crescent. Selina is out at the
Pump Room this morning, but she will be thrilled to know you
are coming round."

"'Til then, H," Kitty whispered as she stood on tiptoe and put
her arms around him.

Was she going to kiss him? Henry would not be able to let
her go if she kissed him. He resolutely kept his arms by his side,
exercising every ounce of self-control he possessed – for if he
embraced her, who knew what might happen? Ah! Kitty!

"H," Kitty said. "I'm so happy you're alive. I can bear *anything*
now I know you have returned. Until this afternoon. . ."

With that, she hastened away, making for the library at last.

Henry leaned back against the wall of the alleyway. He could
not believe that after months and months he had finally seen his
love . . . not that Kitty knew she was his love.

If only he'd had the courage before he left for war to declare
his feelings, to propose but he had thought it would not be fair
when he might never return. Henry had wanted to leave Kitty

free, for who knew what the future might have brought? In truth, it was a miracle he had returned – and it could easily have turned out differently.

"We should leave now," Carter said, coming alongside Henry. "Is your shoulder hurting?"

"I'm fine," Henry said, "but you're right, we should be on our way. 'Tis not entirely safe to be here – especially when we do not know who the enemy is."

"I have good intelligence that the enemy is a high-born gentleman lodging in Bath for the season."

"Yes, 'twas a stroke of good fortune finding that out – although to be honest, that doesn't narrow it down much. And how is it that you have an army of spies at your disposal?"

Carter smirked. "Do not forget all my years in London working for the government before I became your manservant; I have many reliable contacts from those times."

"You must tell me more about your mysterious past one day."

"Possibly! Let's get you back to the Crescent. You need food and rest," Carter said. "You've been hanging around in this alley for long enough gazing at Miss Kitty Honeyfield with your puppy dog eyes."

"I cannot believe I let you speak to me like this! From anyone else, it would be considered insolence, not to say insubordination. I could have you horsewhipped!"

"Just as well I'm not anyone else, isn't it?" Carter said. "And just as well I know you're joking."

"Indeed!" Henry replied. "But I'll never forget what I owe you – my life."

Carter tutted gently. "No need to talk of that. I only did my duty to your family. D'you think I would've been able to forgive myself if I had not found you? I scoured every field and hovel until I came across you in that ditch – and would have stayed abroad as long as it took."

"Even though I know what you think of abroad," Henry said.

"You've told me often enough. The food, the lack of decent ale, the weather. . ."

"I love my country," Carter admitted. "My whole being longed to be back on English soil again."

"How I wish I could remember more details about being dragged to that ditch," Henry said. "I only know it was an English gentleman, not a soldier from either side, who dragged me there."

"That was a good start for my investigations," Carter said. "My sources are helping me narrow it down to find out who could have treated you in this way – like putting fragments of a broken vase together – but we will get there in the end and reveal the offender."

Henry and Carter sidled along the alley, keeping in the shadows. They were in reality gentleman and manservant, one in his early twenties and the other in his late forties, but they would seem more like two close friends or relatives to any casual observer. Henry considered Carter almost as family – perhaps on a par with a favorite uncle.

One thing was certain, Henry owed Carter his life – and would never forget the debt.

Kitty

Kitty hummed as she clutched her library book and made off in the direction of the library; no story she had read had been half as exciting as the account of Henry's experiences at Waterloo! From the moment he had appeared in Milsom Street and hurried Kitty away down a tiny alley, her heart had been leaping like a March hare. Pulling herself together, she slipped back to the steps of the library in the nick of time.

"Miss Kitty, I am sorry for keeping you waiting," Miss Steele said, bustling towards her. "My purchases in the haberdashery took longer than anticipated; I have several lovely ribbons I am sure you will be pleased to see once we get home. Have you managed to borrow the book you wanted?"

Miss Steele was not supposed to leave Kitty alone. However, she was very fond of knick-knacks, so therefore the pair had a mutually agreeable arrangement that when Kitty visited the library each week, Miss Steele indulged in riffling through the colorful wares sold in the shop opposite.

"Yes, thank you, Miss Steele," Kitty said. "I have borrowed an intriguing book recommended by my friend Selina." She looked across the road to the haberdashery. "I can see they have some beautiful things displayed in the window over there, and I sincerely look forward to seeing the ribbons you have purchased when we get home."

Miss Steele adored pretty things; Kitty often found her gazing longingly at some of the trinkets on her mama's dressing table; indeed, once she had even thought she saw her wearing one of her mama's lockets, but Miss Steele had assured Kitty it was merely similar.

"Let me see the book," Miss Steele said. "Mmm. Not heard of this one. I hope it is suitable."

"I think it's quite well known," Kitty said, biting back a giggle. "Selina's mama allowed her to read it, therefore I am sure it will also be suitable for me."

It was amusing that Miss Steele, for all her long years as a governess and companion, was little enamoured of books and knew precious little about them, too. She had frequently cautioned Kitty about the effects of too much reading. Apparently, the activity could lead to frown lines, a pallid complexion, and, worst of all, unrealistic expectations and a tendency to be too clever. None of which men liked.

Whereas for Kitty, reading was her world. It brought solace and comfort when all about her seemed hard to understand. She was eternally grateful to her godmother for paying her subscription to the circulating library, for her papa had told her at the end of last summer there were no longer sufficient family funds for what he termed "this extravagance."

By the autumn, other luxuries had begun to disappear from the household. Cook complained about having to manage on less when ordering provisions, Kitty was told she could expect no new frocks this season, and one of the servants had to be let go, with their work being shared out amongst the others.

Kitty had on occasion tried to discuss the situation with her mama, but Mrs. Honeyfield's health was suffering, and Kitty knew her mama needed peace and quiet if she was to recover her spirits. This made Kitty determined not to worry her or cause her any anxiety. But how she missed being able to confide in her mama, especially with Henry gone . . .

But Henry was gone no longer. He was alive!

"Miss Kitty?" Miss Steele inspected her closely. "Is something amiss?"

"No, merely the wind blowing grit into my eyes."

That, and tears of joy and gratitude that my Henry has returned from the dead!

"Come along then, for Lord Steyne is due to visit soon."

Miss Steele's mouth drew into a thin line, whether of disapproval or anticipation, Kitty could not quite make up her mind.

"Kitty! Kitty! It *is* you!"

Kitty's dearest friend Selina was racing up Milsom Street to catch up with her, joy etched across her face. Selina's maid was running some way behind her mistress, holding a hand to her side.

"Have you been to the library?" Selina puffed.

"I have. Lovely to see you, Selina! Have you been to the Pump Room?"

"Yes!" Selina said. "How did you know?"

"Lucky guess," Kitty said, blushing.

"You must come and see us very soon."

"Of course! I would be delighted. Lord Steyne is to visit us in Russell Street this morning, and we have arranged to take a stroll in Sydney Gardens – but I am free this afternoon. May I come for tea?"

Selina clapped her hands together. "Perfect! There's so much to tell you."

The two girls stared at each other. Kitty knew she must not say anything to reveal she knew Henry had returned, and she realized he would have extracted the same promise from Selina, but it was very tempting to fling her arms around Selina's neck and cry tears of gratitude for Henry's safe return from the dead. Selina must have found this news hard to keep to herself since she had learnt of her brother's return – she had not said a word to Kitty, her best friend! And yet, she had seemed brighter and excessively cheerful when Kitty had seen her recently – this must be the reason! All was made clear now.

I cannot wait to visit the Templetons this afternoon in their home and be able to talk freely and celebrate with them.

Miss Steele began rummaging in her reticule and fiddling with her new ribbons. Selina raised an eyebrow at Kitty, and Kitty raised one back, then they both burst into fits of giggles.

"See you later," Kitty said.

"Can't wait!" Selina replied as she waved her goodbyes.

"Come along now, Miss Kitty," Miss Steele said. "We need to get back, as Lord Steyne will be arriving soon to take us to Sydney Gardens; it will not do to keep him waiting."

In his late forties, Lord Steyne was the darling of the *ton* and was asked to all the best gatherings. Extremely rich, rumoured to be a notorious rake, and single again after being widowed the year before, Lord Steyne was the man that Kitty's father wanted her to marry. He was certainly not Kitty's choice.

For some reason, Kitty felt giggles erupting all over again at the thought of the detestable and pompous Lord Steyne arriving at her home. Did the man not know he had no hope of winning her hand in marriage? Even if he had been her only chance *ever* of making a match, she would have refused him. Why was he wasting his time with these tedious visits?

As Kitty and Miss Steele hastened back to Russell Street, Kitty sobered up somewhat and reflected on Lord Steyne's qualities – or, rather, lack of qualities. The man was arrogant and dull. There was something else too, something Kitty had never come across before – something that went beyond mere self-importance. A sort of aloofness and disdain – and a penetrating stare that had often made her feel uncomfortable and wish she were elsewhere.

I will never marry Lord Steyne! Not if he were the last man left on earth.

CHAPTER TWO

Henry

HENRY AND CARTER took the long route around the city to approach the Royal Crescent, hoping to avoid detection.

"'Twouldn't do to walk round the Circus and along Brock Street," Henry said.

"No, it would not!" Carter replied. "Far too busy and full of all sorts of nosy snobs."

"All right, Carter," Henry said. "I know your views on the *ton*. You think they care for nothing but fashion and gossip."

Carter nodded.

"Well," Henry said with a laugh, "you could have a point, for that is exactly what a lot of them *are* like."

"Not your family," Carter said.

"Very loyal of you," Henry said, "and I agree my parents are nothing like that. My father has true values."

"He is a benevolent employer and runs his estates with great skill and kindness – a rare combination."

"If I can be half the man my father is, I shall be happy," Henry said.

The two men had reached St James's Square now, behind the Royal Crescent. They pulled their hats down over their eyes and their cloaks closely around them, then walked more cautiously to the servant's entrance to Number 1.

"One of the reasons I greatly admire your father," Carter said, "is his steadfast refusal to have anything to do with investing in the plantations and thus with slavery. He could be much richer if he did what many others do."

"He had no choice in the matter," Henry said. "Mama would not agree to marry him unless he said he would never profit from slavery."

"God bless her," Carter muttered. "She cares much for the less fortunate – a wonderful woman."

"She certainly is," Henry said. "Let us make haste to see her."

The two men slipped down the steps at the side of the servants' entrance, making a surprise appearance in the below stairs area, then rushed up into the main part of the house where they discovered Henry's parents and sister sitting in the parlour.

"Greetings!" Henry said.

"My dear!" his mother said. "'Tis a shock to see you every time you arrive! I still can scarcely believe this miracle and thank God every night for your safe return. Come here and let me enfold you in my arms once more."

"I sincerely hope you were careful coming here," Lord Templeton said, coming over to embrace his son, "and thank you again, Carter, for taking such good care of my boy. We will be forever grateful to you for what you did out there."

"Don't I get a kiss?" Selina said, throwing herself at Henry. "Edmund's not here – out gallivanting in the city with his friends – but he will be back later in the afternoon. By the way, I saw Kitty today, and she's coming here for tea at three o'clock. She had to rush away because Lord Steyne was visiting and then they were going for a walk in Sydney Gardens, but she will come to us later. I know she'll be happy to see you – in fact, I have my suspicions you already know of this visit – am I right?"

"Yes," Henry said. "I suggested she visit this afternoon."

"Thought you must have seen her! But how?"

"I waited near the library – if you wait outside the library, chances are, sooner or later, you'll see Kitty."

"She loves books more than anything in the world," Selina said.

But hopefully not more than she loves a soldier back from the war . . .

"I hope Miss Steele will not be accompanying her when she comes to tea," Selina continued. "She kept fiddling with her reticule when I was talking to Kitty, but I had the uneasy impression she was listening to us intently. I am not sure I trust her."

"Carter doesn't trust anyone at all," Henry said, indicating the man himself standing at the side of the room, "which is probably why I'm still alive."

"Sit down, sit down everyone!" Lady Templeton said. "Carter, you know we do not stand on ceremony. Sit down, please. I am eternally grateful to you for rescuing Henry – you must consider yourself part of the family now."

"You're exceedingly kind, Lady Templeton," Carter answered, "but I will go down to the servants' quarters."

Carter left the room.

"You should not embarrass the man," Lord Templeton said to his wife. "He is a treasured servant and saved the life of our dear son, but he isn't part of our family – and never will be."

"There will come a time," Lady Templeton declared, "when all this silly business about upstairs and downstairs simply won't exist, you mark my words."

Everyone laughed heartily to hear this.

"Mama," Henry said, "soon you'll be telling us that women will be able to own property in the future."

"And what would be wrong with that?" Selina said.

"And that ordinary men would be able to become members of parliament!" Lord Templeton added.

"Now that I would not laugh at," Henry said, "because I think Carter would make a very interesting politician. We have had some pretty interesting debates on our journey back across the Continent – and I defy anyone to get the better of him in a reasoned argument."

"He certainly is an uncommon sort of fellow," Lord Templeton said. "I am glad I hired him to work for us as your manservant."

"I think you'll find that was my suggestion," Lady Templeton said with a smile. "I was determined we should have him within our household."

Henry regarded his mother quizzically. She had always appreciated Carter's qualities, and now seemed to hold him in even higher regard after he had heroically helped to restore Henry to his family after the fiasco at Waterloo. However, to learn that Lady Templeton had been the driving force behind Carter's arrival within the household was something Henry had not previously known. 'Twas very curious – but a mystery for another day.

For now, Henry was resolved to relax with his family over coffee and anticipate the arrival of Kitty that very afternoon.

Kitty

On reaching her home in Russell Street, Kitty rushed upstairs, intending to visit her mama in her chamber.

"Make sure you tidy yourself up," Miss Steele called after her. "You need to look presentable to see Lord Steyne. He should always see you at your best."

Kitty put her head round her mother's door. "How are you today?"

"Not too bad," her mother said. She was sitting up in bed, keeping warm with a shawl and night cap. "Perhaps I will try to get up later."

Kitty sat on the edge of her mother's bed and held her hands. "It must be rather monotonous being in bed all day."

"It can be," her mother said, "but I will not complain. If I can but get plenty of rest and sleep, then perhaps I will be partially restored by Christmas time."

"'Tis less than three weeks before Christmas, Mama," Kitty said. "I do hope you make swift steps towards recovery and can at least join us to celebrate on Christmas Day."

"We shall see," Mrs. Lydia Honeyfield said. "Would you pass me my glass, Kitty dear?"

"My word! What's in it? A strange colour. . ."

"Merely something Miss Steele has recommended – a special restoring draught that she says aids sleep and recovery. I find it tastes unusual, but must tolerate it for the sake of my health."

Kitty picked the glass up and sniffed before passing it to her mother. 'Twas a slightly acrid, smoky scent.

"Odd," Kitty said, "and certainly not like anything I have encountered before. Are you sure you should be taking this? What does Doctor Jenkins recommend?"

"Oh," her mother said, "we cannot afford another visit from Doctor Jenkins – you know how tight money is."

"I know that," Kitty said. "I have the evidence in my own bedroom of how much Papa needs to make economies."

They were interrupted by a series of deafening thuds coming from a nearby chamber.

"Yes," her mother said, "I am so sorry about that. Let us hope it is only temporary, but it does save many guineas."

Money! It seemed this was the most important subject in the world.

"Lord Steyne will be here soon," Kitty said. "I do not think much of Papa's plan to marry me off to him, however prudent a financial move it might be. I am fully determined not to accept him."

"I know that," Mrs. Honeyfield said, "and I promise no one is going to force you into an unwelcome marriage – that will never happen to my daughter. We will have to find some other way to manage financially. Perhaps there is someone else of fortune who has caught your eye?"

Kitty looked out of the window. She hated to think in these terms. Henry's family were wealthy, although not quite as wealthy as Lord Steyne, for he was one of the richest men in England – but she knew that if she married Henry, it would be a sound financial contract as well as a love match.

But how unfair that she must think in monetary terms, when from what she could gather, the loss of the family wealth seemed to be caused mostly by her father's fondness for gambling.

"Look at me, Kitty! What are you thinking? You have not fallen for someone else, someone unsuitable and penniless? That will not lead to happiness and a good comfortable life together."

"I have not done that, Mama."

"Promise me!"

Kitty looked her mother straight in the eye. "I promise you, Mama, I have not fallen for someone unsuitable and penniless."

Kitty closed her lips firmly. She had spoken the truth – maybe not the whole truth, and perhaps she had misled her mother in some way, but she had nevertheless spoken the truth.

"Begging your pardon, Mrs. Honeyfield," a voice at the door said. "Mr. Honeyfield asks that Miss Kitty might come downstairs, as Lord Steyne has arrived."

"I'll be down directly," Kitty said to the abigail, then she planted a gentle kiss on her mother's cheek and made her way downstairs to the hall as slowly as she dared, where she found her papa, Lord Steyne, and Miss Steele.

"How charming you look," Lord Steyne said with a deep bow, then nodded at Miss Steele.

Mr. Honeyfield gave Kitty an unusual smile, baring his teeth, and she felt fear stab the pit of her stomach. Why was her papa acting strangely? Oh, that grin! 'Twas like a cat that has got the cream, or is anticipating getting the cream – and is about to be released from a tricky situation. Would Lord Steyne be making an offer for Kitty's hand soon? Mr. Honeyfield would no doubt find this most agreeable, as it would alleviate his distressing financial problems.

But I will never marry Lord Steyne – I only wish for my darling Henry!

"Please! Let us proceed to the parlour," Mr. Honeyfield said.

"Thank you," Lord Steyne said, graciously indicating that Kitty should walk ahead.

Once they were all seated in a semi-circle, there was an awkward silence. Perhaps Kitty should make a remark about the weather? Or take her courage in both hands and ask Lord Steyne what he was doing here when she was determined not to accept any proposal he might be brazen enough to make?

Kitty opened her mouth to comment on the lack of rain and the surprisingly chill wind that morning, but before she could utter a word, Lord Steyne said,

"What in God's name is that strange noise?"

Should Kitty admit what work Papa was having done? Perhaps she ought, for it would underline how little money the Honeyfield family possessed. The knowledge might deter Lord Steyne from seeking Kitty's hand in marriage – he surely would not want to marry into such a lowly family.

Why did he want to marry her, anyway? He obviously wasn't in love with her. Not love, not money – so what?

The hammering increased in ferocity, and Miss Steele began to rub her temples and murmur about getting one of her megrims.

"Napoleon is to blame for the noise," Kitty said.

Lord Steyne curled his lip, displaying yellowing teeth. "Napoleon Bonaparte?"

"Yes. Papa says Mr. Pitt put the window taxes up to help pay for the Wars."

Excruciating thuds now cascaded down through the ceiling. Kitty's mama would be finding it hard to bear.

"Papa is having a window removed to save on his tax bill," Kitty explained further.

Lord Steyne stared in amazement.

"I have heard of this happening," he said, "but have never

known anyone who has actually had it done. Egad, a prudent option, I suppose, for those short of funds. But, if perhaps certain circumstances were to change, if Miss Honeyfield were to make an advantageous match for example, it might not. . ."

"Some call it daylight robbery," Kitty said. "The filling in of windows, that is, not making an advantageous match."

A harsh laugh escaped Lord Steyne, and Miss Steele joined in with a high-pitched whinny.

"Appreciate your wit, Miss Honeyfield," Lord Steyne said, "but beware speaking your mind too freely."

Kitty dug her nails into the palm of her hand. The man was insufferable!

"Time for our walk, Miss Honeyfield," Lord Steyne said, "with your permission, of course, Mr. Honeyfield? And I would be pleased if Miss Steele could accompany us."

Kitty could not think of a reason why she should not be able to go for a walk with Lord Steyne – not one that would be acceptable to articulate. If she lived in a different world and was allowed to speak her mind, she would say she couldn't stand the man and found him boorish and repulsive. And that she would far rather be reading her new book from the library.

The way Lord Steyne was looking at her right now repulsed her! She wished she were wrapped in a large shawl from her neck down to her toes, because he was taking far too much interest in trying to stare through her flimsy muslin frock at her legs and form. And now his eyes were positively dancing with glee all over the skin on show between neck and bodice. Kitty shivered. Why were men allowed to behave like this?

Lord Steyne is no gentleman – not like my dear Henry.

"We shall set off for Sydney Gardens at once," Lord Steyne said. "It will not take us long to walk down there – and the fresh December air will bring out the roses in your cheeks, my dear, and make you even more bonny and attractive."

At least I will be able to wear my cloak – that will stop you gawping at my figure.

Henry

"Selina, did you say Kitty would be walking in Sydney Gardens with Lord Steyne?" Henry asked.

"Yes, I did," Selina said. "Oh no! I know that look in your eye."

Henry tried to assume an innocent expression but failed miserably.

"You can't fool your sister," Selina said. "I know what you're thinking."

"What am I thinking?"

"You want to go to Sydney Gardens and make sure Lord Steyne behaves himself when he's out with Kitty."

"I was thinking no such thing!"

"Was!"

"Wasn't!"

"Henry! Selina!" Lady Templeton reproved. "Stop behaving like squabbling children."

Selina laughed and swatted Henry on the arm. "Ninny!"

Henry winced.

"Oh, sorry! I totally forgot about your poor shoulder."

"We should get Doctor Jenkins to look at your injury," Lord Templeton said. "Check whether there is infection there, in the joint. He's a fine doctor. Very knowledgeable."

"No need," Henry said. "I've almost recovered. My shoulder just plays up now and then – especially when my sister hits me."

"Selina!" Lady Templeton warned as Selina advanced upon her brother again.

"Now you have mentioned Sydney Gardens, sister dearest," Henry said, "I've decided I will take a walk there."

"If you're going," Selina said, "I'm going too."

"I don't think either of you should go," Lord Templeton said. "Henry, you and Carter have spent a long time telling us about the dangers that you faced abroad – and we know you have an unknown enemy in Bath who must not be allowed to know you are returned from the dead. So what the devil do you think you'll gain by going to Sydney Gardens in the daylight, eh?"

Totally ignoring his father, Henry said, "Mama, do you still have the dressing up box?"

"Good heavens," Lady Templeton said. "You haven't asked me that since you were about twelve years old. Selina – do you have any idea where it might be?"

"In the nursery. Come on, Henry. Upstairs, with me."

Ten minutes later, Henry and Selina reappeared in the entrance hall wearing ancient robes, grey wigs, and hats with massive brims covering their faces. Each carried a walking stick and was practicing limping. Mercifully, the door to the parlour was closed and Lord and Lady Templeton were unable to see the comical sight of Henry and Selina wearing clothes that must have belonged to their grandparents or even more distant generations of the family.

"Come on, Henry!" Selina said. "Keep up! Nearly time to set off for Sydney Gardens. No one will recognize us."

"What do you think you're doing?" Carter's voice boomed around the hall. He had come upstairs from the servants' quarters and had deep disapproval etched onto his face, along with something else. Amusement?

"You don't think it's a good idea," Henry asked, "going to the gardens disguised as old people?"

"No! Although I am glad you are having fun."

"But I simply must see Kitty," Henry said.

"You're seeing her this afternoon for tea," Selina said.

"No, you don't understand," Henry said. "I think Lord Steyne is trying to court her."

"'Tis interesting that you care, brother dear," Selina said. "Do you want to court Kitty yourself?"

Henry turned bright red. "None of your business!"

"I tell you what," Carter said, "to put you out of your misery, go and change into the ordinary clothes you were wearing earlier – but keep the very large hat – and I will go with you to Sydney Gardens. From a very safe distance, we'll keep an eye on what's going on there. How does that sound?"

"Sounds like a plan," Henry said. "Let's sneak off before Mama and Papa have a chance to stop us."

Could Carter have his own reasons for wanting to go to Sydney Gardens? He might be trying to sniff out information about the mysterious enemy. Who cared – it was more important to make a quick getaway before Lord and Lady Templeton realized what was afoot.

"Drat!" Selina said. "I do believe I'm to be left out of this plan."

"You'd only give the game away by giggling," Henry said.

"What piffle! I never giggle," Selina said.

Henry snorted.

Carter cleared his throat. "Perhaps we should get going?"

Henry changed quickly, then followed Carter on a very circuitous route through dark alleys and shadowy side streets to Sydney Gardens.

Once there, Carter whispered, "Stay under the trees – and don't look anyone in the eye."

"I can see Kitty," Henry said after a few minutes. "Over there – strolling along with Miss Steele and Lord Steyne."

"No," Carter said as Henry tried to leave the shelter of the trees. "No closer."

Kitty stumbled slightly and accepted Lord Steyne's arm to lean on, causing Henry to grind his teeth.

"Steady!" Carter said. "Don't do anything rash."

"That man!" Henry said.

Lord Steyne's massive bulk towered over Kitty. She looked divine, in her favorite red cloak and a very pretty bonnet. Miss Steele was walking close behind head down.

"Interesting," Carter said.

"What's interesting?"

"How Miss Steele seems in thrall to Lord Steyne. I wonder why this would be."

Carter had a tendency to over-analyze every aspect of human behaviour he encountered; he often said it had saved his life on many occasions.

"You can be very enigmatic, Carter," Henry said.

"I'll take that as a compliment, sir."

"You can take it any way you want."

"Thank you kindly, sir. You are too generous."

Henry sniggered. Carter was the end!

"You've put me in a better frame of mind," Henry said. "And you used to do this when we were abroad, too. How you put up with my low mood for all those months, I have no idea. Why, I didn't even know who I was sometimes, I was that shaken up."

"I would never have given up on you," Carter said. "'Twas a pleasure to be able to look after you in your time of need. Besides, your mother would never have forgiven me if I had not managed to bring you back in one piece."

"Nevertheless," Henry said, "I'm eternally grateful and do not say it often enough. Many apologies."

They watched the others walk towards the Labyrinth.

"Shall we follow them?" Henry said. "I used to love going right to the centre to have a go on Merlin's Swing – before I went to war."

"I think not," Carter said. "We have been lucky so far, but if we go into the Labyrinth, it will be easier for us to be recognized. Those paths inside are narrow! And as for having a go on Merlin's Swing – that would be utterly insane."

"As you wish," Henry said, "but I sincerely hope Kitty will be safe in the Labyrinth with that rake."

"He won't attempt anything inappropriate with Miss Steele there," Carter said. "She would not allow it. Ah! There is Lord Bragg over there and Lord Pratt – oh, and there's Mr. Boyle. Interesting. All of them idiots – and one might be your sworn enemy, too."

"I thought you said before my enemy was cunning – can you be both cunning and an idiot?"

"'Tis a hard task – but some men manage," Carter said. "You could be extremely clever but act like a blockhead to disguise your intelligence."

"I suppose you could," Henry said. "And you're right about it being too risky to go into the Labyrinth. You're always right, Carter, damnation!"

Kitty turned and looked back, and Henry saw her sweet face. He groaned. This was hard! He wanted so much to be with her, to love her, and make her his wife.

But why would Kitty be interested in someone like him? If she knew what he had seen, what he had done abroad, how war makes a man behave, why, she would be shocked and would want nothing more to do with him. Henry wiped his hand across his face as visions of violence and sounds of conflict flooded his mind. He didn't want to think about it, mustn't think about it . . .

How desperate Henry was to close that chapter of his life forever.

CHAPTER THREE

Kitty

WALKING ROUND SYDNEY Gardens with Miss Steele and Lord Steyne, Kitty had the strangest sensation she was being observed. She even turned round at one point to check what was going on, but despite screwing up her eyes, couldn't see anyone except two rather rough-looking fellows standing under a tree in the distance. Her short sight was a real nuisance.

On her return to Russell Street, Kitty was only too happy to say goodbye to Lord Steyne, although she wished he could have bid her farewell from more of a distance, for when he kissed her hand, she felt nauseous. Lord, the man was unattractive! If only she could tell him what she thought of him…but that would anger Papa. Ah, would it not be wonderful if Henry were here right now, kissing her hand? Life was very unfair.

Kitty's father was sitting in the parlour reading the newspaper, and she sat down to join him.

"You can go up to your room now if you want, Kitty," Mr. Honeyfield said. "The men have finished the bulk of the rough work with your window, but will be back in due course to tidy up and make a start on improving the appearance from the inside, plastering and so forth. I am sorry that it has been necessary to take this rather drastic course of action."

Kitty wondered why her room had been the one chosen to

deprive of light. She supposed it would not do that one of the rooms where they greeted guests would have a blocked-up window, as this would be distressing evidence of the lack of family money – although of course her bedroom window could be seen from the street, so everyone would know what was going on regardless. And none of the servants' rooms could have reasonably suffered the loss of a window, as they either already had only one single window or were attic rooms with roof lights.

"Maybe one day," Mr. Honeyfield said, "we will be able to open the window up again, when the family fortune improves – if you catch my drift, Kitty."

"I do," Kitty said. "I know you wish me to make an advantageous match."

But if Kitty made an advantageous match, she would not live with her parents in Russell Street anymore, so of what consequence would the loss of a window in her old bedroom be to her?

"Time is of the essence," her father said. "You are already nineteen, and I have spent much blunt on your clothes and subscriptions for balls, not to mention your education and countless other drains on my wealth; I consider this expenditure in the way of an investment – and I expect to see a return."

Kitty would not – could not – challenge her father. But how dare he! Who was he to talk of investments and his daughter in the same breath? She knew from his constant worried expression and his nightly absences how much he must be losing at cards – and had been losing for some time.

Mrs. Honeyfield's health, never robust, had started to deteriorate noticeably around the time Mr. Honeyfield had begun behaving in this unaccountably disappointing and irresponsible way. Could he not see what he was doing to the family's happiness?

When Kitty's parents had first married, they had been well provided for. Not rich, but certainly comfortable, with enough to see out their days. However, more recently Mr. Honeyfield had become acquainted with certain gentlemen of the *ton* when playing at cards in the Upper Rooms. They had encouraged him to play for bigger and bigger stakes both there and at private gatherings. One thing led to another, until Mr. Honeyfield was wriggling and dangling like a fish on a hook, entirely at the mercy of those who held the rod. In vain had Mrs. Honeyfield and Kitty tried to convince Mr. Honeyfield to quit his gambling and cut his losses. He was addicted.

Kitty sighed. She must do what she could do to help her parents. But not if that meant marrying Lord Steyne.

"I, I . . ." Kitty stuttered.

"Yes, my dear?" her father said.

"I – I do not wish to marry Lord Steyne."

"Has he offered for you?" Mr. Honeyfield asked.

That smile again – the bared teeth. The cat that was about to get the cream!

"If he has," Mr. Honeyfield said, "it is exceedingly good news!" Kitty's papa clasped his hands together. The joy on his face was hard to behold.

"No," Kitty said, "although I think he is interested – but I am telling you that were he to offer, I would not wish to accept."

"What arrant nonsense, Kitty! Have you not been listening to me? Lord Steyne is your best chance in life – and the best chance for our family. You should be grateful for his attention. Lord Steyne has enormous wealth – why, his estate in Somerset is second to none. Imagine living there and being mistress of such a place, eh? Do not forget you are an only child, Kitty, and the future of the family rests on your shoulders. Think about it!"

"But Papa!" Kitty cried. "What if there was someone else?"

"Someone else? There is no one else in your life – I would know if there was."

Then Mr. Honeyfield's mouth twisted. "Tell me you have not fallen in love with some penniless oaf or young wastrel."

Kitty needed to pacify her papa, for the veins in his neck were standing out in a most unhealthy-looking way – poor man. She must remember the pressure his many debts were placing upon him.

"Papa! Of course I have not fallen for an oaf or wastrel! I do not know any such persons – and even if I did, I would certainly not want to marry them. But what makes you think Lord Steyne would make me happy? Do you think he loves me?"

"I am not sure I understand you. Marriage is a contract."

"No, 'tis much more," Kitty said. "Marriage is the union of two loving souls, minds, and bodies. I will not marry a man I do not love."

Mr. Honeyfield gave a bitter laugh. "Love is for those who can afford it, my dear. It seems to me you have spent overlong reading those melodramatic novels of yours."

How dare Kitty's papa criticize her reading matter!

"Yes," Mr. Honeyfield continued, "I picked up one of your novels the other day and dipped into the ludicrously lurid tale. 'Twas very poorly written, with plenty of cliffs and castles, rogues and redemption – and positively bursting with sugary sentiment. My goodness, what sort of drivel and balderdash are you filling your head with? Perhaps you should not visit the library anymore."

"Oh, please Papa, I do adore the library. Look at the book I chose today – not at all like the ones you're describing."

Mr. Honeyfield picked Kitty's library book up from the table.

"*Sense and Sensibility* . . . more likely, *Slush and Silliness* . . . by 'A Lady'. Ha! Too ashamed to put her name to it. And as if a lady would know the difference between sense and sensibility! You, Kitty dear, have too much sensibility and not enough sense."

"Well," Kitty said, "if you have to possess too much of one, and not enough of the other, I think I'd rather have more sensibility."

"You'll learn," her father said, "when you're married."

Did he perchance look a little regretful when he said this?

"Take your book upstairs, my dear – make sure you concentrate on the *sense* part of the story. And you can have a look at the alteration to your room."

Kitty was in no hurry to see how her room had been vandalized – she still considered it the most unfair thing possible.

"And I am sure Mama did not have a hand in this," she muttered as she tarried in the entrance hall.

"What's that?" her father called after her.

"Nothing," Kitty murmured.

She fled upstairs to her chamber only to find that the loss of one entire window had both spoilt the symmetry of the room and increased its gloom.

"No! *No!*" she cried. "This is worse by far than anything I could have imagined. Why, it is positively cave-like!"

Kitty's bedchamber did not receive much light at the best of times, with the Honeyfields' house in Russell Street being situated opposite another tall terrace, but she had at least hoped there might still be light enough to read by. She tried to read as much as she could in the daylight, as Papa frequently reminded her of the price of candles.

Standing by the remaining window, Kitty flipped open her library book, coughing as dust from the building work found its way into her lungs.

Within seconds, she was absorbed in the tale – and read several chapters with her back to the window to try and get as much light as possible on the page.

After a while, Kitty reluctantly closed *Sense and Sensibility*, as her eyes were very tired. It was a wonderful book; who could the author be, the mysterious lady? Fancy! She might even live in Bath. Perhaps Kitty might see her passing by one day? She stared out of the window, then narrowed her eyes to try to focus, as everything looked a bit blurry.

She could probably do with a pair of spectacles, but there was no point in asking her parents, for her papa would say they were a needless expense, and her mama would say they would spoil her beauty. As if Kitty cared more about her looks than being able to see what was going on in the world.

She put the book down on her bed. Perhaps she would have

less need to escape into a book now Henry had returned from the dead, for her own thoughts and imaginings were more vivid than anything she was likely to read between the covers of a book.

Kitty sighed and leant backwards, imagining Henry holding her, nuzzling her neck, kissing her gently, his lips upon hers . . .

"Are you quite well, Miss Kitty?" Miss Steele was standing in the doorway of Kitty's chamber with her head tilted to one side. "Should we cancel your embroidery lesson?"

Henry

On the way back from Sydney Gardens to the Royal Crescent, Henry simply could not resist going past the Honeyfields' house in Russell Street.

"Sheer madness," Carter said, "if you don't mind me saying."

"You can say what you like," Henry said. "I love Kitty, and if I want to go and stare up at her bedroom, I will. Besides, it's on the way home – well, almost – and that means we won't have to go past the Upper Rooms on our way to the Crescent. We can go along Rivers Street, and I can take the chance to look up at Kitty's bedroom as we go past the junction with Russell Street. What do you think? You know if we take the route right past the Upper Rooms, we'll see all manner of the *ton* strutting about."

Carter gave a great bark of laughter. "You might have a point – although the *ton* will mostly be thinking about the effect they are having on other people, rather than staring at a scruffy young gentleman and a grizzled servant."

"But they might be looking for gossip," Henry said, "or recognize me. No, better to go past the far end of Russell Street."

"Why didn't you ask Kitty to marry you before you went to war?" Carter asked. "You could be coming back to a wife and child now. You two are a perfect match – what held you back?"

Henry blushed to the roots of his hair. How could he explain to Carter what had held him back from declaring his overwhelming, all-consuming love?

Kitty had been a friend forever, and Henry valued her friendship more than diamonds. If he had proposed and she had refused him, he would have lost twice over – lost his friend and lost his chance of marrying her.

As long as Henry hadn't declared himself, he could comfort himself with the thought that he would tell her how much he loved her one day – when the time was right.

"Don't miss your chance of happiness, lad, will you?" Carter said. "Regret makes a cold bedfellow."

Trust Carter to hit the nail on the head!

"I have no idea what you think gives you the right to talk to me like this," Henry said, thumping Carter on his back in an awkward attempt at camaraderie, "but I'm jolly glad you do, my friend. Not even my father or brother voice the things you dare – you are always on my side."

And yet I cannot fully tell you how I feel. 'Tis too personal a subject – too difficult to articulate.

There was a mystery to Carter Henry had yet to fathom. In some ways, he was the most straightforward, almost rude man he had ever met in his life – but he was the kindest of people too, treating Henry with compassion and thoughtfulness during his many trials. His devotion knew no bounds.

"Are you coming with me, then?" Henry said. "For I am still determined to go past Kitty's house and gaze up at her window."

Carter crossed his arms. "We will go past the Honeyfields' house, but you must promise to be discreet. After all the trouble I've taken to get you back in one piece, I don't want to lose you to a knife in the back."

"In Bath? A knife in the back? Are you joking?"

"Don't underestimate your enemy," Carter said, "especially when you don't know who he is. There are a lot of folk down from London at the moment – and we all know what London is like."

Henry regarded Carter curiously. "What was your job in London, before you became my manservant?"

"'Twas nothing very exciting – I worked for the government. You already know that."

Henry gave a sharp intake of breath. "You were a spy, weren't you! And I know you can't admit it."

Carter stepped to the side quickly. "Don't you dare slap me on the back again! If I was a spy, I would deny it, obviously – and if I wasn't a spy, I would also say no. So basically . . ."

"Basically," Henry said with a laugh, "you are not going to tell me one way or the other! I'm fairly sure that tells me all I need to know."

So *had* Carter definitely been a spy in his younger days? Henry had suspected as much before, after seeing the way Carter managed to deal with the many problems they had faced abroad. He seemed a master of disguise and had skills that enabled him to deal with almost any problem that arose, sometimes in the most unexpected way. No lock was too secure for Carter, he could defend himself in any fight, and he had the strength and endurance of a much younger man.

Henry knew enough to realize that Carter was a man to be respected, no matter his lowly birth or lack of fortune. But was Carter who he said he was? Was working for the Honeyfield family all these years as Henry's manservant yet another disguise? For the life of him, Henry could not comprehend why a man such as Carter would want to seek employment as a servant unless he was combining the post with active service of a different kind.

Henry shook his head. This was farcical! The possibility of danger all around him was making him harbour strange suspicions. Carter was an unusual man, but he was merely a servant – wasn't he?

Very soon, the pair were standing in the shadows on one side of Russell Street, gazing up at Kitty's bedroom.

"Devil it!" Henry said. "One of her windows has been blocked up."

"'Twill be for financial reasons, not aesthetic," Carter said.

"I know that," Henry said, "but did not think the Honeyfields would have to resort to these measures. I knew their coffers were not overflowing, but I am staggered they felt desperate enough to brick up a window. A lot must have changed since I left for war. Poor Mr. and Mrs. Honeyfield – and poor Kitty."

"Never mind that – you've got five minutes here, not a second longer."

"Kitty's reading," Henry said. "I can see the back of her beautiful head. She's holding the book up to the light. I wonder if 'tis the volume she borrowed from the library this morning. She truly adores reading and once told me her idea of heaven would be a room of her own filled with books."

When they were married, if they were married, Henry would buy Kitty a new book every day. Although, that might mean she wouldn't have time for him because she'd be too busy reading – every week, then – he would buy his darling Kitty a new book every week.

"Time to go," Carter said. "There are some people walking up Russell Street from Bennett Street. We need to be on our way."

"A minute longer," Henry said. "Look! She's turning round – she must be able to see me. She is rubbing her eyes – should I wave?"

"Of course not, sir," Carter said, pulling at Henry's cloak. "Time to leave."

"I don't think she's noticed me. Oh, now she's moving away from the window. Maybe someone has come into the room. Time to scarper."

Kitty

Miss Steele waited in front of Kitty. "Well?" she said. "Shall we cancel the embroidery lesson? You do not seem quite yourself."

Miss Steele had a rather obnoxious stare on her face, the sort of expression that suggested she knew full well what Kitty had been thinking about, and also that she thought she was a complete simpleton – a birdbrain.

"If you don't mind," Kitty said, the blood draining from her face, "I think I might take a rest. I am sure I will be fine to go to tea with the Templetons though, later."

"Have a lie-down," Miss Steele suggested. "You look washed out. Young women should try to look their best at all times. What would Lord Steyne think if he saw you looking sickly and tired?"

I do not exist merely for Lord Steyne – or any other man – to take delight in my appearance. There is more to my life than this! Or should be . . .

Miss Steele cleared her throat. "I will retire to my room for a while if you do not need me."

"Of course! Thank you, Miss Steele."

Kitty stood for a few moments longer at her window, looking up and down the street. Her eyesight was definitely getting worse. She used to be able to recognize people as they passed by, but her vision was becoming increasingly blurry.

She saw a group of young girls with their governesses hastening past, perhaps on their way back from the Crescent Fields; she could make out their colorful cloaks and bonnets, but the faces were indistinct.

There was a gentle tap on her door.

"Only me!"

"Mama! Come in! How lovely to see you out of bed. Are you sure you are warm enough?"

Mrs. Lydia Honeyfield stood in the doorway, her wrapper pulled tightly around her.

"I had to come and see you, my dear. Heavens! Your room is very dusty from the building work and not yet properly put right – I do hope there will be enough money to make good the alterations, for I can see bare brick, and that is not acceptable."

"Do not worry, Mama – 'tis fine. I can live with it a while longer."

"You are a good girl, Kitty. Now, Miss Steele tells me that you feel a little unwell. Are you suffering with your monthly courses?"

"No, Mama."

"Are you sure, my dear? You do look very drawn and pale. Perhaps they are on their way? I myself suffered greatly when I was your age, as you know, and spent much time abed in agony. Perhaps you do not wish to talk to me about it – would you prefer to confide in Miss Steele?"

"No! There is no need."

Kitty couldn't imagine anything more embarrassing than talking to anyone save her mama or one of her close friends such as Selina about the private workings of her own body. As for Miss Steele! The thought appalled her.

There was something about Miss Steele she could not warm to – although she must remember to be grateful that Miss Steele was taking an interest in her mother's health and had given her some medicine, possibly a herbal concoction of her own preparation – especially now that Mr. Honeyfield no longer seemed to be able to afford visits from Doctor Jenkins for his wife.

Kitty longed to tell her mama that Henry was back from the dead, but she could not betray a confidence, and Henry had emphasized the danger of telling anyone about his survival. She also wanted to tell her mother all about her feelings for Henry – but, in a contradictory twist, Kitty also had a fierce desire not to tell anyone in the world about her intensely private imaginings, which she scarcely understood herself. Maybe she might confide in Selina when she went for tea? But it would be hard to find the opportunity, with the whole Templeton family in the same room.

"I'm fine, Mama," Kitty said firmly, "but what about you? We've all been worried."

"I am feeling a lot better after the sleeping draught Miss Steele gave me. Truly, I feel much restored."

"What good news! I am very pleased. Please, Mama, do sit down on the bed. You mustn't overexert yourself."

"Thank you, my dear," Mrs. Honeyfield said. "I believe I would be better sitting down . . . ah, yes, that's better. Come and sit beside me, child. And tell me what you have planned for the rest of the day."

"I'm going to tea with the Templetons soon," Kitty said.

"Are you sure you will be well enough? For Miss Steele seems to think you should not go out this afternoon – should you not stay at home, my dear?"

"I am keen to go and see Selina. And it is always pleasant to see   all the Templetons."

"Poor, dear Selina." Mrs. Honeyfield shook her head. "Such a tragedy for that whole family, losing Henry like that. And of course, Lady Templeton has had her share of difficulty in the past, what with her father and the child . . ."

"What do you mean, Mama? You have never mentioned anything before."

Mrs. Honeyfield put her hand to her head. "Oh, I don't know why I'm prattling on! Please, ignore me. Forget what I said. There's nothing wrong with Lady Templeton, and there has never been anything in her family to be ashamed of, no, nothing . . ."

Kitty looked at her mother curiously. Mrs. Honeyfield had a flushed, feverish look and was not acting with the same propriety as she usually did. It simply was not in her nature to gossip or be indiscreet – nor to be so loquacious. Perhaps the medicine from Miss Steele was reacting within her and causing her to lose her normal inhibitions?

"It happened before Lady Templeton was born," Mrs. Honeyfield said, her eyes glittering in the oddest way.

Should Kitty help her mama to lie down? Try to change the subject? But Mrs. Honeyfield seemed determined to tell her tale.

"I daresay I should not be talking to you of these things, for you are young and unmarried – yet perhaps you should know more of the ways of the world . . ."

It sounded as if this would be interesting – and informative. If Kitty's mother wished to share, what would be the harm in listening?

"Well, my dear," Mrs. Honeyfield continued, "you have probably heard of natural children?"

Kitty blushed. "I believe I have. It is when someone has a child but they are not married."

Her mother nodded. "For a baby to come into this world . . ."

What? Was Kitty's mama about to tell her something she had wondered much about?

". . . it is often said God sends a child to those couples who are married as a blessing, but it happens that sometimes . . . mmm, this is a little difficult to explain."

Kitty felt she should help her mama out – she did have some knowledge of the world, after all.

"I know that sometimes a baby's arrival is a surprise," Kitty said, "and perhaps the child is not born in the best circumstances, even when parents are not married – particularly among the servant classes and poorer people."

"It happens in all levels of society," Mrs. Honeyfield said.

"Are you saying it happened to Lady Templeton?" Kitty felt shocked.

"Of course not," her mother said, "for then Lady Templeton would not have been able to marry Lord Templeton."

"No, I suppose not," Kitty said. "For the sin is always the woman's."

"Indeed it is, at least according to the world," Mrs. Honeyfield said. "But no, this is not directly concerned with Lady Templeton – it is to do with her parents – more specifically, her father. He had a natural child before he was married, the result of an unfortunate liaison with one of the maids when he was but seventeen."

"And the fact that he was a parent at that age did not stop him from making an advantageous marriage later," Kitty said.

Mrs. Honeyfield bit her lip. "You know there is one rule for men and one for women in this life, more's the pity."

"And what happened to the poor maid?" Kitty said.

The maid would doubtless have been blamed for the whole incident, even though she was probably seduced.

"Well, this is where the story gets interesting. Lady Templeton's grandparents were very generous towards the maid. They provided her with a home in the countryside, gave her an allowance large enough for her to be able to live decently and allowed her to keep her baby. They even gave some money for the child to have an education."

"Surely that was the least they could do?" Kitty said. "The maid could not make a marriage after that and would have found it nigh on impossible to provide for her child without support."

"It was more than is usual to give a young woman who has been . . ."

"Taken advantage of?" Kitty finished for her mother. "I see . . . and what happened to the child?"

"No idea," Mrs. Honeyfield said. "When I first met Lady Templeton, many years ago, she told me this sorry tale, perhaps because she was expecting her first baby at the time and her mind was drawn to contemplate the past and her family. She said then she knew she had a half-sibling somewhere, a natural child of her father's, but she doubted she would ever meet them. But she wished to, that was certain. She wanted to draw them back into the family."

"Was it a boy or a girl?" Kitty asked.

"I know not," her mother said. "Does it matter?"

"No," Kitty said. "I was merely wondering. But what a very sad and strange story. I do hope everything worked out all right for the maid and for her baby. It certainly turned out well for Lady Templeton's father, didn't it, because he married her mother and they led a life of distinction and high regard."

"I know it seems unfair," Mrs. Honeyfield said. "And please, I beg of you, share this with no one. I have said far too much – my mind is dancing about now, and I need to go back to bed."

"Let me help you, Mama."

As Kitty helped her mother to her feet, she happened to glance out of the one remaining window onto the street below. Her eye was caught by a figure wearing a red cloak crossing the road and hastening away from the house towards Rivers Street. There was something familiar about the figure – why, could it possibly be Miss Steele? But Miss Steele had said she was going to retire to her room for a while – she said nothing about going out. Wait! There was another figure. The woman was talking to someone on the corner of the street – a stout gentleman who looked suspiciously like Lord Steyne.

Kitty rubbed her eyes. How aggravating 'twas that she could not focus clearly! She determined not to ask her mama to study the figures in the street below, as that could have led to anxiety and agitation. Besides, Kitty had a shrewd suspicion that her mother's eyesight was even worse than her own.

"Lean on me," Kitty said, helping her mother as they walked along the corridor to Mrs. Honeyfield's chamber.

How ridiculous Kitty was, imagining that the couple outside in the road were Miss Steele and Lord Steyne. Why on earth would they be there? Besides, Miss Steele did not possess a red cloak.

Kitty settled her mother back in her bed and then returned to her own chamber, determined to read another chapter of *Sense and Sensibility* before it was time to get ready to go to the Templetons.

But a small nagging voice inside Kitty's head reminded her that the woman in the street had looked more than a little like Miss Steele; there was something about her gait as she had crossed the road. The red cloak was a problem – unless . . .

Kitty ran downstairs and looked at the coat hooks in the entrance hall – only to find that her red cloak was missing.

If Miss Steele is capable of taking my cloak, what else might she be planning to take from my family?

CHAPTER FOUR

Henry

"WHAT'S THE TIME?" Henry said to Selina.

"Henry! That is the third time you've asked in the past five minutes."

Henry got up from the sofa and moved to stand in front of the fire, rubbing his hands.

"I cannot help it," he said. "Kitty will be here soon, and I am looking forward to seeing her very much."

Selina snorted. Was she laughing at him? Henry had been contemplating confiding in his sister about his feelings for Kitty, but now he was not so sure. Did Selina think he would have no chance with Kitty? Was he not good enough for her – or, horrors! – did Selina know that Kitty had feelings for someone else?

"What's the time?" Henry repeated miserably.

"Why don't you look at the clock?" Selina suggested. "You're standing right next to the mantelpiece."

The china timepiece under Henry's nose started to chime three times.

"I think you know what that means," Selina said as she put her head on one side, "if you remember learning how to count as an infant in the nursery."

Sisters could be frightfully annoying!

"To be fair," Henry retorted, "Mama always sets this clock a little fast, to remind guests to leave promptly."

Selina made no answer, merely giggled and buried her head in her embroidery.

Surely Kitty would be here soon?

"I do hope Miss Steele will not be accompanying her, but another member of their household staff instead," Henry said. "There is something about Miss Steele I find unaccountable. Possibly untrustworthy?"

"You are not in love with Miss Steele, then?" Selina said. "Just Kitty?"

"Stop giggling, dash it!" Henry growled under his breath. "And stop your infernal teasing. You don't know anything about my feelings."

"Ah, but I have my suspicions."

But wait! There were sounds from the entrance hall – sounds of a visitor arriving!

"Stay there," Selina said as she stood up. "We do not know who it is yet, and you cannot be seen by a casual visitor. Let me put my embroidery away."

Henry walked over to the window looking onto the Crescent Fields. What a beautiful clear day! He could see right across to the hills opposite and could even make out the Cottage Crescent way in the distance. Did not Selina have a school friend who used to live there? 'Twas an odd sort of crescent, being a distance outside Bath. Apparently men often housed their mistresses there, for it was a fine place, high on the hill, but not situated in a busy area where gossips and tittle tattlers might comment on the behaviour within.

"And don't look out of the window," Selina hissed as she made for the stairs. "You know what Mama and Papa said about keeping out of sight."

Henry did know. He had been subjected to a full lecture from his father on his return from Sydney Gardens with Carter.

"What an unnecessarily foolish risk, traipsing off through

Bath like that," Lord Templeton had said. "I am not sure which of the two of you, Henry or Carter, I blame the most."

Lady Templeton had joined in then. "I know who is most to blame – and I am sorry, but 'tis you, Henry. You must have persuaded Carter to accompany you, or he must have decided that it was his duty to protect you, since you were determined to go. Tell me, Henry – what was the point of Carter keeping you safe all these months if you are going to put yourself – and possibly your family – in danger?"

Henry supposed his mother had a point. It was all very well taking a personal risk – and there had been plenty of those for Carter and himself in their travels abroad – but he had no right to bring the danger back to his parents' doorstep. And what about Kitty? If the mysterious enemy knew how fond he was of her, there was no knowing what they might stoop to.

"Henry!" came a voice from downstairs. "Henry, old chap! On my way up."

Of course! It was Henry's brother, Edmund, returning for tea with his family. Henry's pulse slowed to a near normal rhythm. He would have to wait a little longer to see Kitty.

"Hello!" Edmund said as he came into the room. "I gather we are to have tea up here in the withdrawing room, all because Mama is getting anxious about the fact that passers-by in the street might see into the parlour and recognize you. They will apparently not be able to see into this room – as it is on the first floor."

"What if they brought a ladder?" Henry asked.

"Good point," Edmund said.

"Mama has always been a worrier," Henry said.

"She has – and yet, joking apart, I must tell you, brother dearest, how desperate we all were when we thought you would never come back from war. It was horrible, beyond anything I can express."

"Come here, brother," Henry said gruffly. He gave Edmund an enormous bear hug. "No need for all this – I'm here now."

"Sounds as if our other guest is here as well," Edmund said as excitable girlish voices were heard on the stairs. "I saw Kitty hastening down Brock Street accompanied by her maid as I came to the front door."

Then Selina and Kitty burst into the room, thankfully without the dreaded Miss Steele.

Henry's heart did a somersault when he beheld Kitty. Was it possible that she had grown even more beautiful since he had seen her such a short time before in the alley? Her cerulean eyes locked into his and life paused. How was it that the others could not hear the beating of Henry's heart? To his ears, it was like a military drum. 'Twas thrilling, rousing – and dangerous!

"Here is the tea," Lady Templeton said as she came into the withdrawing room, followed by two maids bearing trays. "I believe Cook has surpassed herself – look at all these delights."

"You have always been very dear to Cook," Edmund said. "I used to get quite jealous."

"Yes, me too," Selina said. "Cook has made your favourite sugar buns."

"Henry started to charm the ladies from about the age of four," Lady Templeton said. "He had the most engaging smile – and still does!"

Everyone laughed, and Selina and Edmund teased Henry mercilessly – but there was only one lady Henry wished to charm now, his darling Kitty.

I wish everyone save Kitty and myself would simply vaporize! For then I could be alone with her, hold her in my arms . . . and show her how much I love her.

Kitty

Would it not be marvellous if everyone melted away and I was left alone with my darling Henry?

Kitty wanted to be safe in Henry's arms; she wanted to feel his lips against hers, to be crushed against his manly chest and to bury her face in his shoulder.

"Kitty," Lady Templeton said, "would you like a sugar bun with your tea?"

"Thank you. Yes, I would."

Kitty nibbled at the soft warm texture, feeling tiny grains of sugar on her lips.

She tried to drive all thoughts of Henry from her mind – she must concentrate, as she did not want her feelings to be known to all and sundry.

Did Henry care for her? She was reasonably sure he had nursed strong feelings for her before he had departed for war, but that was a whole world ago – and how much did she know about what he had been doing since he had left? The people he had met? You heard such tales...and Kitty's charms might seem to be nothing compared to all that he had encountered since.

Granted, he had taken the trouble to find her this morning in Bath, despite the danger to his own person, and he had been most insistent that she come to tea today – but this could be explained by the fact he was one of her oldest friends. It did not necessarily mean that he was in love with her or wanted to marry her. Why would it?

Kitty took a sip of tea from the thin china, willing her hand to remain steady as she returned cup to saucer.

How could she find out what Henry's feelings were for her? She dared not ask him, for what if he were to look shocked and say she was nothing but a friend? Then she would have lost his friendship and also the possibility of anything more.

No, she would wait and see what transpired. If anything did.

Henry sat down beside her, his teacup rattling an irregular rhythm on its saucer.

Could it be that Kitty had this all wrong? Did Henry also feel an overwhelming longing to be one with her – together with an anxiety about losing her friendship if love was not reciprocated?

Would that she could see inside his mind and analyze his thoughts!

"What are your plans this evening?" Lord Templeton asked Kitty. "I have heard there is to be a very fine concert in the Upper Rooms, and we all know how much you love music."

"Is your mama perhaps well enough to accompany you?" Lady Templeton said.

"She is not well enough to go out today," Kitty said, "and Papa is engaged elsewhere."

Papa will be playing cards – and losing money – as he does every night.

The only person Kitty wanted to go to the concert with was Henry, but of course that would be totally out of the question under the present circumstances of his life.

"I do have an invitation to go to the concert, and Miss Steele has offered to chaperone me," Kitty said. "But . . ."

"Who is the invitation from?" Selina asked.

"Lord Steyne."

An invitation I am determined I will not be accepting.

Henry's teacup and saucer fell to the ground with a crash.

"Do not worry," Lady Templeton said. "Was it your shoulder, Henry? Coordination can take time to return to normal after an injury."

Then she turned and said to the maid at the side of the room, "I would be grateful if you could clear this up as quickly as possible. Thank you."

The maid scuttled forward and took the cup and saucer Henry handed her.

"Sorry to make extra work," he said.

The maid put the crockery back on the tray then returned with a soft cloth and began dabbing at the red and cream patterned carpet to remove the tea stain.

"I can do that," Henry said. "'Twas my fault, after all."

He took the cloth and completed the task with great skill, moving his chair and getting down on his hands and knees to press all the damp patches thoroughly to mop up the liquid. It was surprising how far a small quantity of spilt tea could scatter. Then he folded the cloth neatly before passing it back to the maid.

"I say, Henry," Edmund said. "You in training for domestic service, or what?"

"I am used to clearing up after myself," Henry said. "Nothing feels quite the same as before. Different habits now – after . . . after everything."

Kitty's heart ached with compassion for Henry, and for all he had been through. And judging by the silence hanging over the room, she was not the only person to feel this way.

The maid brought Henry a fresh cup of tea and stared at him with – what? It had better not be admiration! Or, worse than that, adoration, for Henry belonged to Kitty. And the sooner he and everyone else realized that, the better.

"I know," Selina said. "Why don't we have some music ourselves – our own concert? Once Henry has finished his tea."

"Delightful!" Lord Templeton said. "I love to hear the pianoforte being played; in fact, I have always wished I could play myself."

"Henry could get his violin out," Selina suggested, "as long as his shoulder's not going to play up again."

"I'd like to have a go sometime," Henry said, "although I am completely out of practice."

"What about a pianoforte duet, then?" Lady Templeton said. "Selina? Kitty?"

"I could play a duet with Kitty," Henry said.

Selina's eyebrows flew up. "Not too out of practice?"

"Not if we play our favourite Mozart sonata," Henry said.

"I would love that," Kitty said.

Ah, the chance to sit right next to Henry, leaning against him, hearing his breath...

"As long as Edmund and I do not have to play a pianoforte duet," Selina said.

Lady Templeton shook her head. "I have to admit that Henry was always the most musical of all my children – the music master who used to visit when you were children always said he had a fine ear and was more than usually sensitive to the beauties of music."

"Settled, then," Lord Templeton said. "Yes, yes . . ." He waved his hand at the maid. "Thank you, yes, clear away if you please. Now, if we can get everyone sitting comfortably, I think it is time for Kitty and Henry to perform one of their Mozart duets."

"The book is right here," Selina said. "I put it out earlier, thinking it might be useful."

A few minutes later, Kitty and Henry were seated at the pianoforte side-by-side on the stool, arms, hips, and legs touching.

"Ready? Good . . . one, two, three, four . . ." Henry whispered.

Kitty's spirits soared as the joyful opening chord of D major rang out. Twenty fingers flew over the keyboard in ripples of sound, with Kitty playing the scintillating melody in the treble while Henry kept the bass part going – strong, confident, supportive and constant.

We are playing in perfect harmony . . .musical soulmates . . . my Henry is the same as ever he was before he left for war . . .

In the slow movement, Kitty swayed gently in time to the exquisite music, her heightened senses fizzing. Four hands performed a subtle dance over the keyboard; they brushed against each other, sometimes connecting, but never constricting. The pulse was flexible, held back by both for a heartfelt moment, then moving forward eagerly as one.

We are joined through the music. Henry is me – and I him.

Henry

This is ecstasy. I will die happy if this is my last moment on earth.

Henry allowed the last chord of the slow movement to die away and breathed deeply, inhaling Kitty's sweet perfume of violets.

He frowned as a memory came to him of inhaling another fragrance – ah! 'Twas not an occasion like this, but something dark – and disturbing. Before he could investigate the recollection, Kitty was nudging him with her elbow, and they launched into the bright chords of the third movement. She was sitting very close to the music, her head right forward, as if intent on leaping into the pages.

"Steady," Henry gasped when Kitty pushed the tempo forward. He willed his injured shoulder not to give out before the end of the piece. "Wait for me!"

"Slowcoach!" Kitty said. "I'm going to go as fast as I want!"

That was the thing about Kitty. Upon first meeting, one could be forgiven for thinking her quiet and shy, but once she knew and trusted somebody, she was irrepressible.

Past memories from childhood flooded Henry's mind – so many glorious days spent playing chase with Kitty and his siblings on the Crescent Fields and scrambling up over the wall of the ha-ha onto the Crescent Lawn. Dressing up sessions, charades, early attempts at pianoforte duets when Kitty was so tiny her feet didn't reach the floor when she sat on the stool – and laughing until the tears ran down their cheeks. Darling Kitty! She meant everything to him.

Henry released his worries and felt his body responding to the optimism of the music as the two of them romped through the sublime musical landscape.

"Bravo!" Lady Templeton said as Henry and Kitty stood to receive their applause.

"Yes, well done, especially you, Henry," Lord Templeton said. "No one would ever think you'd been away for so long without a pianoforte to practice on – and I don't suppose you even had the chance to listen to any music when you were abroad."

"I enjoyed some fine music at a ball in Brussels before Waterloo," Henry said, "but after that, my life began to beat to a different sort of rhythm."

"What about you, Selina?" Lady Templeton said. "Shall we have the pleasure of hearing you sing?"

"Me?" Selina said. "I have nothing to add after that gorgeous Mozart."

"We are sure you do," Lord Templeton said. "Why do you not sing the pretty air I heard you practicing the other day?"

"Yes," Lady Templeton said. "Come here, my dear. I would be delighted to play for you if you would oblige us with a performance."

Selina acquiesced with a nod and walked over to find her sheet music.

Henry and Kitty took the chance to sit together in the corner of the room while Selina performed for her parents and Edmund.

"The Mozart was perfection," Henry said to Kitty. "I felt transported back to life as it was before I went to war."

"I enjoyed it too," Kitty replied, "but was a little worried at the end of the second movement."

"What do you mean?" Henry said.

"You seemed to go into a trance," she said. "We usually wait for about six seconds before we start the final movement, but it was much longer than that. I thought you might have fallen asleep and had to nudge you in the end because I couldn't catch your eye."

"Ah, that!" Henry said. "The funny thing is, it was to do with you."

"Me?"

"Yes. I was smelling your perfume. You still love the scent of violets."

Ah, Kitty dearest, the memory of the fragrance of violets comforted me in my travels and dark times.

"Of course I still love violets," Kitty said, "for did you not give me the scent one past Christmas?"

"I did indeed. And am honored that you still wear it. Anyway, the sweet fragrance you are wearing made me remember another one – but I cannot quite place it." Henry clutched his head. "I am not sure what it was – how tiresome! I simply cannot remember."

"What sort of fragrance was it?" Kitty said.

"Citrus."

"Orange?"

"No, not orange, nor lime," Henry said.

"Lemon?"

"Why, I think, yes! I am sure, 'twas lemon. The sharpness of lemon. But there is something else that I recollect."

Henry put his hands over his eyes. What could he see? A brilliant flash of light . . . a particular shape on someone's hand – perchance something oblong?

"Please, do not distress yourself," Kitty said. "I did not mean to ask you anything to cause you pain."

Lord and Lady Templeton applauded as Selina finished her Handel air. She came over to the sofa and plonked herself between the pair.

"That was lovely," Kitty said.

"I know you weren't listening." Selina chuckled.

"We were," Henry said, "of course we were, but we were conversing as well. I love hearing you sing – and you know that *Let the Bright Seraphim* is one of my favourite pieces."

Selina shook her head. "I know you were not concentrating, brother dearest, but I do not mind at all, for 'tis wonderful to see you two chatting together. Is it not blissful we are all reunited?"

Selina put her arms around Henry and Kitty.

"Now, the big question is, are we to apply pressure to Edmund to force him to sing?"

"I think not," Henry said. "I seem to remember last time he sang, one of the glasses shattered."

"Selina! Henry!" Lady Templeton said. "I heard those very disrespectful remarks; you might have hurt Edmund's feelings."

"Unlikely!" Henry said as he pointed at Edmund who was almost beside himself with mirth.

"And Mama," Edmund said, "'tis all true, except it wasn't only one glass that shattered. When I last sang, a whole tray of glasses spontaneously rearranged themselves into fragments when they heard me growling and caterwauling."

"Well, I think under the circumstances we will probably have to let you escape your duty of performance," Lord Templeton said. "In fact, Edmund, would you mind coming to my study for a while? I have some documents to show you – to do with the purchase of another townhouse. I cannot quite make up my mind about something and would appreciate your advice."

"And I must go and have a word with the housekeeper and Cook," Lady Templeton said. "I need to see if everything is in order for dinner."

Once her parents and Edmund had left the room, Selina said, "Kitty, will you be going to the concert at the Upper Rooms this evening with the odious Lord Steyne?"

"Not if I can help it," Kitty said.

"You do not have to do anything you do not want to do," Henry said, "surely?"

Selina and Kitty raised their eyebrows.

"Henry," Selina said. "You must know that young ladies are not to be trusted to make their own decisions? We are reliant on our fathers and brothers and other members of the family to decide what we do and where we go – and when. Why, I do not believe in my whole life I have ever been anywhere without the permission of one of my betters."

Selina gave a slight cough as she said the word "betters."

"Yes," Kitty said, "this is true for me as well."

"'Tis a shame," Henry said.

"I will do everything I can to get out of going to the concert," Kitty said, "partly because I wish to sit with Mama this evening –

she has not been well."

"And the other reason?" Selina said.

"The other reason," Kitty said, "is that the last time I went to a concert with Lord Steyne, he sat far too close to me. Possibly he could not help it, but I do think he could have refrained from leaning into me quite so much."

"The blackguard!" Henry said. "How dare he! He has no right. I do not like that man."

"Do not worry," Kitty said. "I know how to deal with him."

"Yes," Selina said. "We women have our ways."

"As a matter of interest," Henry said, "how would you deal with him if he was a little inappropriate?"

"We always have a hat pin at the ready," Selina said.

"Yes," Kitty said. "I always carry a spare hat pin in my reticule. If I was a man, I would carry a pistol, but for now a hat pin will have to suffice."

The two girls giggled and mimed thrusting into the air with large pins.

"Now you are joking," Henry said.

Weren't they?

"I'm going to the ball tomorrow," Selina said. "It is a masked one! Do you think you will be able to attend, Kitty? Will your mama be able to be left?"

"I sincerely hope I can attend," Kitty said. "I think Mama's abigail will look after her for the evening and Miss Steele will doubtless chaperone me. I do love going to a ball! If only you, Henry, were able . . ."

Selina grinned. "I have been hatching a master plan for days and have just about worked out how Henry can attend the ball without the danger of being recognized."

Kitty clapped her hands. "Tell me all about it! Now!"

"I need to make quite sure it's going to work first," Selina said. "I do not want to get everyone's hopes up for nothing. 'Tis something Henry and I can sort out later, before he goes back to Beechen Cliff – you know he doesn't sleep here, don't you? A little while after darkness has fallen, he will make his way across the city and up the hill with Carter."

"Yes," Kitty said. She smiled at Henry. "I understand why you have to go back to Beechen Cliff, for there is still the danger you have spoken of, but I think it's a pity because you would be much warmer and more comfortable here with your family."

"Comfort has a different meaning after you've been in the army," Henry said. "As long as I have some sort of roof over my head and food in my stomach, I am content."

Patently untrue . . . for I will not be content until Kitty is mine and I am hers.

CHAPTER FIVE

Kitty

"OH, PLEASE TELL me how you think Henry can attend the ball, Selina," Kitty said. "I can't imagine what sort of plan you are hatching."

"Nor me," Henry said, "and to be quite frank, I'm getting a bit worried because Selina's schemes have a habit of going disastrously wrong."

"Nonsense!" Selina said. "Name me one time when one of my plans has gone awry."

"Where do I start?" Henry said. "What about the time you thought it was a good idea for us to climb out of one of the servant's bedroom windows and walk around the parapet of the house behind the stone balustrade next to the roof, remember?"

"I certainly remember that," Kitty said. "I was visiting that day, but was too scared to climb out after you both, as I didn't think I'd be able to keep my balance. 'Twas bad enough watching you two outside – even that made me feel quite sick. Terrifying!"

"All right," Selina said, "so that was one of my plans that didn't quite work out – but only because Papa happened to be on the Crescent Fields at the time. He looked up, purely by chance, saw us, then made a great fuss about nothing."

"Or," Henry said, "as he put it, he saved our lives."

"Well, I'm jolly glad he did save your life, Henry, and you

too, Selina," Kitty said.

Otherwise, I think I would have pined away from grief. . .to lose my best friend and *my darling H on the same day – unimaginable!*

"Where are you going?" Henry said as his sister jumped up and ran to the door.

"To put my plan into action; I have to collect something from the nursery."

"Should I come with you?" Kitty said.

"Oh no," Selina said. "That would spoil the surprise. You don't need to know anything about this until you are at the ball. That way, you can't give the game away – and besides, 'twill be much more fun if you have to search for Henry."

Heavens! Kitty was to be left alone with Henry – of course, it was her dearest wish to be left alone with her H, but as Selina closed the door behind her, Kitty felt suddenly overwhelmed. To say there were butterflies in her stomach would have been an understatement. 'Twas more like a flock of birds – the massed forces one saw racing through the autumn skies when they are getting ready to migrate.

"Are you feeling all right?" Henry asked.

"Fine," Kitty squeaked. "It's just that we're rarely on our own – and haven't seen each other for such a long time."

Henry laughed heartily. "You're surely not worried because it's not proper? Why Kitty, we are the very best of old friends! Propriety doesn't come into it. Besides, I have no doubt there will be a knock at the door soon and the footman will appear to say your maid is waiting in the entrance hall to take you home again."

Please, God, could that not happen too soon, I beseech you . . . give me some time with my beloved H . . .

Kitty remembered the scene in her bedroom earlier that day when she had imagined Henry holding her, Henry's lips on hers . . .

"You're not quite yourself, are you?" Henry said. "Do you feel faint? Is anything wrong?"

"No," Kitty said. "Nothing."

This was the truth – things were in fact more *right* for Kitty than they had been for a very long time. She had missed H desperately when he first went away, then mourned him, and now, on his return, she had never experienced such happiness in her whole life.

"I missed you," she murmured. "I can scarce believe sometimes that you are here again."

Kitty's arms ached to embrace Henry. Did he feel the same? Worryingly, he was backing away from her slightly on the sofa. They shared a deep friendship, yes, that was obvious, and he had said so on many occasions, but that didn't mean he wanted to take things further, though. Why would he? Was she being a silly naïve girl, imagining H was in love with her? Perchance her own feelings were all in her imagination as well?

But no! Kitty loved Henry fiercely, passionately. She *desired* him. Strange ideas crowded into her head, visions she had only imagined before in the silence of the night in her own bed, when she reached for her H . . . it must be the music that was making her yearn to feel one with him – for when she played the pianoforte with H, she connected with him in a deep way.

"Kitty," Henry said, "I . . ."

"Yes?"

Could it be happening? Was Henry about to declare himself?

"Kitty, I hope I manage to come to the ball tomorrow, for it would be lovely to see you there, but for the life of me I cannot think how Selina is to achieve this miracle."

"No," Kitty said. "It seems beyond reason, does it not? Lord, as you say, it would be a miracle. But Selina is very resourceful."

This was not the only thing that seemed beyond reason – the way Kitty was babbling on, surely, was absurd? Henry's eyes were burning now – and the way he was looking at her! Kitty reached her arm towards him, hesitating as she hovered near his shoulder.

"Is your wound nearly recovered?" she said.

"More or less. A few twinges now and then."

This was the time for Kitty to be brave – for her to take the lead. She must know what he felt. The tension was unbearable!

"So," Kitty continued, "if I were to put my right hand here . . ."

She gently put her right hand on his left shoulder as he sat beside her.

". . .and my other hand on your right shoulder . . ."

"Kitty . . ."

Henry's voice was low, almost a growl – but bathed in sweetness and honey. He put his arms around Kitty's waist. The time for speech was over, and Kitty trembled as emotion pierced her to the core.

"My Kitty, my love," Henry groaned.

Kitty looked at his lips as he gently turned his face sideways and moved towards her, then brushed his lips fleetingly against hers.

"Oh!" she said. "Oh!"

"Forgive me," Henry said. "I could not help myself."

Kitty's answer was to move even closer and put her hands around Henry's back. His breath was hot against her cheek, and she could feel his heart beating. Henry took her lips with his again – more firmly this time. And Kitty felt as if she were in heaven. It was as she had imagined, but so much more. Every tingling nerve ending shot sensations right through her.

Henry lifted Kitty onto his lap, then kissed her again, probing and pressing with his tongue as Kitty parted her lips in surprise. She felt she had gone through a door into a beautiful sunny meadow where nothing bad would ever happen and where she and Henry would be happy forever. Nothing else mattered, save the sensation of being in his arms, being with him, connecting in this strange new way.

Then she sensed Henry's hesitation.

"Kitty, dear . . . this is not . . ."

This would be it! Surely now he would declare himself? They had kissed!

"You do not need someone like me – I, I am not the man I was before I left. I have done things I can never tell you about . . ."

There was a knock at the door, and Henry and Kitty sprang to opposite ends of the sofa.

"Begging your pardon, Miss Kitty," the footman said, "but your maid has arrived and is waiting downstairs to walk you home to Russell Street."

"Thank you," Kitty said. "I will be down directly. In fact, I will come straight away with you now."

Was it Kitty's imagination, or had the footman looked shocked to find her and Henry alone together?

Henry

A kiss! A kiss sent from heaven – and then Kitty could not get away fast enough. She did not want to hear any details of Henry's experiences abroad. Damn that maid for arriving back at the house when she did, and damn the footman for interrupting them!

Henry had been desperately trying to explain to Kitty that if she was in love with his personality from before he went to war, it was his duty to let her know he had returned a different man – because of what he had seen and what he had done. He pressed his fingers into the corners of his eyes. The sufferings of war, the heat of battle, the viciousness of dog eat dog, kill or be killed . . .

He swallowed hard. For had he not dispatched a few souls from this life to meet their maker? Yes! To his eternal shame, he had killed – and maimed. How cruel! But was that not what he and his fellow soldiers were there for, to fight the enemy, defend Britain, and defeat Napoleon?

The question was, why did that necessitate killing and injuring young men in their prime – bright-eyed, vigorous and vital –

merely because they happened to wear a different uniform?

And the terrible sight of an injured horse lying on the ground unable to walk . . . Henry shuddered. He had known how to deal with that, for sometimes mercy killing was the best way for animals. There were plenty of soldiers lying on the ground in conditions from which he knew they could never recover – and yet he could do nothing but give them water and pass by. Soldiers calling out for their mothers, begging their comrades to deliver a death blow to release them from their suffering . . .

Henry started to pace angrily around the room. If he had been given but a few minutes more with Kitty, he would have been able to explain to her in what way he felt a changed man. He would have asked her acceptance of him as he was now, warts and all.

He did not want to deceive her, for her to think he was exactly the same as before – because he *had* changed, he certainly had. His love for her had never wavered – but now he was back, she needed to get to know the new him.

Who was he kidding? Henry didn't even know himself, so why would the sweet and innocent Kitty be interested in getting to know his new persona? He was seriously thinking of resigning his commission, for he never wanted to go to war again. Would this change the way Kitty felt about him? Was it important to her to be married to a soldier? If so, would Henry be able to put his reluctance for bloodshed aside and fight once more for king and country?

But the kiss! Henry would never forget the kiss. And if that was the closest he ever got to Kitty in his life, he would treasure the memory forever – his lips upon hers, their arms entwined, feeling as one with the love of his life.

And there was still a major stumbling block to consider – maybe Kitty would be better off without him? She could never enter his world, after all he had seen. Would she not be happier looking for a marriage partner among the *ton* of Bath? But not Lord Steyne: he was far too old. Besides, the man's reputation . . .

rumour had it that he had a mistress in London and a mistress in Bath and, what's more, had done so even while his young wife had been alive. No, Lord Steyne was not the sort of man that any young woman deserved, least of all the precious, the incomparable Kitty.

And other candidates for her hand, such as Lord Bragg and Lord Pratt, though rich, were far the inferior of Kitty. As Carter had so aptly put it when they had spotted these gentlemen in Sydney Gardens, the men were idiots. Including Mr. Boyle – though he was already married, so at least that would save Kitty from his attentions – honourable attentions, at least. There were always the other sort of liaisons favoured amongst rich entitled gentlemen – but heaven forfend Kitty should ever fall victim to a rake who did not intend marriage.

No, Boyle, Pratt, and Bragg were off the menu. As were other men of Henry's acquaintance, such as Mr. Vane and Lord Rash. Neither would suit. Mr. Hart was a good chap, though. Henry had been at school with him, and Hart had always been kind. Well, mostly. But he had a rather annoying laugh . . .

Now, Lord Knightly would be a good catch – for he owned half of Suffolk and was said to be fond of reading, as Kitty was. Henry put a finger to his lips. What was Knightly fond of reading? Ah! The English Stud Book. Perhaps Lord Knightly was not entirely Kitty's cup of tea.

Lord Truelove was a romantic soul who was always writing poems. Might Kitty like him? But he was also a comical figure, wearing flamboyant cravats, high pointy collars he could scarcely see over, and absurdly tight pantaloons. He was even rumoured to polish his boots with champagne, as his idol Beau Brummel did. No! Lord Truelove was already in love with himself and would not suit the generous, warm-hearted Kitty.

Henry made his way over to the pianoforte and started improvising a wistful piece in a minor key. He might have to face the fact that the best thing he could do for Kitty would be to explain to her that she must look elsewhere. But who to suggest?

Perhaps Edmund might be suitable?

But no! Henry would not be able to countenance the thought of Edmund with his beloved Kitty, however much he loved both Kitty and his brother. 'Twas far too close to home. Imagine having to spend family time with Edmund and Kitty, to watch their married bliss, the arrival of children . . . Henry shuddered. If Edmund married Kitty, Henry would stay in the army and ask for a posting far, far away – and be glad if he lost his life on foreign soil.

"Henry!" Selina said as she bustled into the room with a heap of garments slung over her arm. "I've just said goodbye to Kitty on the stairs, and she seemed a little distracted. You haven't been rude to her, have you?"

"Of course not," Henry said.

Had he?

"I am glad to hear it," Selina said. "Maybe she was worried about her mother and wanted to rush home to see her? Anyhow, you'll be very excited when you see what I've got here, for you *will* be going to the ball – and these are the clothes you will be wearing."

"I cannot go to the ball," Henry said. "Everyone will see me and know who I am."

"Not if you go in disguise," Selina said.

"But whatever I wear, I'll still look like myself, won't I?"

"Wait and see," Selina said. "I brought your violin down from the nursery as well."

"My violin?"

"Yes! Your violin. A possibility has occurred."

"A possibility?"

"Henry! You are beginning to sound like a parrot, repeating everything I say."

"But you are not making any sense."

"Listen, then!" Selina said. "You know I am friends with Mama's abigail and always have been."

"I know you're a terrible gossip and will chat away to anyone."

"Stop interrupting! Mama's abigail is being courted by a young man who plays the violin in the musical trio due to perform at the Upper Rooms tomorrow night."

"Yes, and?"

"He is not well – not well at all," Selina said. "The organizers of the ball are going frantic looking for someone else to play, so naturally enough, I put your name forward."

"You put my name forward?"

"Well, not exactly me," Selina said. "Mama's abigail, through her young man, was able to put your name forward – and of course it is not your real name, but a false one. You are expected tomorrow evening half an hour before the ball begins."

"This sounds mighty suspicious." Henry wrinkled his nose. "And I am not sure I believe you."

"It's true!"

"What part of it?"

Selina sighed. "Most of it."

"Don't tell me," Henry said. "Let me guess; the part that is not true is that the young man who plays the violin is ill. You and Mama's abigail have persuaded him to say he feels ill, and that is why there is a sudden vacancy."

Selina nodded. "Correct."

"And exactly how was he persuaded? Why would he do this for you?"

"Easy!" Selina said. "I spotted him sneaking away from our house at the crack of dawn recently – and he does not wish me to say anything, obviously."

Henry smiled. Selina was rather admirable; with all her sub-terfuges and scheming, she would have made a good spy – like Carter.

"But I don't fully understand about the clothes," Henry said. "I'll still be recognized, won't I?"

"You'll understand in a minute. Start getting changed – that's it! Hurry, for we don't want Mama or Papa to discover us."

Henry quickly shed his outer garments and began trying on the breeches and jacket that Selina gave him.

"I didn't know we had these in the dressing up box," he said.

"Oh no, these belong to the young man who is courting Mama's abigail. I have borrowed them. Mm. I do believe he is shorter than you are – but the fit is not too awful. Turn round and let me see from the back. You'll do! At a pinch."

Pinch was indeed the operative word. Henry felt constrained in the tight jacket which pulled uncomfortably across the shoulders.

"I hope I can manage to lift the violin bow high enough to draw it across the strings," he said. "This jacket is a poor fit."

"Fuss pot! You are mightily ungrateful," Selina said. "And after all I have done for you! It has taken a great deal of my time in the last few days; indeed, I have been planning for this since first you returned to us."

No one likes being called a fuss pot – so Henry decided not to complain about the breeches being too short and rather strange in design. They were not too tight, though, as Henry had lost much weight on his travels. Henry was grateful for that, for if there was one thing he could not abide, it was skin-tight pantaloons that were impossible to sit down in.

"Now," Selina said, "I need to know more about what tran-spired between you and Kitty when you were left alone. Please tell me you have not declared your love and she has rejected you."

"No."

"No? You mean no, you won't tell me, or no, that's not what happened?"

"No – that is not what happened."

Selina tapped her foot impatiently. "Oh, Henry! 'Tis almost impossible to get the full story out of you. Tell me everything, from beginning to end."

"Never!" Henry said. "Some things are private."

Selina pursed her lips. "I think I know what happened, then.

You kissed each other, then you said something stupid, she misunderstood you because you didn't finish your conversation, and now she's gone home upset."

This was indeed an astute observation; Selina was wise beyond her years, despite the fact that she had limited experience of life outside the home. Her words offered comfort too, for when Selina described the situation in this way, it did not sound quite as bad as Henry had feared – or quite as final.

"And it won't be as bad as you think," Selina said.

Good Lord! His sister was a mind reader now.

"I have a scheme to get you into the ball," Selina said, "and I'm sure all your difficulties with Kitty will be able to be sorted out there. You two were made for each other, and I'm very pleased that something romantic has happened in this very room. I am also sure Mama didn't really need to go downstairs to see the housekeeper or Cook, by the way, nor did Papa need to go to his study with Edmund. Everyone has been trying to give you and Kitty some space, but you've been too noodle-headed to make the most of it, and now you have had a silly misunderstanding. Am I right?"

Henry nodded. What else could he do?

"Now, try your violin," Selina continued. "Can you still play?"

Henry slid the bow over the open strings to tune up. Thank the Lord the jacket did not rip across the shoulders, for he could swear the stitches were groaning and protesting under the strain.

"I might be recognized, you know," Henry said. "I still look like Henry Templeton, despite changing clothes."

"The one thing I have not yet mentioned yet," Selina said, "is that it is a masked ball."

Henry felt rather dubious about this. "A mask does not cover the face that much, does it? Just the eyes. I know people pretend they can't recognize each other when they're wearing masks, but they can."

"Yes, I know," Selina said, rather impatiently, Henry considered. 'Twas quite unfair, if one thought about it, because she was bombarding him with all manner of surprises, and he was doing his very best to be logical and point out the possible pitfalls.

"This is your mask," Selina said, holding up a full-face mask. "You have suffered from smallpox."

"Have not!" Henry said.

"You have suffered from smallpox," Selina insisted, "your name is John Greenwood, and you are a very shy musician only recently come to Bath. What is more, you are exceedingly self-conscious about your premature baldness, and thus you always wear a large hat. This one is from the nursery."

"Ah! Yes, I recognize the hat. Let us hope this is going to work," Henry said as he placed the full-face mask over his head and covered his brown curls with a very wide brim. Then he lifted his bow, played the opening of a lively country dance and started tapping his feet.

"Better!" Selina said. "I knew I'd be able to cheer you up. There's always hope, especially when affairs of the heart are concerned."

And my heart definitely is concerned! I will go to the ball – even if I have to look like a nincompoop who has grown out of his clothes – and I will endeavour to find time to talk to Kitty secretly, for I must clear up our unfortunate misunderstanding without delay.

Kitty

Kitty could not get away from the house fast enough. She still burned with the memory of the kisses she had shared with H – but afterwards! How shocking! What was it he had said?

"You do not need someone like me – I am not the man I was before I left . . ."

What could he have meant by this? He also said he had done things he couldn't tell her about. What, exactly? Did he mean he had met someone else to love when he was abroad?

He would not simply have been referring to fighting, for it was obvious he had been fighting. He was a soldier at war, a captain in the army. Kitty did not want to think about the violence, and she was sure the soldiers did not want to do it either, but everyone knew that soldiers had to fight – kill or be killed. 'Twas the most terrible thing ever, almost beyond imagination, but it was a soldier's duty, and the safety of England depended upon it.

Someone has to stand up to that bully Napoleon – although I think Henry has done enough fighting. He's done his duty, and I for one would be over the moon if he left the army.

"Miss Kitty," Mrs. Honeyfield's abigail said as they reached the end of Brock Street and entered The Circus, "are you all right?"

"I am, of course I am fine," Kitty said, "but I would like us to walk a little faster for I am very keen to get home and see my mother."

"Yes, Miss Kitty," the abigail said, quickening her pace.

Kitty allowed the back of her hand to trail across the iron railings as she hurried round The Circus – sneaking a look down into the basement rooms as she had many times as a child on her way to and from the Templetons' house.

"How do you think my mama is?" Kitty said.

A silence – perhaps Kitty should not have asked? Then the maid asked, "What exactly do you mean, Miss Kitty?"

"You are with my mother a great deal – how do you think she is? Is she sleeping well? Is she making light of her illness? With Christmas round the corner, I long for Mama to take a turn for the better, but do not always know how to help her."

"In my opinion, and this is only my opinion Miss Kitty, Mrs. Honeyfield is a little up and down these days."

"Perhaps because Doctor Jenkins does not visit?"

"'Tis interesting you should mention that, because I was with your mother only an hour ago when Miss Steele mentioned that there was to be a new doctor attending quite soon."

"A new doctor?" Kitty said.

"Yes, and that no one was to worry about the expense, because Lord Steyne was to foot the bill and would hear no argument to the contrary."

Had Kitty misjudged Lord Steyne? For this was a most generous offer. Perhaps Kitty's distress at her mother's condition had led her to think less well of Miss Steele too? Was this what Miss Steele and Lord Steyne had been discussing when Kitty had seen them out of her window but a few hours ago? That was, if it had in truth been them, not some other people chatting on the pavement.

But if it was Miss Steele I saw, I don't think she should have taken my cloak!

Miss Steele was a conundrum. She had become Kitty's governess when Kitty was about twelve, and then as Kitty had grown up, her role had altered to that of companion. Sometimes it seemed as though she still thought she was Kitty's governess – and responsible for more than a companion usually was.

She will be employed by my parents until I marry – or until my father gives up hope of an advantageous match, and that will not be to Lord Steyne. Never! However kind he is being to Mama.

Kitty and the abigail were approaching the bottom of Russell Street, opposite the entrance to the Upper Rooms, when lo and behold, the man who was in her mind doffed his hat from the other side of the road. Lord Steyne!

Kitty nodded and smiled. Then she blushed deeply – for no good reason, for it was not as if the man could see inside her head and inspect her thoughts about not wanting to marry him.

Where was Lord Steyne going? Perchance he had been visiting one of his lady friends – news of Lord Steyne's many lady friends had reached even Kitty's ears – and was now on his way back to his lodgings in The Paragon?

The Paragon seemed such an unsuitable address for a man like Lord Steyne. He was certainly no paragon of virtue – in fact quite the reverse, if the rumours Kitty had picked up were true. Although she had to admit that the man was not an out-and-out villain, for had he not offered to help her poor mama by hiring a doctor?

Once inside her home at the top of Russell Street, Kitty handed her cloak to the maid. She had been very pleased to see that it had been returned after its mysterious disappearance earlier in the day. Had Miss Steele taken it? Kitty would probably never know for certain.

Unless, unless . . . of course! It could have happened like this. Miss Steele might have noticed Lord Steyne passing by and picked up the first cloak she could find before running out of the house to beg him for help with Mrs. Honeyfield's health. This might have acted as a catalyst and encouraged Lord Steyne to make his generous offer to fund the medical treatment for Mrs. Honeyfield.

Kitty bit her lip; this sounded a trifle far-fetched, even for someone as generally optimistic and positive as she was. Miss Steele wasn't impulsive; she would not suddenly run out of the house to beg for help. Would she?

"Miss Kitty," Miss Steele said, sweeping downstairs to the entrance hall.

Lord! Kitty only had to think of someone these days and they appeared before her! Kitty made a mental note to refrain from thinking about Lord Steyne and Miss Steele as much as possible.

"Miss Kitty," Miss Steele repeated, "do you intend to go to the concert tonight?"

"No. And yes, I do know it will be a very interesting program, but I intend to spend the evening with Mama. She will appreciate my company. I might read to her, and besides, I've had my fill of music for the day. Why, I have been playing pianoforte duets all afternoon at the Templetons."

"How delightful."

Why, oh why did Kitty have to go on burbling like a demented dullard about playing duets – and *all afternoon*? And wasn't a lot of the afternoon spent with H indulging in a duet of a different sort?

"Pianoforte duets with Miss Selina? I always thought her musical talents were vocal rather than at the keyboard."

Too late, Kitty realized she had dug herself a massive hole. Wait! Everyone knew what a fine pianist Lady Templeton was.

"I played duets with Lady Templeton."

Oh, and now I have lied! How mortifying.

"I see." Miss Steele put her head on one side. "Well, if you do not need me to accompany you to the concert this evening, I think I will go to my room."

"What's this, Kitty?" Mr. Honeyfield said, coming out of the parlour. "I heard the last part of what you said. Do I understand you are not going to meet with Lord Steyne this evening?"

"I'm very fatigued from my day and wish to sit with Mama this evening."

"Admirable," Mr. Honeyfield said. "What exemplary behaviour – well done, my dear."

Thank the Lord Mr. Honeyfield felt such compassion for his wife and put that feeling above his wish to marry Kitty off for financial advantage – at least for this evening.

Kitty loved her father. She knew his weaknesses but also knew that, deep down, he adored his family. His wife's illness affected him greatly – and, of course, added to his financial worries. 'Twas a vicious circle. And one that needed to be broken.

Perhaps Mr. Honeyfield might consider suggesting to Miss Steele that she seek employment elsewhere? It would save some money, though admittedly not much. Kitty had been far too old for a governess for a long time, and she did not consider that she needed a companion, at least not one like Miss Steele. Surely there was someone else who could chaperone Kitty?

For I do not altogether trust Miss Steele, particularly as far as Mama's health is concerned . . . the strange draught she gave Mama worries me still, and yet all could be in my imagination.

A little later, after dinner, Kitty sat with her mother in her bedchamber reading to her from *Sense and Sensibility*.

"This is an intriguing tale," Mrs. Honeyfield said. "What a tangled web! I am wondering how all the various threads will work out – but feel confident that love will conquer all."

I want to feel that confidence too, that love will conquer all. Darling H, how I long to be yours.

CHAPTER SIX

Henry

HENRY AND CARTER waited until it was dark before making the journey up to Beechen Cliff from Number 1 the Royal Crescent, the Templetons' family home.

"I look like a numbskull," Henry said.

"You look like the young musician John Greenwood," Carter replied, "which is not quite the same thing."

"I am not sure why you insisted I wear these clothes to walk across the city," Henry grumbled. "These breeches Selina found me are more than a smidgeon short and the jacket's too tight."

Carter snorted. "I don't think we're going to be too concerned about fashion, do you? You are no Beau Brummel. Instead, you are a young impoverished musician who is about to have the chance of his life tomorrow, playing his violin at a masked ball in Bath. You must be incredibly excited!"

"Yes!" Henry said, pitching his voice oddly. "I simply can't wait to make my debut performance in the Upper Rooms."

"What sort of accent was that meant to be?" Carter said.

"Don't rightly know – I was trying to sound a bit different, that's all. I've got my violin here right now – do you wish me to strike up a tune?"

"Certainly not!" Carter said. "First of all, it would draw everyone's attention to you. People will start flinging open their windows to see what's going on. And secondly, I think it might set off the neighbourhood cats."

"Spoilsport!" Henry said. "But I might do some practice once we get up to Beechen Cliff, for I could do with brushing up a few of those dance tunes."

"Perish the thought!" Carter said. "We are supposed to be staying discreetly at the house, remember? I think the next-door neighbours might have something to say if they heard your dreadful playing wafting through the walls."

"Very funny! Anyway, 'twas kind of Cook to give us the bag of food. I'm starving."

"You're always hungry," Carter said. "Although I must say, I wouldn't turn down another slice of that venison pie."

"Which way should we go here?" Henry asked. "Past the theatre?"

"We had better not. You never know who might be hanging round. 'Twould be best if we take the path down to the river's edge and walk along until we can cross the bridge."

"How I am longing for the time when I can go about openly in the daylight," Henry said. "I wouldn't even mind going to the Pump Room and tasting the disgusting water."

"We need to find out who your enemy is first," Carter said. "'Tis not worth taking a risk."

The two men looked about and up and down the river path before scurrying across the bridge.

"I will feel safer once we're hidden by trees," Carter said.

"'Tis not long now."

On they went, up the steep hill and then they both bounded up Jacob's Ladder two steps at a time.

"I have never been this fit," Henry said.

"Army training and the last six months have toughened you up."

"Mostly the last six months," Henry said. "The training I got when I joined the army didn't prepare me for what I faced at Waterloo."

"Quiet!" Carter whispered suddenly. "And stay still."

"What is it?" Henry mouthed.

A few seconds of silence followed, then the wind in the trees, a carriage on a distant road, horses' hooves, the hoot of an owl . . .

"Nothing," Carter said. "I thought I heard something – but no."

At the top of the steps, the two men followed a narrow path and slipped through the back door of the terraced house where they had been hiding out.

"Let us get down to business," Henry said.

Carter drew the curtains, lit some candles, and grabbed a couple of platters from the side, while Henry unwrapped the food from Cook and cut generous slices of venison pie and fruit cake.

"'Tis not worth lighting a fire," Carter said as he tucked in. "You look tired and should go to bed soon. How's your shoulder?"

"Not bad," Henry said. "Perhaps a little sore after my sister thumped me earlier."

And my darling Kitty touched my shoulder too, shortly before we kissed . . .

"Bed. Now," Carter said. "You're nodding off."

LATER, AS HE lay in bed, Henry's thoughts ran over the events of the day – and what a day it had been, from seeing Kitty near the library in Milsom Street until now.

Would he escape detection at the ball tomorrow by dressing up as the fictional John Greenwood? An owl hooted outside, answered by another.

"Henry!" There was an urgent whisper from the doorway.

"Carter?" Henry sat up in bed. "What is it?"

"There are too many owls. I don't like it."

"What do you mean, you don't like it? I thought you enjoyed nature."

"'Tis no time for jokes," Carter said. "I have to be wary in my line of work."

Good grief! *"In my line of work?"* Carter was more or less admitting that he was much more than a manservant. How interesting this was – but perchance 'twas not the best time for a discussion.

"I'm going outside," Carter said, "to have a snoop around. Come downstairs and bolt the door behind me."

Henry yawned. "I suppose I have to stay up until you come back?"

"That's the idea," Carter said, "and would be exceedingly kind of you. Or put it another way – I'll be downright furious if I have to sleep in the garden because you've gone back to your bed when I return."

Henry grinned. "What do you expect you're going to find out there? What makes you suspicious? Apart from being a spy, of course."

"I'll ignore that comment! And what's making me suspicious is the amount of hooting going on. We have not heard this many owls any other night, have we?"

"No – we've seen some bats, though – can't hear them because apparently their sounds are too high for the human ear to pick up."

"Fascinating though this lecture on natural history is, I believe I must get going. Come on!"

Henry shivered as he leapt out of bed and padded after Carter down to the ground floor. He did as he was told and bolted the door securely, both top and bottom.

Once Carter had left, Henry looked around the kitchen. There was nothing for it – he would have to eat another piece of cake and maybe have some ale too.

And I'll while away the time thinking about you, dearest Kitty, and wishing you were waiting for me upstairs, lying in my bed.

Sometime later Henry was roused from his half slumber at the kitchen table by a sharp knock at the door.

"Only me," Carter said. "Let me in."

"Anything to report?" Henry asked as he opened the door.

"No," Carter said "No evidence of anything, not that I could find, anyway. If there was anyone there, they've gone now."

"Maybe you were being overly cautious?"

Carter's mouth was set in a grim line now. "I'm not so sure. Just because I didn't find any evidence doesn't mean there weren't people out there looking for us – or even following us, God forbid."

"What does it mean, then?" Henry said.

"It could mean our enemy is cleverer than I had thought."

Kitty

Kitty too was finding it hard to sleep that night. She had tried reading in bed by candlelight, but this made her eyes tired without the rest of her body feeling sleepy.

Next, she tried lying on her side and relaxing every part of her body from the top of her head down to the ends of her toes – followed by tensing every part of her body then releasing it. Neither of these techniques had the desired effect, so she drew her knees up to her chest and tried to think about nothing, absolutely nothing at all. Her mind would soon be a blank and she would drift off into peaceful slumber . . .

Only this was not what happened. Instead, her mind became crowded with images – her father's disapproving face when she had told him she did not wish to marry Lord Steyne, Miss Steele's unexpected appearance in Kitty's bedroom when she had been thinking about her beloved Henry, her mama's pallor and lack of energy when Kitty had read to her the previous evening, and tea with the Templetons – the fun, laughter, music . . . the kiss! Her feelings . . .

And holding everything together, acting as the framework for Kitty's musings, was the beautiful Mozart pianoforte duet and the feeling of being at one with Henry as they journeyed through the musical landscape. Four hands, two minds and hearts, joined as one in the performance.

Fragments of music from the duet escaped from inside Kitty's head – whirling spirals of semi-quavers danced across the ceiling, on and on, with snippets of melody wafting through her bedchamber. Could no one else in the household hear it? 'Twas so loud! Would her mind never find rest? And what were the notes trying to say?

Then silence fell on the other side of the music, and there was a vision of Kitty and Henry – not seated at the pianoforte this time, but lying in her bed.

Kitty floated on the ceiling looking down at herself with Henry. They were so close; it was paradise. Henry started kissing her, as he had done in the Templetons' withdrawing room. Kitty moved her lips, remembering, remembering . . . Henry's soft lips were upon hers, two mouths moving in perfect time with each other, then his probing tongue was joined by hers as they melded together, deeper and deeper . . . and what would have come next if Henry had really been in her bedroom?

Kitty was a little hazy about the mechanics of love. When she was sixteen, her mama had spoken to her about marriage and about what it meant, but she had made such veiled references that Kitty had been none the wiser after their conversation.

"Your husband will lie next to you in bed," Mrs. Honeyfield had said. "You will climb the heights together – you will be as one. Many will tell you that this is something for a woman to endure, but I have heard some find it an enjoyable experience rather than a duty."

"And which of these was it like for you," Kitty had asked, "endurance or enjoyment?"

Mrs. Honeyfield had turned bright red at that point and said that it was time for Kitty's pianoforte lesson and she was sure she had just heard the music master arriving at the house.

Kitty had thought about what her mother had told her – and

hoped very much that she herself would fall into the enjoyment category rather than endurance.

Marriage and what went on between a man and wife was something that had been a frequent topic of conversation between Kitty and Selina. There had been one hysterically funny occasion many years ago when the two girls had been in the nursery at the Templetons' and Selina's governess had overheard Selina and Kitty speculating about what might happen when they were married. The governess had then told the two girls the most extraordinary tale, which was obviously patently untrue, about what happens between a man and a woman in holy matrimony.

"The man has a certain appendage between his legs," she had said, "which is usually small and insignificant."

This much the girls already knew – but they remained silent, wondering what might be revealed next.

"Under certain conditions," the governess had continued, "the appendage becomes aroused and hard, and is then placed inside a lady to give her pleasure and to relieve the man's need."

Selina and Kitty had laughed so much to hear this nonsensical tale that Lady Templeton had come into the nursery to find out what on earth was going on. Neither Selina nor Kitty were capable of rational speech at that point, and the governess had become flustered, mumbling something about the fact that she thought girls should not be ignorant, for would that not make them into victims? And was it not her duty to educate young ladies about what they would face in the future?

Lady Templeton had ordered the governess to go down to the parlour with her, and shortly after that Selina was told that her governess had left to seek alternative employment.

Kitty had not thought of what the governess had told them for years and years, but now the details came back to her mind.

Was it a nonsensical tale? Kitty now recollected that when she had been sitting snug on Henry's knee in the Templetons' withdrawing room, she had been surprised by a change occurring in a part of Henry's body – a certain *stiffening*, for want of a better word. This might suggest there was some truth in the governess's story. And it had not seemed funny, but natural, although admittedly unexpected.

And if Kitty combined the matter-of-fact nature of what the governess had told her and Selina, with the more whimsical account of marriage from her mother, ah, was it then possible that Kitty was getting nearer an understanding of what it might mean to be joined to a man? To experience married love?

At last, I begin to understand . . . from Henry's sublime kisses, on and on, until . . . ah, Henry, my darling!

Kitty must have fallen into a light sleep at that point, for the next time she awoke, in a tangle of bedsheets, she was conscious that time had moved on – together with her understanding of what it was to love a man, physically.

But my Henry is not here – all is but a dream.

She coughed and reached to the side of her bed for a sip of water to ease the tickle in her throat. The stuffed-up feeling persisted, and Kitty became desperate for a nip of fresh air.

Despite the chill in the room, she decided to open one of her windows – but because she was still half asleep, she had forgotten that the windows in her room were no longer plural and she was mistakenly trying to pull back a non-existent curtain from a blank wall.

Oh no! How could she have forgotten the daylight robbery and the modifications to her room? Not to mention the choking dust and lack of air . . .

Kitty stumbled over to her remaining window in the gloom, stubbing her toe in the process, which increased her low spirits. She pulled back the drape and one side of the shutter, then lifted the lower sash of the window. Ah! The December night air was chilly – but refreshing.

". . . have to be quick," a woman's voice murmured from the shadows far below. "Who knows who might overhear us . . ."

"What have you to report?" a male voice said.

Kitty knew that confident drawl – Lord Steyne! He must be

talking to one of his women. But why outside her house?

"You said before when we met that you thought you saw . . ." Lord Steyne continued. "I have men checking it out as we speak . . . and what of the other situation?"

". . . cannot be sure . . . the quantities . . . I am not much experienced in these matters . . ."

And the woman sounded like Miss Steele. This was confirmed when there came forth a high-pitched whinny. That insufferable woman had better not be wearing Kitty's red cloak again.

"Zounds!" Lord Steyne said. "You need to learn to do your job, woman."

". . . I have tried . . ." Miss Steele said.

Kitty strained forwards, whilst taking care not to be detected – a delicate balance! Why couldn't they speak up? Miss Steele was generally very keen on diction.

And now they were talking about Easter. Why? For it was not long before Christmas.

"I need to attack fast," Lord Steyne said, "on all fronts. . ."

Kitty could not believe her ears! This sounded like some sort of threat – but to whom?

". . . but if they don't want to . . .?" Miss Steele said.

Kitty sat down on the floor beneath the window and put her head in her hands, feeling the blood pounding away. Had she fallen headlong into one of her dramatic novels? What was going on? She was convinced Lord Steyne wished someone ill, but who? It could not be to do with her or her family, for did Lord Steyne not wish to marry her, however repellent the idea was to her? And had he not recently said he would pay for a doctor to treat her poor ill mama?

Should Kitty tell someone about this? She could talk to Papa, and felt sure he would be concerned, but he was still out playing cards in one of the gambling dens. And Mama was far too ill to be bothered with this. Miss Steele was someone to whom Kitty was supposed to able to turn – and yet she was a part of the mysterious problem!

Kitty groaned. She would have to wait – and perhaps confide in Henry tomorrow when she saw him at the ball.

Henry

Henry woke early the next morning. He lay on his bed staring out at the dark sky. Had someone really been looking for them last night? Following them, even? Perchance he should not have gone into Bath in daylight to meet Kitty and then to his parents at the Royal Crescent, and on to Sydney Gardens? Thence to the Crescent again. Oh dear. Carter had urged caution, yet Henry had insisted.

But there was nothing to be gained from crying over spilt milk – what was done was done. Henry clenched his fists. What if, by his own foolish behaviour, he had put his family in danger? He would never forgive himself. And as for Kitty! If anyone tried to harm his darling girl, he would not be answerable for the consequences.

Henry's heart nearly burst out of his chest at the thought of Kitty. The kiss! He had wanted so much more . . . although he would never disrespect Kitty in the way he had heard some of his friends talk about their women. Why, even Edmund boasted openly of his conquests.

Lord and Lady Templeton had always been keen for Edmund to settle down and find a suitable wife and had dropped many hints about this, for Edmund would inherit the Templeton land and estates, and must make a good match. It was his duty to produce an heir and a spare, both of them male, or preferably an heir and several spares, to inherit the Templeton title and wealth in due course.

Henry's parents had been able to have a more relaxed attitude to Henry's matrimonial prospects. There had been no pressure for Captain Templeton to choose a wife before he left for war – in fact quite the reverse.

Lady Templeton had always told Henry how important it was to choose wisely and that he was lucky because he could choose for love, whereas Edmund must choose his marriage partner in a more strategic way. Indeed, Edmund himself thought of marriage more as a business contract than as an occasion for romance.

"I will marry to please our parents," Edmund had once told Henry, "and I will take a mistress or mistresses to please myself."

Henry shuffled in his bed uncomfortably. He had never wanted to take a mistress. He had loved Kitty for as long as he could remember, and although there had been temptations along the way, he had never succumbed.

Once Edmund had said to him, "Come out with me tonight, and I can show you all the pleasures Bath has to offer – and believe me, they are many and varied."

"No," Henry had said. "I am not going out to look for these casual encounters. Nor am I interested."

"I respect you for that, Henry," Edmund had said. "You are a better man than I am – and I know why you feel this way, too."

"Why is that?" Henry said.

Edmund had laughed. "Henry, if you think that anyone in our family does not know how much you love Kitty, and have always loved Kitty, then you're an even bigger dunderhead than I had taken you for previously!"

Henry's friends had not been so admiring of what they called his puritanical behaviour.

"For God's sake, man, you're not going into the church!" one of them had said.

"Something wrong with you?" another had suggested.

Other remarks had been more crude.

In the end, Henry had simply ignored his friends' comments and told them it was his business, and his business alone – and they had stopped teasing him.

Truth be told, I am not the only one of my friends not to have lain with a woman yet, but they are too scared to admit it openly.

There was another reason, too, why Henry was reluctant to "sow his wild oats," as many of his friends put it. Once, his mama had taken him aside and explained that if a man was to behave in a certain way, then he should be willing to accept the consequences.

"Consequences?" Henry had said.

"Yes," his mama had replied. "Consequences for the woman – and for any offspring resulting from the union."

Henry had bitten his lip before venturing to suggest, ". . . there are methods, whereby . . . are there not?"

His mama had looked amused and said, "Whatever your friends have told you, there is no completely certain way to ensure the woman does not become with child."

Henry had no answer to this.

"And seriously, Henry," his mama had continued, "these situations can result in great hardship and suffering for the woman and her baby. I know of what I talk, for in my own family, there is an example, which happily worked out better than some – but which was nevertheless far from ideal or fair, especially for the woman and her child."

"But . . ."

"No, Henry!" Lady Templeton had held up a warning hand "Our discussion is at an end. The tale is not mine to tell. I merely wanted to alert you to one of the facts of life that young gentlemen are often misled over."

Realizing he was not going to be able to get back to sleep, Henry hopped out of bed and went down to the kitchen and started to make some tea. By the time it was brewed, daylight was beginning to peep through the windows, and yet there was still no sign of Carter. He must be particularly tired after his nighttime jaunt along the cliff looking for phantom owls or gang members that might or might not have been pursuing them.

"Here you are, Carter," Henry said, going into Carter's

chamber. "I've brought you a cup of tea."

Carter sat up in bed and scratched his head. He was still wearing his clothes from the day before.

"Good Lord! I'm supposed to be your manservant, remember? What business have you bringing me a hot cup of tea? But I am mighty grateful that you have."

"There is still some venison pie down in the kitchen – would you like me to fetch you a slice for breakfast?"

"Thank you, but I'll wait until I go downstairs to eat," Carter said. "There are enough mice in this house – I don't want to leave pastry crumbs for them to feast on in my chamber."

Henry sat down on the chair beside Carter's bed. "The house is getting in a bit of a mess – makes me appreciate how much the maids do in my parents' house."

"Talking of maids," Carter said, "when are you going to declare yourself to your favourite young woman in all the world?"

"And who might that be?" Henry said.

Carter guffawed. "I am going to say something to you – but do not want you to take it the wrong way."

"Why would I do that?"

"You might think 'tis not my place to interfere – but I want to offer guidance."

"Ah, 'tis the sort of advice you're always giving me," Henry said. "I know you're going to start prattling on about Kitty again and ask why I didn't ask her to marry me before I left for war."

"Not quite," Carter said. "As you are hinting, I've probably said enough about that missed opportunity already."

"More than enough!"

"But it is about Kitty – and your future together."

"What, then?" Henry asked.

"First, I want your solemn word you're not going to take offence."

Henry took a few more gulps of tea then set the cup down on the floor. "Why I should take any advice on affairs of the heart from a grisly old bear like you that has never been married, I have no idea."

Carter sat bolt upright in his bed. "What makes you think I've never been married?"

"You dark horse!" Henry said. "What happened? Have you really been married?"

"I married my childhood sweetheart," Carter said. "She lived in the village where I grew up."

Henry let out a long, low whistle. "How old were you when you were wed?"

"We were both eighteen – then she died a year later from consumption. And before you ask why I did not marry again, that's simple – I never found anyone to compare with her."

Carter, a romantic! Who would have thought it?

"And how long ago was this?"

"Too many years," Carter said. "Her death made me restless, and I moved away from the village where I had grown up and made my way to London."

"And became a spy?" Henry said.

"I worked for the government."

"Same thing?"

Carter regarded Henry with grave eyes for a considerable time before sighing deeply and saying, "My good friend, you are correct in your assumption. Many years ago, I became a spy for His Majesty's government. 'Twas not the sort of work I would ever have undertaken as a married man, but being widowed made me reckless."

"You and I have been together for a long time now, through thick and thin," Henry said, "and yet this is the first I've heard of your marriage or anything this personal."

"In my line of work, we learn to be reticent. I have told you more than I have told most people. There is one who knows my whole story… but that is a tale for another day."

"Thank you for trusting me enough to tell me as much as you have," Henry said. "As for the rest of your story, I respect your privacy – but whenever you feel like telling me that tale, I'll be ready to listen."

"Thank you! And I think I'll have that slice of venison pie now," Carter said. "Let us go down to the kitchen."

"But first, ask me what you wanted to. You know, the thing I might not want to hear."

"'Tis quite personal . . ."

"You have just shared much that is personal with me," Henry said, "so I will try not to over-react."

"Here goes, then: do you perchance occasionally feel too frightened to love Kitty because of what you have gone through in the war and afterwards? Scared, because she will have to get used to the new you? I mean, what if she cannot cope with the person you have become?"

"Are you asking if I am a coward?"

"You are no coward!" Carter said. "But I have known many soldiers who on return from war were changed characters. It can happen when men have been through unspeakable times, when they have been ordered to be more aggressive than they would ever want to be. An officer of my acquaintance was at the sack of Badajoz, and he told me that living through that, seeing how the soldiers behaved – and being powerless to stop them – will stay with him to his grave. For many years after he returned from war, he was unable to stop reliving the past – and this had a detrimental impact on his relationship with his family and friends. It took a long while for him to recover from the great shock to his mind."

"Ah, I see what you mean – and you are right. Life seemed straightforward before the war, but after the horrors of battle, followed by lying in that ditch, I sometimes find my courage deserts me. Kitty deserves a better man. One that has not taken life. One that does not wake at night reliving savage scenes of great suffering . . ."

"You scarce knew who or where you were when first I found you," Carter said gently. "In the grip of a raging infection, you struggled to speak, let alone walk – and yet you have come a long way since then, and the passage of time will continue to help. You should not be afraid to declare yourself to Kitty. Do not let the war sap your spirit. You do want to marry her, don't you?"

"I love Kitty with my whole heart," Henry said. "And yes, of course I want to marry her. But am I still deserving of her? Sometimes I have my doubts. And then on top of my own unworthiness, there is the predicament I find myself in now, with an unknown enemy. Nothing can happen between us before this is resolved, for I will not put Kitty in danger."

Carter smiled. "However changed you are, you are still the perfect match for Kitty. I am glad we were able to talk in this way, for now I am all the more determined to discover and get rid of your enemy – to clear the way, so that you and Kitty can have your happy ending."

A happy ending with my darling Kitty – more than I deserve but everything I long for . . .

CHAPTER SEVEN

Kitty

'T IS THE DAY *of the ball!*

Kitty sat up in bed while a maid drew the curtains and opened the shutters. Selina had promised to do her best to make it possible for H to attend the ball – but how would this be achieved? If he was not to be noticed, he would have to be in some sort of disguise – but Kitty would make it her business to find him. Even if he was disguised as a cook in the kitchen, she would seek him out – discreetly, of course.

Her spirits fell when she remembered what she had heard the previous night. Lord Steyne and Miss Steele were plotting something unpleasant, and that meant danger – for persons as yet unknown. Kitty should tell someone – but who? Her papa would not be out of bed before noon. He rarely rose in the morning if he had been immersed in one of his long nights of gambling and cards. Kitty bit her lip. If only her papa had possessed some good friends willing to steer him onto the right path and help him fight his bad habits – then he would not have these money worries, and life would be much easier. And her mama would be able to be treated by Doctor Jenkins again.

Kitty went downstairs and was soon joined at the breakfast table by Miss Steele.

"Good morning, Miss Steele."

"Good morning, Miss Kitty. Did you sleep well?"

"Yes," Kitty lied. "And you?"

"I slept soundly the whole night through, thank you," Miss Steele said.

Another bare-faced lie! For had Miss Steele not been outside Kitty's window in the small hours, talking to Lord Steyne? But there was no point in challenging her.

"Would you mind passing the coffee pot?" Miss Steele asked.

"Of course I would not mind," Kitty said. "Allow me to pour."

Her hand trembled as the hot stream of fragrant liquid filled Miss Steele's cup. "Oh, sorry, there are some drops in the saucer."

"Pray do not concern yourself. You must be excited about going to the ball this evening and seeing Lord Steyne."

"I am excited about going to the ball tonight," Kitty agreed.

Suddenly, Kitty noticed that Miss Steele was wearing a new brooch – a very showy and somewhat inappropriate creation for the breakfast table. Where could she have found the money for that? Generally, in common with others in her situation, Miss Steele rarely had much money to fritter away on ornaments and trifles; spending a few pence on ribbons once in a while was the most Kitty had been aware of before.

The brooch could have been a present – or she could have been given it in payment for some sort of service. Did Lord Steyne have anything to do with this?

Miss Steele put her hand over her mouth and gave a genteel cough. "As your father is still asleep, I feel I should tell you that there is a doctor's visit for Mrs. Honeyfield planned this morning. This appointment is a generous gift from Lord Steyne."

That was quick!

"I knew Lord Steyne had offered to send a doctor for Mama," Kitty said, "but I am amazed 'tis so soon."

Miss Steele grimaced. "It seems that although the doctor is very popular and busy, he is nevertheless prepared to come at short notice, as Mrs. Honeyfield's case is urgent."

"But Mama seemed a little better yesterday, for she rose from her bed for a short while, and she enjoyed the book I was reading to her in the evening. Has she now taken a turn for the worse?"

"'Tis nothing to alarm you," Miss Steele said, "but you cannot be too careful at her age, especially when there is a weakness in the constitution."

It was true, Kitty's mama was no longer in the first flush of youth, and her constitution was not as strong as it had been. She had suffered from various complaints, mostly female in origin, for a number of years and frequently had to rest. And Mr. Honeyfield's obsession with gambling and the resultant loss of much of the family wealth had not aided Mrs. Honeyfield's recovery – quite the reverse, for nowadays she found it increasingly difficult to restore herself and spent much time in her bed.

But Doctor Jenkins had been very understanding and had helped Mrs. Honeyfield enormously. 'Twas such a pity he no longer attended her.

"And there is a weakness in her mind, too – the melancholy she suffers from," Miss Steele said. "She had been much afflicted recently and has told me she has had strange imaginings."

"Melancholy? Mama has never displayed signs of melancholy! She has borne her ill health with great fortitude and resolve – for the most part, at least. And these strange imaginings you mention. What are they?"

"Imaginings are when you see things that aren't there, Miss Kitty. You must have heard of them – even if only between the covers of one of your library books."

Miss Steele tried – unsuccessfully – to hide a smirk.

How dare she! Miss Steele's new paste and foil brooch twinkled on her bodice in the morning light. How unutterably vulgar!

"I have never heard Mama complain of imaginings or melancholy," Kitty said. "Doctor Jenkins never had cause to treat her for any such conditions."

"Excuse me, Miss Kitty," Mrs. Honeyfield's abigail said. "There is a gentleman in the hall wishing to see Mrs. Honeyfield;

he says he is the new doctor."

"Ah, yes," Miss Steele said, rising to her feet. "Doctor Voss. We were expecting him. Please go upstairs to your mother, Kitty, and make sure she is ready to receive our visitor. I will bring him up when you are ready."

Kitty was so surprised by this development, and so used to automatically obeying Miss Steele, that she abandoned her toast and coffee and ran upstairs to her mother's bedchamber.

"Mama?" she said gently. "There is a doctor downstairs to see you. No, sadly not Doctor Jenkins, but a new doctor."

Kitty could hear Miss Steele and the doctor outside in the passage as they had already come upstairs. This was indeed speedy – and perchance a little inappropriate.

"Here is Doctor Voss," Miss Steele announced as the door was flung open.

A tall, gangly individual of middle years entered the bedchamber; his eyes darted furiously around the room, and he cracked his knuckles in a most disconcerting way. 'Twould be hard to imagine a person less like the family's trusted Doctor Jenkins, and Kitty felt alarmed.

"Thank you, Miss Kitty," Miss Steele said. "I will take it from here."

"Mama?" Kitty said.

"You go downstairs, my dear," Mrs. Honeyfield said. "I will be fine with Miss Steele and Doctor – what did you say your name was?"

"Doctor Voss – at your service, dear lady."

The doctor gave a deep, sycophantic bow and Kitty scuttled away. She would find her father this instant. Something was not right.

Her father lay flat on his back in the next room, snoring loudly, and it took Kitty a good ten minutes to rouse him and get any sense out of him.

"Everything is fine," he pronounced. "Doctor Voss sounds a good man. As long as I do not have to foot the bill, I am content.

Oh, my poor head! I have such a megrim . . . I must rest.”

There was no point in Kitty trying to tell her father about her concerns over the conversation beneath her window last night – he simply wasn't in the mood.

By the time Kitty went back to see her mama, Mrs. Honeyfield was alone.

“Doctor Voss has this minute left,” she said. “A brief, introductory visit.”

“How did it go? What did you think of him? He seemed a touch strange to me.”

“I believe he is a little unusual, but I found him a sympathetic man. He asked all sorts of questions, and I answered him as truthfully as I could.”

If only I had been in the room . . .

“He said the sleeping draughts Miss Steele has been giving me are exactly what I need, and he suggested I take them much more frequently, for they can do nothing but good.”

“Did you ask him what was in the draughts?”

“Oh no! I would not dream of questioning a medical man. He is the expert – I am only the patient.”

“If you are sure,” Kitty said.

“I'm sure, my dear. And the doctor mentioned perhaps I should go away for a prolonged rest sometime, somewhere quiet. He has a private hospital not far from here where he can offer special treatments to his patients, and he has affected some miraculous cures.”

“But this sounds expensive...” Kitty began.

“There is no need to worry. Miss Steele said Lord Steyne would be happy to foot the bill for whatever treatment Doctor Voss suggested. In fact, she said Lord Steyne was hoping that I would be sent away for treatment, as that is one of the best ways to recover without being a burden to your family. Is that not particularly kind and thoughtful of him?”

Kitty felt rather dubious about this, but her mama seemed very positive after the doctor's visit – and it was fair to say that when one loved someone as much as Kitty loved her mama, one could be overanxious. Kitty had little medical knowledge, and Doctor Voss must have trained for years to have built up a successful career in medicine. The man could not help his rather unusual appearance and manner – and as Kitty's mama had said, he was the expert.

Hopefully, all would turn out well. A rest cure in a hospital might be exactly what Mrs. Honeyfield needed. And the perfect time for her to go away for a few nights would be well after the Christmas festivities were out of the way – to help her get through the often-dismal month of February.

The abigail came into the room.

"Madam, a note has arrived for Miss Kitty – from the Templeton household,"

"It's from Selina," Kitty said. "I recognize her handwriting."

She unfolded the paper and read with delight that Selina would be calling for her at around 6:45 that evening with her parents and Edmund in the carriage. It was proposed they would all go to the ball together, if this was agreeable to Kitty.

"The ball!" Mrs. Honeyfield clapped her hands. "How exciting, my dear! You must make sure to come and see me once you're dressed up in your finery. And I have looked out a lovely necklace and a pretty mask for you to wear tonight. See, here!"

Mrs. Honeyfield reached out to the table beside her bed and picked up a double string of white beads with a pink cameo at the throat, and a delicate white and gold eye mask.

"I have them both ready for you. What do you think? They go together rather well. I wore them many years ago when I attended a ball in London with your papa."

"Thank you, Mama. They are perfect! But I wish you could come to the ball too."

"Is there a reply?" the abigail said. "The footman from the Templetons is waiting downstairs."

"Of course," Kitty said. "Please say that I will be delighted to see them here and I look forward to travelling with them."

"You are going in their carriage!" Mrs. Honeyfield said, once the abigail had left the room.

"A little comical, is it not?" Kitty said. "For 'tis but a short step down to the Upper Rooms from here – the end of the road, no more! Granted, a little further for the Templetons, but not much."

"Appearance is everything," Mrs. Honeyfield said. "'Tis better to be seen arriving by carriage rather than on foot. There will not be room for Miss Steele to travel with you, but I am sure she will enjoy walking down – she can join you outside the Upper Rooms."

There would be a few blissful moments without Miss Steele – a rare gift as far as Kitty was concerned.

"And I have to admit my dancing slippers will wear out less quickly if they do not get scuffed on the pavement," Kitty said.

"Dear Kitty! Ever practical." Mrs. Honeyfield said.

KITTY SPENT SOME time in the afternoon lying on her bed with slices of cucumber over her eyes. Apparently this was very restorative and could result in fascinating, sparkling eyes which were impossible to resist. How Kitty hoped this would prove to be true . . .

Then she carefully applied Milk of Roses to her face. Kitty knew Selina would be doing the same, for it was generally agreed by all the young ladies of their acquaintance that this was the best treatment for the complexion.

Her ball dress was hanging ready on her wardrobe door – white silk and gauze, with gold braid and delicate pink flowers on the bodice. There was a headband with matching pink flowers, and her mama's double string of beads and dainty eye mask completed the outfit.

Kitty lay on her bed and breathed deeply, trying to relax. As long as Selina's plan worked out, she would see H this evening.

I wish H were here with me on my bed now . . . what bliss that would be.

She sat up and tried on her long white kid gloves, admiring the delicate frill. They were as soft as cream. Then she slipped on her white leather slippers and practiced a few dance moves on the rug in her bedchamber, in the arms of an imaginary Henry.

What if he proposed tonight? What would that be like? Would Henry perhaps kiss her gently as he had in the Templetons' withdrawing room yesterday? Hopefully he would not hesitate this time, nor say that Kitty would be better off without someone like him, or suggest he was not the same man that left her to go to war all those months ago. These were disturbing thoughts – Kitty would have to face them sometime – but not now, not while she was resting before the ball. And not while the unknown enemy was still a danger.

Ah, imaginary Henry would press Kitty's hand to his heart and declare he loved her far beyond anything he could express, or could be envisaged by anyone in the whole history of the world. He would say that loving her had driven him almost to the point of insanity, such was the depth of his manly feelings. His whole being cried out to be joined with her for ever, and if she turned him down, he would be compelled to find the nearest cliff and fling himself over the edge as there would no longer be any purpose to his life . . .

No, this would not do. Kitty stopped swaying to the rhythm of the music in her head. This would definitely *not* be how Henry would propose! The very idea was ludicrously over the top and very un-Henry-like. True romance was unexpected and personal. Kitty would have to wait and see how – and if – it might unfold.

If I am lucky enough to have a proposal from Henry, I care not where or when it happens…it will be enough to know that he loves me and wants me to be his wife . . .

Dinner was a dull affair with Papa and Miss Steele at five o'clock. Kitty chased a piece of meat round her plate for a while, but was far too excited about the ball to be able to eat anything much, despite her papa exhorting her to build up her strength for dancing by stoking up with food.

"You should do as your father commands and eat a hearty meal," Miss Steele pronounced, "for it is a long time before supper in the Upper Rooms, and you want to have plenty of energy for socializing, do you not? You need to look your best with rosy cheeks for Lord . . ."

Kitty stopped listening.

Not this again! I do not care how I appear to Lord Steyne.

She would have welcomed the chance to talk to her papa about what she had overheard Lord Steyne and Miss Steele discussing, but Miss Steele was right there, and besides, Papa seemed more than usually morose and disgruntled today. He must have lost heavily at cards again last night.

At last the tedious meal was over, and Mr. Honeyfield retired to his study while Kitty escaped upstairs to dress for the ball.

The abigail was already in Kitty's bedchamber, ready to assist.

"Shall we do your hair first, Miss Kitty?"

"Thank you."

The abigail dipped a tortoiseshell comb into a little water, then tamed Kitty's curls, section by section. Finally, she coaxed her locks into shape with her fingers and secured the creation with the headband.

"Lord, Miss Kitty," the abigail said, "you have the easiest hair! Many maids of my acquaintance have to be busy with the papers and tongs for hours with their ladies to create the sort of curls that are natural to you."

"You do not think my hair is too much?" Kitty asked. "I worry sometimes it is a little wild and unruly. My friends at school sometimes teased me."

"I hope you took no notice! They must have been jealous. Now, shall I arrange a few tendrils round your face?"

"If you think it would suit me," Kitty said.

"I do. Here we go."

The abigail carefully took a few strands and wrapped them round her fingers to make light spirals.

"What do you think?"

Kitty looked in the mirror. Would Henry like the way she looked? Would he notice?

"I like it!" Kitty said. "Thank you."

"Now for your frock, and all the rest of the bits and pieces," the abigail said. "Here we are . . . ah! You look an absolute picture, Miss Kitty. You make sure you have a wonderful time this evening. Go and enjoy yourself. Oh, and do not forget to wear your lovely mask! Here. I will help you tie it at the back. You look properly mysterious now!"

"Thank you," Kitty said. "I am very grateful for your help and feel like a real lady this evening. Now I must go and show Mama. I promised I would let her see me before I went to the ball."

Outside in the corridor, Miss Steele was going up the next flight of stairs to her room. Had she been in Mrs. Honeyfield's chamber?

"Mama!" Kitty whispered softy as she went into the room. "Here I am!"

But her mama was fast asleep, with the curtains already drawn for the night. Her plate of dinner lay untouched on a tray beside her bed.

"Miss Kitty!" the abigail called. "The Templetons have arrived!"

Kitty planted a soft kiss on her mama's forehead.

It is time to go to the ball! So why do I feel this sense of dread?

Henry

"John Greenwood!"

Henry looked behind him. Who were these men talking to?

"John Greenwood?"

Then he remembered. "Oh yes, that's me. I'm John Greenwood."

These days, it was quite hard to remember who you were

meant to be. Henry pulled at his breeches, trying to lengthen them. He must look a complete chump.

"We need to get up to the gallery," a man holding a flute said. "Come on! I'll show you the way. Rehearsal starts in five minutes. I hope you're experienced with these sorts of events – we cannot put up with shoddy playing."

Henry raced after the man. He would have to play his very best to convince him that he was an adequate substitute. Inside the ballroom, servants were positioning chairs round the edge of the room and sweeping the dance floor.

"This way!"

Henry climbed the stairs to the musicians' gallery where another man was strumming a few cheerful chords on the pianoforte. Henry looked out over the balustrade. 'Twas strange to see the familiar room from a different perspective. The five magnificent crystal chandeliers ablaze with candles were even more amazing from this higher vantage point.

The pianist played the note "A" for the flautist and Henry to tune up, and Henry quickly opened his violin case, sending up a silent prayer that his playing would be good enough to pass muster.

"Take your hat off man, for God's sake!" the flautist said. "I can hardly see your face with that ridiculously old-fashioned headgear! And the mask – you didn't have to wear a full-face mask! Eyes only would've been sufficient, like ours. You look scruffy – and untrustworthy."

"Leave him alone," the pianist said. "You know what we've been told. He's sensitive about his smallpox scars – and missing hair. We needed someone at short notice. Beggars can't be choosers."

"Yes, indeed," Henry said. "And I can't abide anyone seeing my bald pate. Baldness runs in my family. 'Twas all very well for my father and my grandfather because they could put on a wig like everyone else, but these days everyone wants to display their natural hair. So sad."

The flautist began to play a soulful melody, and the pianist strummed a few minor chords.

"This could be our new piece," the pianist said. "We could play it tonight if you want – it's a lament for your missing hair."

"A melancholy *hair*, instead of a melancholy *air*?" the flautist suggested.

Henry joined in, improvising a full-throated mournful tune on his violin and throwing in some fake sobbing for good measure.

This broke the ice between the three musicians, and they indulged in some hearty laughing before settling down to practice the dance pieces.

"The Sussex Waltz," the pianist said. "We always start with this."

The three musicians rattled through the first line.

"That will do," the flautist said. "Don't want to exhaust ourselves."

"Or peak too early," the pianist said.

"What next?" Henry asked.

"Quadrille," the pianist said.

Barely two phrases were played before the pianist declared, "Enough! You're going to fit right in, John."

"What a relief!" the flautist said. "For a moment there I thought we might have to have a proper rehearsal."

"How about a drink before we start," the pianist said, producing a hip flask.

The flautist waved his own supply in the air.

"I'm afraid I haven't brought a flask," Henry murmured.

"Fret not," the flautist said. "You may share mine."

This was indeed true acceptance! And in such a short space of time. Music has many powers.

"Let's go outside," the pianist said. "We can wet our whistles – and see who's arriving for the ball."

Henry was grateful the other two musicians seemed friendly chaps, after an admittedly shaky start, particularly with the flautist. They hadn't asked too much about his weird disguise, and he had passed the musical test. Now they could all indulge in a stiff drink before they had to play at the ball.

Henry followed the men outside and stood by the colonnade in Bennett Street. People were arriving in carriages on both sides of the Upper Rooms. Others came in sedan chairs, and on foot, in excited chattering crowds.

"Here," the flautist said to Henry, passing his brandy over. "Have a swig – go on! You look as if you're gasping."

Henry unscrewed the top, held the flask to his lips, and tasted the sweet fruity liquor. A hint of oak too – just as there had been when the man . . .

"'Tis not bad standing here," the flautist said, wiping away Henry's curious recollection. "We can see all the young ladies arrive."

"Yes," the pianist said. "We usually give them a rating out of ten. What do you think of this one?"

Henry frowned. He wasn't keen to play this sort of game, but he did not want his cover to be blown by making a reasoned argument about why they should not treat women as objects in the way farmers rate cattle in the market. Therefore, he wisely decided to keep quiet, merely nodding as a parade of young ladies walked past.

"Five for that one," the flautist said. "Look at her complexion!"

"Seven out of ten for the next," the pianist said. "Nice figure – but too tall."

"Can't abide tall women," the flautist said. "Shouldn't be allowed. Oh, there's an eight. Spoilt by frizzy hair."

"Six for the next," the pianist said. "Looks too sharp and clever for her own good."

Hell and damnation! Who gave these knuckleheads the right to be judge and jury? And it wasn't as if either of them were the answer to a maiden's prayer.

Another carriage arrived in Bennett Street – one Henry recognized – and he moved back slightly, taking shelter in the curve of a pillar.

"Ten! Very tasty," the flautist said.

He was talking about Selina! And now Kitty was getting out. She looked stunning – and her hair was a little differently styled too, with spirals framing her lovely face.

"Top marks for her friend! Another ten! Whoa! Those beautiful dark curls!" the pianist said.

"If I could give an eleven, I would!" the pianist said. "I can see a pair of fine blue eyes, despite the glittering mask. If only she were mine . . ."

The flautist gave a coarse laugh and took a swig of brandy from his hip flask. "Wouldn't she be something to wake up to in the morning?"

Henry ground his teeth. Kitty was his! Or would be, once he had summoned up the courage to declare himself. Once he had finally rid himself of the feeling she would be better off without him . . .

"I am not sure about this lady, though," the pianist said as Miss Steele hastened to join the Templeton's party.

"Indeed! Look at her brooch," the flautist said. "Far too large! Tawdry."

"Yes, 'tis definitely over sparkly. Perhaps she is not quite a lady?"

"Kitty!" Miss Steele pulled the skirt of Kitty's dress straight. "You want to look your best for Lord Steyne, don't you?"

"Ah! She's a lady's companion," the pianist said. "And I pity that pretty young lady if Lord Steyne's after her. No good will come of it."

Henry felt a boiling rage building up inside him. How dare these two jackasses talk about Kitty? And was she in danger? He wanted to throw off his wretched hat and mask and declare to the world that Kitty was his. Changed man or not, he and Kitty were the perfect match – was that not what Carter had said so recently?

But if he made a scene now, it would ruin everything. No, he had to play the long game.

"Shouldn't we be getting back?" Henry said. "If the guests are arriving, we'll be playing soon."

"Quite right," the pianist said, and the three of them raced back to the musicians' gallery.

"Time for the Sussex Waltz," the flautist said.

"Want another 'A?'" the pianist asked.

"Thank you," Henry said as he checked the tuning of his violin.

As the dances followed one another in quick succession, and more and more revellers took to the floor, Henry made every effort to keep his hat and mask in place and play the right notes. He also tried to look down at the dance floor to see where Kitty was – and with whom she might be dancing. If he could also avoid his borrowed jacket splitting across the shoulders while he played, 'twould be a bonus.

Hopefully Lord Steyne would be too busy in the card room to pester Kitty as a dance partner. Interestingly, Carter had said he'd heard Lord Steyne was leading Mr. Honeyfield into bad ways, encouraging him to gamble for large sums he could not afford at the gaming tables many nights a week. Henry resolved to warn Kitty about this. There were apparently rumours that Lord Steyne cheated at cards – he was certainly staggeringly successful and, according to Carter, that meant he was cheating, for no man could win every time as he did and not be practicing some kind of deception, surely?

Then there were all the young men on the dance floor to be concerned about, many of whom Henry recognized as friends and acquaintances. Were they like Henry's fellow musicians? Did they rank ladies by their assets and regard them primarily as potential bedfellows, nothing more than pieces of flesh? While Henry fully appreciated Kitty's alluring physical beauty, he was not going to have anyone ogling her or pawing her in a slow waltz. That was not on!

No! Kitty was Henry's, and Henry's alone – he loved her for

her beauty of character, mind, and spirit, as much as for her physical beauty. Henry felt his courage growing – he would declare himself very soon, as Carter had advised, not just kiss her as he had yesterday then blather on about how he wasn't the man she used to know. She must be thoroughly confused and disappointed with his behaviour – as he was himself.

At one point Henry felt himself being observed. He looked down – straight into the eyes of Selina, who was mightily amused. Henry attempted a little wave with his elbow while he was playing, which caused a slight hiatus in the melody – and resulted in the worrying sound of a stitch ripping in the jacket. Selina continued dancing, shoulders shaking with laughter.

"Next piece, John!" the flautist said. "You've not put the right piece of music on your stand yet. Concentrate!"

"What is it?" Henry said.

"The quadrille."

This was one of Henry's favourite dances, and as he played the lively melody his feet shuffled and tapped. Now, if he were down on the dance floor with Kitty – what fun they would have! And then, in a quiet moment in the tea room later, he could whisper in her ear what he felt.

I long to declare myself, dearest Kitty – and I long for you to be mine!

Kitty

What a treat to be collected by carriage and taken down the length of Russell Street – which admittedly was a very short journey. Miss Steele seemed a little put out that there was no room for her in the carriage, and she set off at a brisk walk, only arriving a minute or so after the Templetons and Kitty. There were great crowds of people making their way into the Upper Rooms and quite a lot of people standing about near the entrance, including some characters dressed in matching jackets by the colonnade.

The ballroom looked as glorious as it always did, the candle-light softening the pale icy blue walls.

Selina pointed out some of the details of the decorative plaster work on the walls and pillars to Kitty, but sad to say, it was all rather a blur.

"You need spectacles," Selina said.

"What's this?" Lady Templeton said. "Can you not see, dear Kitty?"

"My sight is merely a little fuzzy," Kitty said, "more than it used to be. Possibly I have been reading too much."

"Ah," Lady Templeton said, "I did notice you rubbed your eyes a little when you were playing the pianoforte yesterday and had to sit very close to the music. 'Tis a problem that is easily remedied! Spectacles are needed. Not all the time, but just put them on when there's something particular you want to see in the distance, and of course for reading, and it will help you greatly, my dear."

Kitty had nothing to say to this. She knew her mama would not wish her to be seen in spectacles. The other problem, the ever-present obstacle, was her papa's lack of money.

Lady Templeton rummaged in her reticule and pulled out a quizzing glass. "For now, try this. Even if you had spectacles, they would not be of much use this evening, because you have your mask on, as do we all, but a quizzing glass is an excellent accessory at a ball for those of us whose eyes need a little help. I have two such items in my reticule, and you would be doing me a favour if you accepted one, for Selina is always telling me I carry too much in my reticule. Are you not, Selina?"

"Am I, Mama?" Selina said. "Oh, oh, yes, I remember now."

Kitty held the glass up to one eye. Suddenly, she could see the delicate mouldings and filigree decorations with crystal clarity.

"Ah!" she exclaimed. "I had quite forgotten all this detail. All so fine!"

"This quizzing glass will not be the correct prescription for you," Lady Templeton said. "We can get a much better one for you if I take you to see an optician."

"But . . . but . . ." Kitty said.

"'Tis my treat for you," Lady Templeton said. "Christmas is on its way, and I can think of no better present for you, my dear."

This was not the first time Lady Templeton had shown her generosity to Kitty since Mr. Honeyfield had become short of funds. She was an extremely kind and thoughtful lady, and always tried to make the gifts of a very practical nature.

"And I will get them to make you a pair of spectacles too, which I hope you will find useful."

"Thank you so much, Lady Templeton, but I simply cannot accept."

"Hush! You will accept. And no need to say another word. I will make an appointment for you very soon and accompany you to the optician in Milsom Street."

What could Kitty do but accept graciously and thank Lady Templeton profusely?

And even though the quizzing glass was not the perfect prescription, it would be useful for trying to find out exactly where Henry was.

Lady Templeton gave a beaming smile. "I am going to sit down at the side with Lord Templeton – I see some of our friends over there – and we will have a chat and enjoy watching you two young ladies dancing. Look! There are already hordes of men looking as if they are going to request the pleasure of a dance. Your duty is to enjoy yourselves! This way, Miss Steele. You shall sit over there with the other companions and chaperones."

Kitty and Selina were certainly not short of dance partners. Some trod on their feet – one lumbering individual even fell over – while others danced with grace and agility.

But none of them are Henry – how I long to be in his arms!

A few of Kitty's companions made witty entertaining remarks – but others droned on about horses and the size of their houses in the country.

"The size of the estates seems to be in inverse proportion to the size of their brains," Kitty whispered to Selina as she passed her in a reel.

And how much Kitty enjoyed the music! Most of it was already known to her. In fact, she felt there was something extraordinarily recognizable about the melodies played by the violin this evening. Had she heard this musician at a previous ball? Or was he perchance playing one of the tunes she used to play on the pianoforte when she had accompanied Henry on his violin years ago? Ah, those had been sweet times indeed, when they had made music together.

"Ladies," Edmund said, "there is to be a short break in the music – a chance to go to the tea room for refreshment. What d'you say? Shall I accompany you both?"

He held out an elbow to his sister and to Kitty. "Papa and Mama are already there."

"Should I wait for Miss Steele?" Kitty said.

"Maybe," Edmund said. "Or at least we should tell her where you are going."

"But where is she?" Kitty said, screwing up her eyes. "How strange! She was sitting over there with some of the other companions – but now I cannot see her."

"She is definitely not there," Edmund said, looking in the same direction as Kitty.

"I thought I saw her setting off towards the Octagon card room earlier," Selina said, "when we were dancing."

"Never mind," Edmund said. "We will do our own thing. Miss Steele knows you're fine with me. I am the perfect chaperone."

The tea room was even more crowded than the ballroom, and it was a while before Edmund managed to bring cooling glasses of lemonade for Selina and Kitty.

"Oh look," Selina said. "I do believe, yes, the musicians are coming in here for a break as well."

Kitty peered in the general direction that Selina was pointing and then decided to whip out her quizzing glass. "Ah! The group of men who were standing next to the colonnade when we came in."

Goodness! Now Kitty could see better, she could recognize the distinctive hat from the dressing up box in the Templetons' house. But what a strange full-face mask the individual was wearing! And the figure himself . . . what was it about him? He was wearing a pair of breeches that were a little too short and strangely cut, but she would recognize those shapely thighs and calves anywhere. Henry! Now she understood why the violin playing had a familiar tang – for Henry had a special way of pulling back the last few notes of a phrase, to extract every last ounce of emotion.

The figure nodded to her, beckoned, then slowly walked away.

'Tis Henry, for sure! I will follow him – we will have our time alone . . . my sweet Henry, returned from the dead after so long. Changed by the cruelty of what he has experienced, yes, but in essence the same man I have adored since childhood . . . he tried to explain before but I was not listening . . .

"I must away to the ladies' retiring room," Kitty said to Selina, "but will be back directly."

"I'll come with you," Selina said. "Let me put our drinks down first."

Once the two young ladies were outside the tea room, Selina said, "Quick! Go after Henry now and snatch a few minutes together. If Miss Steele or anyone else asks where you are, I will cover for you."

"Thank you, dearest Selina. Henry and I must talk – we have much to resolve, and this opportunity is truly heaven sent."

Ah! How I ache to be with my love – and to remove his ridiculous hat and mask so that I can kiss him.

CHAPTER EIGHT

Henry

HENRY'S LEGS WERE trembling as he walked towards the entrance, hoping to find a shady spot outside where Kitty would join him unobtrusively. They would not have long, for he was due back in the musicians' gallery in ten minutes.

"Beg pardon," Henry said as he walked into someone of his own age outside – a man he recognized.

Henry had been at school with Lord Rash, but there was no danger of being discovered, for the man did not recognize him in his strange getup. But the gentleman accompanying him – heavens! 'Twas Lord Steyne! Henry chewed his lip, but again he was lucky, for Lord Steyne took no notice of a man he considered to be an inferior, not even glancing in his direction.

"We must go back to the tea room," Lord Steyne said. "Come on, Rash. Let me advise you on which ladies you might ask to dance with you later, then we will try our hands at cards again, what?"

As Lord Steyne spoke, he waved his hand with an extravagant flourish, and the diamond ring he wore on his little finger flashed in the moonlight. Henry had seen that distinctive oblong shape on someone's hand before! And then the smell of lemon perfume wafted towards him on the cool night air. The pieces of the puzzle were falling into place at last! The ring, the lemon scent . . . memories from the battlefield.

"I will go straight to the card tables," Lord Rash said, "for I am not really one for the ladies – and am anxious to win back the guineas I have lost."

"As you like," Lord Steyne said with a laugh as he walked away briskly, "but you do not know what you are missing. I'm going to have a good look at the merchandise – there is one girl in particular I am desperate to get my hands on."

A few seconds later, Kitty appeared outside on the flagstones, flushed and a little breathless – her beauty as bewitching as ever. Her curls shone round her darling face – a halo of loveliness.

"Henry! I am here."

The white ballgown clung like a soft cloud to her exquisite shape, with the pink flowers on the bodice drawing Henry's eyes to her delicious curves.

Henry swallowed hard, then linked his arm through Kitty's and walked her briskly down Alfred Street, turning right down the passageway that led to Bartlett Street. They would not be disturbed there and could snatch a few minutes of conversation together. He had much to warn her about.

Before he could reveal his discoveries, Kitty moved closer to him and held her enchanting face up to his.

"Are you not cold?" Henry said. "You are not wearing your cloak."

Kitty's arms were bare, save her gloves, and the diaphanous dress she was wearing could not provide much warmth. Henry put his arms around her – purely to keep her warm.

"Please take that hat off," Kitty said, "and that dreadful mask. We are safe here."

Henry obliged and said to her, "I will remove your mask too."

Much better! Now he could drown in the full beauty of her sparkling eyes set like twin jewels in her divine countenance. If he were her husband, he could remove further items of her clothing . . . her long gloves first, pulling gently at the soft white leather, freeing each of her fingers in turn . . . then he would release her abundant curls from the headband restraining them, allowing his hands to run through the glorious texture . . . next the frock would slip from her shoulders and slide to the floor . . . and her stockings, slowly, one by one . . . ah!

But this was not right. What in God's name was Henry thinking of, at a frighteningly dangerous time like this? He must warn Kitty – and tell her what he had discovered since last they met.

"I have remembered about the scent," he said.

"The scent?" Kitty wrinkled her nose.

"Lemons – I said yesterday, when we . . ."

Shortly before we shared our first kiss . . .

". . .when we were in the withdrawing room," Henry said, "I mentioned a hazy memory of a lemon smell – well, it is coming back to me, the full story of what happened on the battlefield. And all because I have smelt the lemon perfume in reality – and I have also seen a diamond ring."

"At Waterloo?" Kitty said.

"Yes. And here! I remember now what happened after I was shot. I have had but a partial memory 'til now. The lemon smell and the sight of the ring have restored the missing pieces of the puzzle to my mind."

Kitty's eyes widened. "I cannot bear to think of the time you were wounded." She took a sharp intake of breath. "But tell me everything you now remember – please, I beg you."

"I will try to be brief," Henry said.

And I must not alarm Kitty more than necessary – she will never hear from my lips the full ghastly details of the battlefield – of what men do to each other in the name of national honor and so-called glory.

"I fell off my horse from the force of the bullet from a French musket, then must have been knocked unconscious, for much time passed and when I awoke, all was dark." Henry put his hand to his head. "I could hear men shouting in the distance, then a few scavengers appeared. You already know my outer garments were stolen – and how one ruffian tried to remove my teeth."

"Makes me feel quite queasy to think of it," Kitty said. "Thank heavens they did not succeed."

Henry flashed a grin at Kitty – showing his intact set of teeth.

"Yes! 'Tis a relief to me too, I can assure you! But I must tell you the missing part of my tale."

"To do with the ring and the lemon?"

"Yes! Much time passed, for I remember sleeping fitfully on the ground, and night turned to day and then to night again and possibly more . . . to be honest, I have no firm recollection even now of how much time passed, for I must have been unconscious for much of it. But it was long enough for the visitors to arrive – the *battle tourists* we called them in the army. Have you heard about these people?"

"Visitors? To the battlefield? No."

"I will spare you a detailed account, only know this, that people travelled from Brussels in their hundreds to make their way to the battlefield. Some were looking for the bodies of loved ones – some found them still alive and were able to save them. Others, sadly, including members of the *ton* who were already abroad, merely thought it would be amusing and interesting to view the carnage firsthand."

Kitty's eyebrows rose almost up into her hair to hear this.

"Amusing? And interesting? Merciful heavens! And did you see some of these *battle tourists*?"

"I saw a group in the distance – I could not hear what they were saying exactly, but I recognized a few English words. The group came closer to the pile of corpses I was lying amongst and I tried to call out, to let them know I was alive – but I was beyond the power of speech by then, such was my low state. The group wandered off, but not long after, one of the men returned. He had a scarf obscuring his face, as many did, clearly afraid of contagion. He stared at me but said nothing."

"Oh, Henry!"

"He put his hand against my mouth, perhaps trying to see if he could feel my breath. As he did this, something scratched my cheek – more of this later. Then he dragged me from where I lay – pulled me by my feet! At first, I thought he wished to save me, but he uttered not a word of comfort, simply grunted with the effort of moving my body along the great distance. Once we were far, far away from where I had lain, he kicked me into a deep damp ditch and covered me with branches and mud and left. Not a crust of bread nor sip of water nor comforting word did he give me. I drank some foetid water from that ditch – did not do me much good, for I felt very ill afterwards."

"Henry! You had to drink from a ditch, like an animal!"

"I lay there until Carter found me. He rescued me – were it not for his kindness and skill, I would have perished. I scarce knew who I was or where I was. Carter looked after me as you would a small child, feeding me, treating my wound and protecting me until I recovered. He sensed foul play from the very beginning – which was why he did not inform anyone I had survived until we returned to England many months later. And even then, he only told a few trusted army officers. The less people that knew, the better. For all the while, Carter was concerned an attempt would be made on my life if it was known I was still alive."

"But Henry," Kitty said, "this is terrible. Let me kiss it better . . ."

Dear God! Kitty's lips were moving towards Henry's . . . what joy! Bliss!

Henry put his arms around Kitty, and they once again enjoyed a sweet kiss. He pulled her closer and felt her soft body against the hated borrowed jacket he had been obliged to wear this evening. Then he kissed her neck tenderly and placed a series of quick kisses across her collarbone.

"Careful of the necklace," Kitty said. "Mama will not be pleased if the beads become loose."

"I will be careful," Henry said. "So very careful."

He gently lowered his lips onto hers once more, this time for a deeper, more intense experience – then took a step back.

"Don't," Kitty whispered. "Do not move away, as you did before – when first we kissed. For now I understand more."

"Understand?"

"Yes. You said I did not need someone like you because you were not the man you were before you left. But I accept you as you are, darling H."

"Even though I have lived through experiences I will struggle to tell you about? Even though my mind is oft disturbed by past events?"

"I am changed too," Kitty said. "You cannot mourn someone for six months and then see them return from the dead without your view of the world shifting…"

"I have been thinking too much of myself, and not enough of what you too have endured." Henry buried his face in Kitty's neck, and they clung to one other.

The world stood still; Henry forgot about the danger, forgot about his past sufferings, and was on the point of dropping to one knee when Kitty gently disengaged herself from his embrace.

"Henry, my dear one; we must finish our conversation, for I still do not understand the significance of the ring and the lemon."

Thank God she had broken the spell, for 'twas vital that Henry reveal to Kitty all he had discovered. Her safety was the paramount consideration now.

Pray God there will soon be another occasion for me to declare myself.

"Yes, the ring," Henry said. "I have just seen Lord Steyne's, and 'tis is the same oblong diamond ring I saw at Waterloo – on the hand of the man who dragged me to that ditch. When he put his hand over my mouth to check for my breath, the ring scratched me – and I had the chance to see the oblong diamond close up. I would know it anywhere.

"And the man who abandoned me to die smelt of lemon cologne – I have this evening smelt lemon perfume when Lord Steyne walked past."

"So you think Lord Steyne was on the battlefield with the other battle tourists?"

"I do," Henry said. "I know he was in the area, for he was at the Duchess of Richmond's ball, the night before the battle. You have heard of this ball?"

"Yes," Kitty said. "It was much talked about after the news reached England of the great victory. We heard many who attended the ball perished, because of wicked Napoleon. Did you go to that ball?"

"Yes," Henry said. "There were many army officers invited, and it was a very splendid occasion – although it ended somewhat abruptly when we were told we must all make haste to march, as Napoleon had moved earlier than had been expected. I did not manage to finish my dessert!"

"But why was Lord Steyne at the ball?"

"He had been travelling on the Continent – most inadvisable in wartime – but he had been visiting one of his, er, ladies . . ."

"You mean one of his mistresses?" Kitty said. "You can say these things in front of me, you know."

"One of his mistresses, then! Lord Steyne happens to be a good friend of the Duchess of Richmond – and I can only presume she was happy to invite him to her festivities. Whatever we think of him now, he is highly regarded in society for his wealth and influence."

"But why did he show such animosity towards you?" Kitty said.

"I think you know the answer to that," Henry said. "He wants to marry you and must have heard through the gossip vine of the deep friendship between our families. He spoke to me at the ball and asked if I had a sweetheart. I would not normally have spoken as I did, but my tongue was loosened by wine, and I said there was one young lady in particular, a sweet girl I had known all my life, that I intended to declare myself to on my return. When he came across me on the battlefield, the temptation to dispose of a rival must have been too much to resist for a person with such loose morals."

Kitty looked ecstatic – could it be that she was thrilled at the thought of a declaration of love from Henry and longed to become his wife? How wonderful!

The blessed time when I feel 'tis perfect to declare myself cannot be too far away now, surely?

Then Kitty frowned. "How wicked Lord Steyne is! He left you for dead – when he could have helped you and restored you to your regiment. My poor Henry – and if it had not been for Carter . . . and to think, I was beginning to be grateful to Lord Steyne, as he has offered to pay for a new doctor for Mama."

"Kitty, promise me that when you go back to the ball, you will be careful. Lord Steyne must not know that we have discovered his secret. I will consult with Carter, and he will know what is best to do. At least now I know who my enemy is."

And I know that I must do everything in my power to protect Kitty from Lord Steyne, now I know the depth of his wickedness.

Kitty

"I will be cautious who I confide in," Kitty said. "You know that I cannot bear the thought of you being in danger – it is imperative that Lord Steyne does not know you are alive."

"It is imperative that Lord Steyne leaves you alone," Henry said. "I do not like to think of him anywhere near you."

"I will avoid him as much as I can," Kitty said. "I am beginning to wonder why he wanted to engage a doctor for my mama."

"To get on the right side of you," Henry said. "He has little enough to commend him, save his fortune, and he must have reasoned if you thought he was kind to your mama, you would think better of him."

"I would never have married Lord Steyne," Kitty cried passionately, "even had you not returned from Waterloo. I used to dislike him intensely – now I hate him!"

"I must go back," Henry said, "although I wish I could stay with you all evening. Time is pressing on, and the other two musicians will be wondering where I am."

Was this the time for Kitty to mention her concerns about the conversation she had overheard between Miss Steele and Lord Steyne?

"I know that look," Henry said. "You are bursting to say something. Kitty, please, spit it out. If I'm late back, I am late back, that's all there is to it. 'Tis not as if I mind blotting my copybook, for I'm not looking for a career as John Greenwood the musician, am I?"

"Ah, you are called John Greenwood now, are you?" Kitty said.

"Yes! I have smallpox scars and suffer from premature baldness, hence the full mask and bizarre hat."

"I will be sure to call you John Greenwood whenever I want to tease you."

"And I have a feeling that will be a frequent occurrence."

"I'll try not to take too long," Kitty said, "but I happened to overhear a conversation the other night when I could not sleep – I opened my window, desperate for some air, and overheard Lord Steyne and Miss Steele talking in the street. And I thought I had seen them together before, too, during the day."

Henry frowned. "What did they say – at night, when you overheard them?"

"Miss Steele said she had to talk quickly, and Lord Steyne asked her what she had to report, then they were conversing about Miss Steele having seen someone earlier – and that some men were checking it out."

Henry gritted his teeth.

"Then they referred to something else – quantities? I couldn't quite hear what they were saying, so it was difficult to understand. I crept as close as I could to the window, but I did not want to be discovered, as I'm sure you can imagine."

"I can indeed," Henry said.

"And Lord Steyne mentioned Easter which I thought very strange."

"Easter?"

"Yes! The time of rejoicing, when Christ rises from the dead – oh, my!" Kitty put her hand over her mouth. "Are you thinking what I'm thinking?"

"That Miss Steele thought she'd seen me . . ." Henry rasped.

". . .because it was as if you had risen from the dead," Kitty said.

"We probably took a careless risk meeting near the library yesterday morning," Henry said. "Carter certainly thought so – I had no end of stick from him when he thought I'd stayed too long in that alley."

"Carter always has your best interests at heart," Kitty said.

Henry nodded. "But now we have more to worry about than I had thought. Carter suspected someone might have been following us recently – oh, do not look alarmed, Kitty. We will be fine. Just tell me – did Miss Steele and Lord Steyne say anything else?"

"That was it – no, wait! Something about attacking on all fronts. What do you think he meant?"

"Not sure," Henry said. "I have an uneasy feeling, though. I know he wants to kill me and marry you – but maybe someone else is in danger. I cannot work it out."

Kitty flew into his arms.

"Promise me, Kitty, that when you go home after the ball, if anything bothers you, or if Lord Steyne is there and he tries anything, anything at all, make your way on foot up to Beechen Cliff where Carter and I will be waiting. It will be dark and you might be frightened, but I know you can manage the journey. Promise me!"

"Promise," Kitty said. "And do not worry about me, for I could make my way up to Beechen Cliff blindfolded, particularly when I know you will be waiting for me. I doubt I will have to do a midnight flit, but if I do, why, I still have the box of dressing up clothes in my closet at home, ones we used to wear when you came to play – you, me, Selina, and Edmund. Since you have dressed up so beautifully in a disguise this evening, I don't see why it shouldn't be my turn. Now you must go back, before you lose your job!"

Henry put his mask and hat on again, and the pair hurried back to Alfred Street. Henry melted across the road into the back door of the Upper Rooms, while Kitty raced round to the front where she found Selina standing just outside the main door.

"You've been gone for ages," Selina said. "Hope it was worth it."

"It was worth it!" Kitty said. "I've been standing in an alley-way with Henry – or should I say, John Greenwood?"

"Ah ha!" Selina said. "So he told you his new name?"

"Yes, he did. And it suits him!"

"I think I did rather well to create John Greenwood, I must say," Selina said, "especially with that full-face mask. No one could possibly recognize him."

"Yes," Kitty said, "and that is vital, because from what Henry and I can work out, Lord Steyne is his mysterious enemy – and what's more, he knows Henry is alive."

"Lord Steyne! Well, I am not that surprised, for I never liked the man," Selina said. "He held my hand far too long once during a dance and stared at my chest. I told him to desist."

Kitty shuddered. "He's the vilest man imaginable."

"Tell me everything you know," Selina said. "Henry has been slow to speak of his time abroad beyond the fact that he has an enemy in England and would have to lie low for a while. In truth, the family find it hard to understand. We have quizzed Carter since his return, but of course he does not know everything that happened to Henry before he found him. Perhaps we will never know the full truth of how Henry ended up in that ditch."

"Henry did not know the full truth of what happened – until

this evening," Kitty said. "Two things have helped jog his memory – an oblong diamond ring and the smell of lemons."

"How bizarre!" Selina said. "You must tell me more."

The two young women reached the ballroom.

"Where is Miss Steele?" Kitty asked.

"I have not seen her for ages," Selina replied. "Not since I thought I saw her going into the Octagon, and that was a while ago."

How strange – and very unlike Miss Steele, who usually breathed down Kitty's neck on every outing and at every social event.

"I am a little perturbed at the thought of what she might be doing," Kitty said.

"Do not concern yourself," Selina said. "She has probably got caught up in the excitement of the cards and is still in the Octagon. Does she perchance have a beau?"

"Not as far as I know," Kitty said. "But she does have a new shiny brooch which she's wearing this evening – perhaps she has made a new friend."

"Well, I for one am glad she is not here," Selina said, "for it gives us the chance to sit this dance out. You can tell me all about the ring and lemons. Oh, my poor brother. He has suffered greatly."

Kitty looked up at the musicians' gallery. Henry, with his hat slightly askew, had lifted his violin bow and was about to launch into the next dance – a jig.

"Do nothing to draw attention to Henry," Selina cautioned.

Kitty understood. Despite wanting to gaze at the object of her affections for the rest of the evening – the rest of her life – she must feign indifference.

But in my heart, all I do is think of you, dearest H.

Henry

Henry enjoyed playing the jig. His foot tapped, and his shoulders moved with the rhythm. What a pity Selina and Kitty were sitting this one out. He could see them clearly from the gallery – they were talking animatedly, as if they had not seen each other for months, not merely ten minutes. There were no prizes for guessing what they must be talking about – the new discoveries concerning Lord Steyne. Henry sincerely hoped they had the good sense to keep their voices down to avoid being overheard by any of the more indiscreet members of the *ton*.

Henry flushed with apprehension. Kitty and Selina were close confidants – please God, let them not be discussing every single detail of what had transpired in the alleyway. There were certain things that should remain private between two – what should Henry call himself and Kitty? They were not merely friends, but not yet lovers . . . two young people who were on the threshold of something unbelievably special.

Henry knew he was deeply in love and had been for a considerable time – and he thought Kitty probably loved him. Probably? Of course she did! She must, surely? For she gave him such enchanting smiles . . . and kisses . . . ah! Kitty's kisses were like ambrosia from the gods above.

But until the two of them could enjoy undisturbed time together, without the ever-present danger looming, until they were able to declare their love for each other without reservation, then nothing was truly settled.

"John!" the flautist said. "Concentrate, man! Next piece is coming right up."

"Oops, sorry!" Henry said. "Is it the jig next?"

"We've just played the jig," the pianist said. "You know, for someone who calls himself a musician, I cannot believe you have so small a grasp on reality and such a pitiful memory. We are playing the reel next."

"Yes," the flautist said. "'Tis almost as if your mind is elsewhere. With someone else."

The pianist raised one eyebrow.

"I have heard you were spotted near Bartlett Street during our break – with a young lady," the flautist said.

"Come on," the pianist said. "Spill the beans. Who was she, this mysterious beauty?"

"Yes," the flautist said, "and two questions: number one, why would she be so interested in you? And number two, does she have a sister for me?"

The flautist started cackling and the pianist guffawed loudly – so much so that strange glances shot up from the dancers down below. When would they be able to start the next dance? Why were the musicians laughing?

"One and two and. . ." the pianist said – and they were off.

No! Lord Steyne was dancing near Kitty! He was not partnering her – but he was very near and kept staring in her direction. How dare he! There were plenty of other beautiful young women on the dance floor – why could he not ogle one of them instead?

Hell's teeth! Now Lord Steyne was standing at the edge of the room facing away from the dancers – and holding what looked suspiciously like a jealousy glass. He was spying on Kitty! Checking up on her by using one of those dratted glasses that could see round corners. How dare he!

Henry was extremely troubled by Lord Steyne's preference for Kitty. Could the man not detect when his advances were unwelcome? Or was that more of a challenge for him, a challenge that he enjoyed perversely – in a twisted way? Kitty was the most perfect young woman in the world, and anyone would want her as their wife – but surely someone as worldly and snobbish as Lord Steyne would be looking for someone from a higher family than the Honeyfields of Russell Street? The daughter of a duke or viscount would seem more appealing to him, wouldn't they? A conundrum, to be sure.

Lord Steyne disappeared at the end of the dance, and the

musicians moved on to one of Henry's favorites – the country dance he had practiced with Selina in the withdrawing room at home when he was in training to become John Greenwood.

The dancers lined up for the country dance, and the couple opening it were – merciful heavens! – Lord and Lady Templeton, Henry's parents. They generally preferred to sit out the dances these days, but Henry was thrilled to see them lead off, and he played the jaunty dance tune with great vigour and gusto – perhaps too much, for Lady Templeton turned and stared into the musicians' gallery, then shook her head. Had she recognized Henry's inimitable style on the violin, the playing that was so familiar to her ears? Henry pulled his hat further down over his face. It would not do if his parents knew that he was up there in the gallery.

"Stop showing off," the flautist said. "I've got the main tune there – let me shine."

"A thousand apologies," Henry said.

After that, he played in a much more restrained way.

"Only joking," the flautist said at the end of the piece. "You can play as loudly as you want. Lord! I am running out of puff and cannot wait for supper – will not be long now. We are nearly at the end."

"Yes," the pianist said. "'Tis Sir Richard de Coverley to finish off, as usual. I love this one."

"'Tisn't my favourite," Henry said. "I think the Sussex Waltz has a far better tune."

The pianist laughed. "I only love it because it's always the last dance – once Sir Richard de Coverley is over, 'tis time for a drink."

"Yes," the flautist said. "I'm gasping for wine. And John, you've nearly finished your first evening with us. Did you enjoy it? Care to join us for a drink? John?"

Henry was silent – until he remembered that his name that evening was John.

"I would love to," he said. "But I need to go straight home."

"Another time, then? Where are you staying?"

"The other side of the city," Henry said. "Yes, another time. Promise!"

Once the dances were finished, the crowds made their way to the tea room for refreshments and supper. Henry had already decided he was not going to join the throng there, for he was far more likely to be discovered than he had been high up in the musicians' gallery. He had been lucky thus far – why tempt fate? There were very many people of his acquaintance in the Upper Rooms, and it was beyond reason that his disguise would fool every single one of them.

However, he could not resist a peek into the Octagon before he made his escape. On his way there, he nearly collided with Miss Steele, who shot past him in the corridor on her way to the tea room. What was she in such a hurry for? No matter. At least she had not recognized him.

What a lot of card games were in progress in the Octagon; in a far corner, Henry spotted four players, including Lord Steyne and Mr. Honeyfield. Kitty's father had his head in his hands. Lord Steyne, on the other hand, had a wolfish expression and was collecting money owed.

"So that's his game!" Henry whispered between gritted teeth. "He's trying to relieve Kitty's father of what little blunt he has left."

But why was he hellbent on destroying Honeyfield's dwindling wealth? Could it be that once Honeyfield had finally run out of money, he would not be able to say no if Lord Steyne asked for Kitty's hand? Carter had said Lord Steyne was a cheat at the card table. If this were true, it made his actions all the more heinous. Was there no end to the man's crimes?

You fiend! I long to challenge you to a duel and send you to hell!

Henry melted away, deciding that now was not the time to challenge Lord Steyne – but he would sort this out if it was the last thing he did. Lord Steyne would not be allowed to ruin Kitty's family and steal Henry's love away.

I will go back to Beechen Cliff where Carter is waiting, and I'll seek his advice about the best way to defeat Lord Steyne.

CHAPTER NINE

Kitty

KITTY LOOKED FOR Henry at supper but was not surprised he was not there. 'Twas far too risky now, with Lord Steyne on the premises. And hopefully Henry was on his way to Beechen Cliff and to safety.

And he said if I were ever in danger, I must make my way to join him there.

"Another lemonade?" Edmund asked Kitty. "'Tis very refreshing."

"So why are you not drinking lemonade, brother dear?" Selina teased. "I see you are still on the wine."

"Wine is for gentlemen and lemonade for young ladies," Edmund said. "And you can stop laughing, Selina!"

"No wonder you gentlemen behave badly sometimes, if all you drink is wine," Selina said.

"And no wonder we young ladies stick to our lemonade," Kitty added, "for we must deal with the bad behavior of the gentlemen."

"Perchance 'tis time for me to go and fetch us all more drinks before you mock me further," Edmund said with a grin. "I will see you at our table over there in the corner – Mama and Papa are sitting nearby with some of their friends. And by the way, I saw your Miss Steele when I was first at the buffet. She said she had a megrim and was going home, but promised faithfully to be back at the end of the ball to escort you home – until then, I am apparently to be trusted as your chaperone."

"She will not be missed too excessively," Selina said, "and has been absent most of the evening, anyway. Do you remember I thought I saw her going to the Octagon? Would she have been playing cards? Are companions allowed in there? Who knows. She is an odd woman. Now, Kitty and I will go to the buffet for desserts. And we might even pick up something for you too, Edmund – a portion of trifle, perhaps. But only if we think you deserve it! Or have room for it – you think I did not notice how you stuffed yourself with cold ham and turkey but five minutes ago? Slices of pie and chutneys, salads and potatoes – is there no end to your gluttony?"

"Most unjust," Edmund said. "A man must eat."

Once Edmund had disappeared in search of wine and lemonade, Kitty and Selina could talk more freely.

"Lord Steyne behaved shockingly after Waterloo," Selina whispered.

"Yes, indeed," Kitty murmured. "The man is pure evil. Why, he could have helped Henry, tended his wounds, given him some water and called for help – then dear Henry would not have been lying outside in the rain and cold."

"But 'tis one thing not helping," Selina said. "That is bad enough. Passing by on the other side, like the story in the Bible. But Lord Steyne actively made things worse for Henry by dragging him into a ditch and covering him with mud and branches . . ."

". . . hoping that by his wicked actions, no one would ever find Henry until it was too late and he was dead," Kitty said.

And for that, I will never forgive him.

"He had better not come anywhere near us," Selina hissed, "or I will spit at him."

There should be some authoritative figure they could consult about Lord Steyne, a magistrate or suchlike – but how did one go about this? And would it be wise? Besides, Kitty could not tell any outsider the full truth – that she knew Henry was at that very moment making his way back to his father's house on Beechen Cliff. The fewer people who knew that, the better.

"The situation is more fraught with danger than we had realized," Kitty said.

"Yes," Selina said. "Now we know that Lord Steyne has discovered Henry is alive, we must be very cautious."

And Lord Steyne knows that we all know Henry is alive too . . . how complicated!

"We should not be talking about this here in public," Selina said.

"And we should endeavour not to look worried," Kitty said, "but instead, we must pretend we have not a care in the world."

Selina threw her head back and laughed. Kitty tried to do the same but started coughing, sudden tears flooding her eyes.

"Here," Selina said, handing Kitty two plates, laden with biscuits, cake, and fruit. "Take this to our table. I will follow with ice cream and trifle. This has been hard on you, Kitty."

"Please do not make more of my suffering than yours," Kitty said, "for Henry is your brother and, and . . ."

It was no use – her eyelids were bulging now, tears threatening to spill down her cheeks.

Selina grabbed at more desserts, her impeccable society manners for once forgotten. Then, laden with trifle and ice cream, she steered Kitty away from the buffet. "You need to sit down! Try to smile as we walk. And dry those tears!"

"I cannot reach my handkerchief, not while I am carrying the plates. Oh! A piece of cake's slipping."

"Miss Honeyfield," a voice said. "How delightful you look this evening."

"Thank you, Lord Steyne." Kitty held her head up and gulped the tears away. The cake, miraculously, stayed on the plate. She would stand up to this brute – and never reveal where Henry was.

"I have a request, Miss Honeyfield," Lord Steyne said.

"Pray, what is it?"

"Might I ask that you stay at home tomorrow morning, so that I might visit? I have a particular question to put to you – and I anticipate a favorable answer."

If I was near the buffet again, I would seize one of the jellies and hurl it at you!

Kitty took another gulp. "I believe I am at home tomorrow morning, and you would be most welcome."

Her nails dug into the underneath of the china plates she was carrying until she thought her fingers might burst through and appear sticking out of the piece of dry cake – or perhaps one of the biscuits or some grapes.

What was more, Kitty immediately resolved that she would not be seeing Lord Steyne the following morning. She would be far too busy attending to her mother in her bedchamber to be able to go down. One of the servants would have to give him her apologies at the front door.

Selina moved closer to her – for reassurance? Of course, Kitty could always make her way to the Templetons tomorrow morning and throw herself on the mercy of Lord and Lady Templeton. Lord Steyne would never dare go there and demand to see her.

But for now, Kitty was safe, for was not Edmund already seated at the table, waving and raising a glass of wine?

"Please excuse us," Selina said. "I believe my brother is waiting for his dessert."

Lord Steyne bowed. "Until tomorrow, then."

"Horrid man!" Selina said as they settled down at the table with myriad desserts. "You are not to worry about a thing, Kitty."

"Man trouble?" Edmund said. "You will let me know if anyone has disrespected you. I fancy challenging someone to a duel tonight."

"Edmund!" Selina said. "As if that would ever happen! You have never fought a duel in your life – and never would. You are far too much of a coward."

Edward snorted. "That is a touch harsh, Selina, even from you."

"I wish I had a brother to protect me," Kitty said.

"You will have a husband soon, I wager," Edmund said, "and I can guess who he will be."

Kitty took a sharp intake of breath. "Surely you do not mean Lord Steyne?"

"Lord Steyne? Credit me with some judgement, Kitty," Edmund said, "as I credit you with sense. I know you would never marry that man, no matter his position and rank – we have been friends since you were virtually an infant, and I – and my whole family – know whom you should marry. There is one man alive that is perfect for you. Henry!"

This was a bold way to talk! Granted, Edmund had been a friend since childhood, but this was too much.

"Selina! Do you not discuss such matters with Kitty?" Edmund continued. "And Kitty, has that brother of mine declared himself yet? If not, why do you not declare yourself to Henry?"

"Edmund, you take your teasing too far," Selina said. "Poor Kitty is embarrassed now. And you would do better to talk to Henry – for as you know, it is the man who declares, not the lady. We are bound fast by the rules of society – more's the pity."

Kitty put a large piece of shortbread into her mouth to cover her embarrassment. This would obliterate the need for her to answer Edmund's questions – for etiquette forbade her to speak with her mouth full.

If Henry declared his love and proposed, I would be elated.

Henry

Henry kept to the shadows and the smaller streets and alleyways as he made his way through the city and across the river, on his way to Beechen Cliff. Would Carter be sitting up in front of the fire, waiting for him to return, ruminating in that middle-aged way of his? It was late, so perhaps he had gone to bed. Henry patted his pockets. He had managed to acquire some cuts of meat, fancy biscuits, and some fruit from one of the maids on her way into the tea room with trays for supper. Carter should be pleased! He probably would have liked Henry to have picked up a bottle of wine too, but that could have excited attention and been too risky.

Halfway through climbing Jacob's Ladder to the summit of the hill, Henry turned and looked at the city spread out before him in the valley. Soft lights from houses were visible, and a full moon illuminated the beauty of the Abbey standing proud amidst the fine buildings surrounding it.

Henry could hear horses' hooves and the rattle of wheels on Holloway, the road below him.

He had heard horses' hooves and the rattle of cannon wheels on the battlefield . . . and other sounds too, that now he could not bear to think of . . . and then afterwards, afterwards . . .

And now I know it was thanks to Lord Steyne that I ended up in that ditch.

Henry turned and trudged up the remaining steps, left right, left right, like a soldier marching to the beat of a military drum.

He must tell Carter how the sight of Lord Steyne's ring and the smell of lemons had brought back the memory of Lord Steyne standing over him as he'd lain wounded on the battle-field – and all that followed. Moreover, there was the disturbing news that Lord Steyne knew Henry was alive.

Carter would be able to decide what to do – now that the danger was heightened.

Henry paused at the top of the steps to gaze once more at the cityscape. What camaraderie he had enjoyed with the musicians that evening! And it had been mighty kind of the flautist to share his liquor before the ball. Henry closed his eyes as the curious recollection struggled to surface again. When had someone else given him brandy? Ah, he had been lying on the battlefield, not long after being injured. A French officer had appeared and offered him brandy for the pain; he had left him his flask and a few dry biscuits. The gifts had been a real comfort – and had probably helped to save Henry's life.

Was that French officer still alive? How cruel it was that soldiers were forced to fight each other – people who in different circumstances could have been friends – and all because the men at the top could not reconcile their differences and thus resorted to bloodshed. The deaths of soldiers were merely collateral damage.

But 'twas no use dwelling on the past and trying to relive the complicated events of the last six months. Although Henry was still in danger, he was back in England – he had his family, Carter, and Kitty.

Sweet memories of the kiss he had shared with Kitty earlier that evening outside the Upper Rooms floated into Henry's mind. He put the back of his hand against his lips. How soft her mouth had felt. How tender.

This would not do! 'Twas time to talk to Carter.

"Hello!" Henry shouted as he entered the house through the back.

"What sort of time do you call this?" Carter said. "Did you enjoy the ball?"

"I did, and even saved you a few treats from the supper table. Here we are."

"Thanks," Carter said, "and since you're always hungry, would you like to share them with me? I'll pour some ale."

"Good idea. And you must listen to what I have to say – I am afraid 'tis not good news."

Henry revealed all that had passed – the ring, the lemons, the conversation that Kitty had overheard.

"I knew we should have been more careful!" Carter thumped the table.

"I am truly sorry. You were right all along. I should not have lingered near the library . . . it's just that . . ."

"You were keen to see Kitty," Carter said. "I know – and cannot blame you."

"The question is, what do we do next?"

"Nothing," Carter said, "for we do not want to draw attention to ourselves in any way whatsoever. I think we are pretty safe up here."

"This is not what you said the other night when you went chasing off after some owls."

"I was probably mistaken. I am suspicious of everything and everyone, as you know."

"I do know!" Henry said. "'Tis possibly what has kept me alive this long. No doubt you developed your suspicious nature during your previous work as a spy."

"No doubt!" Carter took another gulp of ale.

"There is a mystery you can clear up for me," Henry said.

"What?"

"I am not saying I don't appreciate what you did for me, Carter, rescuing me, nursing me back to health, shielding me from danger – but why did you do it?"

"Why did I do it? What sort of a question is that?"

"Yes," Henry said. "Why did you do it? I know *how* you did it – you've already told me you decided to follow me when I went to war. You joined the camp followers – in disguise, of course, not as my manservant. 'Tis one of your favourite occupations, pretending to be something you are not! But it cannot have been easy for you, camping out in all weathers just so that you could be near me. And all the time I had no idea."

"'Twas not the most civilized time I've ever had," Carter admitted.

"If I had known you were around, perchance I could have gotten you an invitation to the Duchess of Richmond's ball."

"What makes you think I *wasn't* at the Duchess of Richmond's ball?"

"No!" Henry said. "Were you there? Surely not! In the ballroom?"

"Not exactly in the ballroom – or among the musicians, as you have just been. No, I spent some time in the kitchen at the Duchess of Richmond's ball, chatting, gathering information, the usual sort of thing. I managed to taste some of the dishes before they went in – and sampled a few of the wines."

"I've heard it all now!" Henry slapped his thighs. "I am surprised you didn't dress up as a soldier and fight alongside me."

"I did not want to fight – but when I finally found you after the battle and realized you had been hidden away to die a slow death alone, I swore I would find your mortal enemy, and so…"

"Carter, I repeat, I want to know *why* you looked for me, not *how*. Why did you take such great pains to find me? Why undertake a dangerous and possibly futile search?"

"Don't rightly know," Carter said. "Must have had nothing better to do."

"A typical evasion of an answer from you! You are an expert at keeping secrets. Look at how you managed to conceal the fact of my survival from everyone while we were still abroad – and once we got back to England."

"But I did agree to confide in some trusted army officers in London," Carter said. "I knew they could be relied on to keep things quiet – they'd never have been indiscreet enough to blab about you."

"I suppose not. And though it irks me to admit it, they totally agreed with you and said I should remain incognito until the whole mystery was cleared up."

"Which it has been," Carter said. "We know it was Lord Steyne. But we have to be even more careful now – so that he does not find you."

Henry balled his fists. "If he ever hurts my Kitty!"

"But she's not your Kitty yet – because you haven't declared yourself. More's the pity."

"I believe you have mentioned that before," Henry said. "I also believe you're trying to deflect me from probing as to why you have done so much for me. Admit it, man! You're trying to change the subject, aren't you!"

Carter stared into the fire, his fingers raking the legs of his breeches. "I will tell you one day. Promise."

"Tell me now! My curiosity is overwhelming. You have behaved towards me as if I am precious to you, not merely your master. After all, not content with looking after me abroad, you then found us discreet lodgings in London where we lived for a long time, you helped me talk to my superiors in the army – and what am I going to do about that, by the way? They said I was not ready for active service, but would be happy to find me a desk job once I was feeling up to it – and if I wanted it."

"You can do whatever you want – 'tis up to you. You're a man. Make your own decisions – do what you want to do."

"I do not know what I want to do," Henry said, "but am damned sure I don't want to go back to war. I am thinking of resigning my commission, for I am not keen on the desk job idea, to be honest. Maybe I could get a job with the musicians who play in the Upper Rooms? Would they employ me on a more permanent basis, d'you think?"

"I am not sure your parents will think that's such a good idea. You need a profession." Carter held his glass out. "Cheers to whatever you do!"

"Cheers! And you have done it again! Deflected my question. God damn and blast you, Carter, why have you been so good to me? You've acted almost like a father."

Carter gave Henry a curious look.

"No, no . . ." Henry said. "That's simply not possible . . ."

"Absolutely not," Carter said. "I worship your mother – she would never do anything immoral, and I would never disrespect either her or your father. Besides, it would be unthinkable! Look, this is hard, but I'm going to have to tell you, to avoid any more unsuitable speculation – and so that you can understand the deep affection and feeling I have for you. Truth is, I'm . . ."

Carter's revelation was interrupted by an unwelcome sound.

"Owl!" Carter leapt to his feet. "We had better check – cannot be too careful."

Kitty

Kitty heard an owl as she stepped into the Templetons' carriage after the ball. Edmund had offered to walk home to the Royal Crescent to make room for Miss Steele in the carriage this time. Kitty sat opposite her and stared in fascination as Miss Steele's new brooch sparkled with odd flashes when a moonbeam happened to shine in the window of the carriage.

Selina took off her eye mask and yawned deeply, bunching her fists and raising her arms over her head.

"My dear!" Lady Templeton said. "Remember your manners – at all times. Just because we are no longer in society but *en famille* does not mean . . ."

"I sympathize with you, Selina," Lord Templeton said. "Certainly has been a long night. I hope you young ladies had fun."

Lady Templeton delicately stifled a yawn. Ah! Yawns were terribly catching! Kitty felt one creeping up on her.

Once the short journey to the top of Russell Street had been completed, Selina and Kitty left one another with many promises to catch up soon to discuss every detail of the ball.

"But not this morning," Selina said. "I am going to have a good lie-in."

"Me too," Kitty said.

And I will dream of Henry's kisses – and try to forget Lord Steyne and the danger we are in.

Miss Steele coughed. "I think, on this occasion, it would not be improper to miss your pianoforte practice before breakfast."

Lady Templeton raised an eyebrow. "Do you still supervise Kitty's daily timetable? She is nineteen years old and an excellent musician – I cannot imagine she needs to be reminded to practice or otherwise, surely?"

"A young lady's life cannot be too regulated," Miss Steele said.

Oh, yes it could! Kitty was getting far too old for the stranglehold Miss Steele placed on her activities – and more so recently, since Lord Steyne had taken an interest in her.

"Lord Steyne will be calling to see you later this morning," Miss Steele reminded Kitty. "He never tires of hearing you play the pianoforte."

Kitty rolled her eyes, then jumped out of the carriage and gave a wave as she stood on the pavement. It would not do to display any emotion or fear when Lord Steyne's name was mentioned – but she would *not* be receiving him later this morning, or any other day. Ever.

For I hate the man for what he has done to my darling Henry . . .

How Kitty wished she could stand up to Miss Steele – why was she allowed to dictate what Kitty should be doing with her time? But 'twas important not to raise suspicion at a tense time like this.

Mr. Honeyfield's hat was not in the hall when Kitty went into the house.

"Your father is still out," Miss Steele said, "in case you're wondering. No doubt he's throwing the last of his fortune away at cards as I speak."

This was impertinent! How dare Miss Steele?

"'Tis time for bed, Miss Kitty," Miss Steele continued. "Straight to your chamber – if you please."

"I am going upstairs to see Mama first," Kitty said. "I have been out for hours and need to make sure she is sleeping well."

"No need. Do not waste your time going up to her bedroom."

What on earth could Miss Steele mean? There was a new strange attitude from her that Kitty did not find appealing – in any way. It was never a waste of time for Kitty to go to her mama, for even if Mrs. Honeyfield were asleep, Kitty could stand beside her bed, stroking her cheek and listening to her soft, gentle breathing.

No time with a sick person was to be regretted. Even if they did not seem to know their visitor was there, they might perchance sense their comforting presence. And if Mrs. Honeyfield were awake, then Kitty would be able to talk to her. There was a lot to discuss – and much that Mrs. Honeyfield could advise on.

Mama! Never have I felt more in need of your warm embrace and good counsel.

Kitty opened the door to her mother's bedchamber. Oh, no! What was going on? The covers were pulled back, the bed was empty, and the wardrobe doors were open. Had someone been rifling through Mrs. Honeyfield's clothes? The drawers of the dresser were not completely closed, and various trinkets and jewelry lay on the floor.

"I told you there was no point in visiting your mama." Miss Steele was at the door. "She is no longer here, but has been taken away by Doctor Voss for treatment. Did I not warn you her nerves were getting the better of her? Now you do not have to worry, for she is in a comfortable place, getting the very latest medical treatment."

"This cannot suddenly happen with no warning," Kitty said. "Why was I not told? I need to find Papa to tell him what has happened."

"I am here, my dear, lately returned from cards." Mr. Honeyfield swayed slightly on his feet as he entered the chamber.

"Did you know about this, Papa?"

"Did I know that your mama was going to receive the finest of care, paid for very generously by Lord Steyne? Of course I did."

Tears sprang to Kitty's eyes.

"Hush child, do not alarm yourself," Mr. Honeyfield said, placing a hand on Kitty's shoulder. "I know how much you love your mama and how you will miss her – but it has become necessary for her to go away for a while for treatment. Lord Steyne has recommended an excellent place in the country."

Miss Steele's triumphant smirk in the background was highly vexing. *Told you so*, it seemed to say. *You didn't believe me – but you were wrong, as you are about everything.*

"Mama mentioned possible treatment," Kitty said, "but I did not think she meant she was going today."

"You mean yesterday," Miss Steele said, "for we have passed midnight. I received an urgent request from Doctor Voss to come back to the house while you were at the ball – I was needed to help pack a few belongings for Mrs. Honeyfield's hospital stay."

Miss Steele came back to the house because she had an urgent message that she must pack for Kitty's mama? She told Edmund she left the ball because she had a megrim. Both tales could not be true. What a liar! And she had disappeared earlier at the ball too – perhaps to meet with Lord Steyne? Carry out some tasks for him? Deliver messages? Kitty shivered. There was more going on than she knew about, that much was certain. She could smell danger in the air.

And why were Mrs. Honeyfield's trinkets and jewels all over the floor of her bedchamber? Someone must have been going through her valuables after she had left.

As if we do not all know who that person is!

"I confess I am surprised that Doctor Voss managed to find a place for her so quickly," Mr. Honeyfield said, "but 'tis all to the good, for the sooner your mama is treated, the sooner she will be back amongst us – hopefully in time for Christmas, or if not that, the New Year."

"But I would have liked to have said goodbye," Kitty said.

"Yes, my dear," Mr. Honeyfield said, "I would too. There, there. Perhaps Miss Steele thought it would be for the best, for partings can be difficult."

"That is true," Miss Steele said. "I am pleased to have been able to spare you both the pain of saying goodbye to Mrs. Honeyfield."

This was preposterous – what about the pain of coming home and finding that her mama had disappeared?

Mr. Honeyfield was incapable of feeling pain at the moment, as he was deep in his cups, but when he recovered, Kitty had no doubt that he too would regret not saying farewell to his wife and wishing her well for her treatment.

"Doctor Voss took every pain to make sure Mrs. Honeyfield was fit to travel," Miss Steele said, "and he gave her a sleeping draught to make the journey more comfortable. With God's help she will make a full recovery and return to us ere long."

A sleeping draught? Was Kitty's mama drugged, unconscious even, when she left the house? That would have been the easiest way to affect a swift, silent removal, without fear of the servants rising from their beds and posing awkward questions.

"Perhaps your mama will be back with us for Christmas," Mr. Honeyfield said. "Would that not be an occasion for joy, to think she might be restored to health by the time the festivities start? I think I will go to my room now, for I need to lie down."

The way had been cleared, then. Kitty saw now that the whole business of sending Doctor Voss to tend to her mama had actually been part of an elaborate plan. Kitty's mama would never have forced Kitty to marry Lord Steyne against her will – therefore she had to go.

Kitty must be very cautious now. She must not betray from her demeanour her revulsion at the wickedness of Lord Steyne. And what was Miss Steele thinking of, to be supportive of him in his evil aims?

No, Kitty would go to her room meekly and quietly, without further argument.

But I know what I must do next!

Once she had reached the safety of her own chamber, Kitty turned the key in the lock and ran to her wardrobe. Her best dress was missing! And a pair of satin shoes. Could Miss Steele have taken them? But why?

Pushing her hands through the remaining muslins and silks, Kitty reached for a long-neglected pile of oddments, clothes that she, Selina, Henry, and Edmund used to don when dressing up for amateur theatricals in years gone past.

Within ten minutes, she slipped out of the house dressed in an old pair of breeches and a shirt, her hair hidden under a cap and a long jacket covering the motley ensemble. The quizzing glass from Lady Templeton was in Kitty's pocket, in case she needed to look closely at anything in particular.

An owl hooted as she hared down Russell Street – the feathered creature must have been amused at the comical sight of Kitty dressed as a boy. Then she turned right to run across the Circus, down Gay Street and through Queen Square, on and on through the city until she reached the river, feeling thoroughly out of breath – both exhilarated and terrified, all at the same time.

The climb to Beechen Cliff was steep, but Kitty ran up the steps of Jacob's Ladder as if possessed. Henry was but minutes away – he would know what was to be done, surely?

Then the rain started, great fat drops lashing down, the water seeping through Kitty's clothes until she was wet through. The trees around her whispered and moved, some stretching out ghostly fingers to pull at her jacket.

Henry! I long for the comfort of your arms.

CHAPTER TEN

Henry

"IT WAS AN OWL," Carter said. "A real one!"

"Yes, a relief to know there's nothing to worry about," Henry said, "but better safe than sorry."

Henry and Carter had just completed a thorough search of the clifftop area after hearing the sound of an owl hooting. Now they were on their way down the path back to the safety of the house on Beechen Cliff. They had found nothing to concern them – and had enjoyed making the acquaintance of a large feathered creature perched on a high branch of an oak tree.

"You were about to tell me something important," Henry reminded Carter, "before we left for our ramble."

"Ah, yes!" Carter said. "Well, you should know that I am – hang on!"

There was a tiny figure standing next to the back gate.

"We have company," Carter said.

"Kitty! My Kitty!" Within seconds, Henry sprinted ahead and swept Kitty into his arms. "My darling! I'm thrilled you're here! We must get you inside and out of the rain and cold. Come – into the house at once."

"But Henry! There is much to tell you!"

"Evening, Miss Honeyfield." Carter grinned at Kitty and doffed an imaginary cap before winking at Henry. "You two lovebirds need time to yourselves – once we get inside, I'll go upstairs, and you can sit in the kitchen and dry off. It seems safe enough up here on the Cliff, but we must continue to be cautious, so don't put too many logs on the fire. Draw the curtains – and speak softly!"

Henry melted as he thought of all the things he could do alone in the kitchen with the curtains closed. Speaking was not top of the list – and although Kitty was wet through and needed warmth, maybe there were other ways to generate heat that didn't involve sitting by a fire?

"Come on you two," Carter said. "Hurry up and get inside the house. You cannot be . . ."

". . . too careful! We know!" Henry said.

Once the three of them were safely inside, Henry bolted the back door. Carter was as good as his word, instantly disappearing upstairs with another irreverent wink at Henry.

And he has still not revealed his secret to me . . .

Henry put his arms around a shivering Kitty.

"You're soaked through! Let me warm you."

Henry was trembling himself, but that had less to do with the cold and more to do with the fact that he had his love in his arms at last.

Now was the time! He would brook no more delay.

"Kitty! My sweet Kitty! I love you . . . I've loved you for years."

Kitty smiled broadly and snuggled closer. Henry pulled the sodden cap from her head and ran his fingers through her damp curls, encouraging them to spread out over her shoulders and down her back. Her jacket was open, and her bosom was partially visible through the wet shirt. Ye gods! Henry struggled not to reach out and explore her goddess-like form.

Never had Kitty been more beautiful to him. Forget all the expensive jewels and all the fancy silk and satin ballgowns in the world – how much more wondrous was his Kitty, standing there before him clad in ancient garments garnered from the Honeyfields' house – a reminder of the childhood fun and friendship that had led so naturally to deep love.

'Tis time to seize the moment – and embrace this perfect opportunity . . .

"Kitty! My darling!" Henry dropped onto one knee. "Be mine? Will you marry me? Do me the honour of becoming my wife?"

Kitty gave the most delightful smile. "I thought you would never ask! Darling H, I love you so much. Of course I will be yours – 'tis all I have ever wanted."

"But will you be able to take me as I am?" Henry said. "There is much that has happened. I don't even know if I wish to be in the army any longer. How would you feel if I resigned my commission?"

Kitty put a finger to Henry's lips. "Hush, hush. I love you for yourself – as you are now. I do not care if you are in the army, a servant, or a musician in the Upper Rooms. I want to spend the rest of my life with you."

"As I do with you," Henry murmured as his lips sought hers.

The kiss was different this time. 'Twas no more a kiss between two people who wondered if the other cared as deeply as they did – but a full sensual kiss after a loving pledge has been made.

After a while, the two of them gently broke apart, and Henry gazed into Kitty's cerulean eyes.

"What next?" she whispered.

I wish we could unite here and now – be joined to one another . . . and I know my Kitty feels the same.

Henry would be forever grateful that Kitty had run across the city to find him and they had both finally managed to break through their natural reserve and declare their love for one another. But now he had to act responsibly – for there was danger in the air.

"First, we need to talk," Henry said. "You haven't told me what led to you running up here yet. Are things bad in Russell

Street – or did you perhaps fancy some exercise after the ball?"

Kitty bit her lip. "Things have taken a turn for the worse. This is what I discovered when I returned home after the ball . . . and Miss Steele has grown increasingly insolent and hostile. I had no choice but to leave immediately."

This was worrisome news – and how shocking that Mrs. Honeyfield had been removed from her house in this way, without Kitty being able to say goodbye. There was a distinct smell of danger – and too many unanswered questions.

"There is much to consider," Henry said, "and Carter's advice must be sought. Also, you need to get out of those wet clothes."

Kitty raised an eyebrow and giggled.

"Seriously!" Henry said. "You do not want to catch a chill. I have some spare things upstairs – they are much too big for you, but needs must."

"The breeches you are wearing are too short for you," Kitty said. "Shall I try them?"

"Ah, my John Greenwood breeches. Yes, they are far too short and thus might fit you. But you need another shirt and jacket – and I will need more breeches if you are going to wear these. Stay here, my darling, while I go upstairs and collect some clothes – and tell Carter what has been happening in your parents' house."

I will not be telling him everything that has been happening between Kitty and myself, that is for sure!

"Do not be long," Kitty said. "I cannot bear to be away from you!"

"Same for me," Henry said, making for the stairs.

"I have much to tell you about my journey across the city," Kitty called after him. "Extraordinary – I heard such a great quantity of owls that I thought I was in an aviary!"

Henry froze as an icicle of fear pierced him. Coming to his senses, he ran back to Kitty.

"What did you say? Owls?"

"Yes, so much hooting! I have never heard the like. Why,

whatever is the matter?"

"Carter," Henry shouted. "Carter, get down here now!"

"What is it?" Carter rasped, appearing downstairs, instantly alert, a pistol in one hand. "What's going on?"

"I was just telling Henry about the owls I saw on the way here," Kitty said. "What is going on? Heavens! What are you doing with that gun?"

"Did you see owls, or hear them?" Carter said.

"Does it matter?" Kitty said. "In point of fact, I did not see any – but I heard so many owls, I actually thought they were following me. Listen – there they are again."

Carter put his finger to his lips, and the sound of hooting – mixed with the distant shouts of men's voices – could be distinctly heard.

"They were following you!" Carter said. "Not a moment to lose. Henry, gather a few things. We must be away from here. 'Tis best to go out the back where 'tis darker and then up the cliff path. Quick as you can – see you back here in one minute. No more!"

"I don't understand," Kitty said.

Henry put his arms round her. "Trust me! We have to do this – I will explain all later, but for now we must get ready to go."

Kitty picked up her cap – it might be useful if she needed to disguise herself again.

Suddenly, there was a sound from the back garden.

"There are already people out there," Carter said. "Change of plan: no time to collect anything. Exit via the front door – now."

The three of them rushed out of the house and stood on the deserted road.

"Which way now?" Henry said. "Back into Bath or further on up the road towards Coombe Down?'

"Away from the city, if you agree?" Carter said.

"Agreed," Henry said. "Round this corner, then straight along, that's it. Keep away from the streetlight."

"Where do you think you're going?" a voice drawled.

Lord Steyne! Hell and damnation! They were done for. Henry pushed Kitty behind him and Carter reached for his pistol, but they were hopelessly outnumbered. A crowd of ruffians appeared from the shadows, spreading their arms out so that the three were caught in a trap, like lobsters in a pot. One of them knocked Carter's pistol from his hand, and two others sent him crashing to the ground, then kicked him savagely. Henry was held fast while an ugly brute made free with his fists, pounding into him without mercy. And, worst of all, they dragged Kitty away screaming – and bundled her into Lord Steyne's waiting carriage. The hands of a woman could be seen helping to pull her into the coach – must have been that traitress, Miss Steele!

The abduction was over in seconds, leaving Carter unconscious on the ground and Henry limping after Lord Steyne's speeding carriage, howling in anguish.

Kitty, my Kitty! What danger have I put you in? I will never forgive myself if anything happens to you . . .

Kitty

Henry, my Henry – those men have hurt you. I cannot bear it.

"Stop your snivelling," Miss Steele said as she shoved Kitty back in her seat, "and what in God's name are you wearing?"

Kitty pushed back against Miss Steele, trying to reach her face with her nails. She wouldn't stay in this coach a minute longer than she had to. She would . . .

"I would not attempt anything foolish if I were you, missy," Lord Steyne said.

He was sitting opposite Miss Steele and Kitty, a haughty expression on his face. "I do not fancy your chances if you fell from the carriage travelling at this speed."

"How dare you treat me like this!" Kitty shouted. "I will

report you! I will tell my father –”

Lord Steyne gave a discordant laugh. “As if he would be interested! For he is far too busy sitting at home missing his wife and feeling sorry for himself on account of how much money he has lost over the last months.”

“You serpent!” Kitty said. “You deserve to go to hell.”

“Perchance I do – but wherever I am going, you are coming with me.”

“What do you mean?” Kitty said.

“What do you think he means, silly girl?” Miss Steele said. “Why, you are to marry Lord Steyne. You are to be his wife – you will be together forever.”

“I will never marry you,” Kitty hissed. “Never in a million years! I will slit my own throat before I give myself to you.”

Lord Steyne licked his lips and gave a long, low laugh.

Merciful God! What a bumblebroth Kitty found herself in! She slumped back in her seat. 'Twas not possible she could be forced to marry a man she did not love – was it?

How could things have gone wrong so quickly? And why did Lord Steyne want to marry someone who loathed him? The man seemed obsessed with making her his wife, to the point of trying to kill Henry and forcing her mama into a hospital. But there must be some serious reasons behind this beyond a mere physical attraction, surely?

Kitty would not risk angering Lord Steyne but would sit quietly while her brain went into a flurry trying to work out how she would escape – how she would get back to her beloved Henry.

And Carter? What about Carter? The last time Kitty had seen him, he had been lying seemingly lifeless on the ground.

Dear God, let Carter and Henry not be too badly injured – and let them come to my aid as soon as possible!

“'Tis not long now,” Lord Steyne said as the horses galloped up a steep hill.

Kitty tried to work out where they were. They had not travelled that far from Beechen Cliff yet – perhaps they were going to Coombe Down? But no, for they had taken a right fork some while back if she was not mistaken.

Kitty tried looking out of the window for clues, but everything was mostly dark, with a few glimpses of vegetation. The road was a good one – they must still be on a main route. That was something. She would not lose hope! She would trust in God – and her H.

"I expect you're hoping that useless article Captain Henry Templeton will be chasing after you," Lord Steyne said. "Well, you can forget that! There's no way on earth he can know where we're going. And unless he can run as fast as my horses, he's not going to be able to follow us, is he? His manservant Carter would normally have been able to make a better job of tracking me, I suppose, for he is an unusual character, with considerable skills and ingenuity." Lord Steyne adjusted his gloves. "But my men have made sure Carter has gone into a deep sleep and will not wake for some time – if at all."

"Henry and Carter are better men than you will ever be!" Kitty said.

"Very possibly," Lord Steyne replied, "but you're not going to marry either of them, are you? You're going to marry me. That is for definite."

"I am not!" Kitty screamed.

I wish I had one of my hat pins handy to attack this ogre.

Lord Steyne lunged forward. "Any more lip from you, young lady, and I'll ask Miss Steele to give you a dose of laudanum, eh?"

"We're nearly there." Miss Steele took some rags from her bag. "I don't think laudanum will be necessary, but I think I should . . ."

"Yes, yes," Lord Steyne said. "If you think the girl will not be quiet, you must do what you have to."

To her great shock, Kitty found her hands tied behind her back and a gag placed over her mouth.

"Blindfold her as well," Lord Steyne said, "then she won't

know where we are."

Miss Steele looked shocked at this request. "I think that will be going too far – what does it matter if she knows where we are? She cannot do anything about it, can she?"

"A fair point," Lord Steyne said. "But make sure you keep an eye on her once we get inside."

They had reached their destination. The driver got down and led the horses through an archway, round to the last house of a crescent and round the side entrance and across a courtyard. Then Lord Steyne jumped out of the carriage, leaving the door open.

"Get out," he said to Kitty. "Look sharp!"

She shook her head, unable to speak because of the gag. Her cap felt a little loose when she moved her head – which gave her an idea.

"Do not refuse to get out – for he will only make you," Miss Steele said. "And that will hurt. Better for your sake if you dismount without any fuss. Now!"

Miss Steele's voice was not as acidic as it had been. Was it possible that she did not entirely approve of the way that Kitty was being treated? It might even be possible that Miss Steele herself was being used by Lord Steyne. Did he have some sort of hold over her? Or maybe she had started to help him for money and had got drawn in deeper than she had intended.

Maybe she is in love with Lord Steyne and will do anything for him – this would help to explain why her feelings towards me have turned to hatred, for she was never like this when I was younger.

Kitty stumbled out of the carriage – 'twas hard to be graceful with her hands tied behind her back – and her cap fell to the floor without being noticed by the others. With any luck, the discarded cap could be the beginning of a trail for H to find – would that not be marvellous? There was but a slim hope this would work, but Kitty was determined not to lose faith.

"In through the back door – hurry!" Lord Steyne said. "Do not turn round or try to attract attention."

Kitty knew where she was! She was going into the end house in the Cottage Crescent, high above the city. She recognized this side of the Crescent, with the gardens all overlooking the valley. One of her school friends used to live here for a short time – a house further along, in the middle – and Kitty had visited her once.

Sadly, Kitty knew there was no point in trying to seek help from that family, as they had not stayed in the house long at all – in fact they had moved out extremely quickly, saying it was an unsuitable, odd sort of place – and they had been happily residing in Sydney Buildings now for many years.

But why was Lord Steyne bringing her here? It made no sense. Unless . . . ah, Kitty could understand more now what someone might mean by an "unsuitable, odd sort of place" – a house where a mistress might live? Or a house of ill-repute that might be used for gambling and riotous parties? Presumably Lord Steyne owned this house, and, and . . .

Lord! I know not what wickedness I have been pitched into.

Kitty half-tripped over the step into the house. "Let me untie your hands," Miss Steele said. "We can't have you falling over. And I will remove the gag . . ."

"Thank you," Kitty said when it was done.

Miss Steele was being considerate! Was there hope?

"It wasn't for your sake I untied your hands, you little fool," Miss Steele said. "We cannot have you with a bruise on your face when you get married later today."

"Later today? I am to marry later today? You cannot make me –"

"I should not have removed the gag!" Miss Steele moaned.

"Get the laudanum," Lord Steyne said. "I cannot listen to this nonsense. I need my sleep. There are pitifully few hours of the night left, but I will have my sleep!"

"No, no," Kitty said, sobbing, "not the laudanum! I will be quiet. I apologize – and will be no further trouble."

She had to get a grip on her emotions. She must not show

fear, she must not show anger, but what she did have to do was find an escape – as quickly as possible.

"One last chance," Miss Steele said. "Get upstairs."

A few minutes later, Kitty was standing in a top attic room at the back of the house with Miss Steele.

"I've had your room prepared – hope you like it."

There was a bed with a rough blanket and a wardrobe with a dress hanging on the front.

"My best dress!" Kitty said. "What . . . how . . . I knew it was missing, but . . ."

"I've been busy," Miss Steele said. "I picked out your favourite dress, the one I knew you would like to be married in – your shoes too, and a few bits and pieces from Russell Street so that I can do your hair and help you with your toilette. You will make a very beautiful bride. I arranged for all this to be brought up here in readiness while you were dancing with those young gentlemen at the ball."

"So that is why you were missing during the dancing!" Kitty exclaimed. "We thought you were playing cards in the Octagon."

"I was there for a while, but then slipped away to Russell Street. I went back to the ball later and told that bonehead Edmund Templeton I was going home with a megrim."

"Whereas in fact you were returning to help Doctor Voss take Mama!"

"You're catching on quickly," Miss Steele said. "I managed to get back for the end of the ball, then later that night the plan was that Lord Steyne would arrive in his carriage and bring you here, to the Cottage Crescent, in readiness for your marriage."

Miss Steele came closer to Kitty and hissed, "You nearly ruined everything by running away! 'Tis just as well Lord Steyne has men all over Bath and you were spotted and followed. In the end, it was no trouble to pick you up at Beechen Cliff. And here we are."

Kitty had never stood a chance. Lord Steyne and Miss Steele were prepared to use any underhand methods to get what they wanted – she was always going to end up in this attic room, on her way to a forced marriage. But she would not give up without a fight! However, she must tread carefully – perhaps appeal to Miss Steele's softer side, if she still had one.

"But I don't want to marry Lord Steyne," Kitty protested. "It is wrong that you are trying to make me. Do you not realize it is not what I wish for – marriage to someone I do not love, however wealthy or well connected they are?"

Miss Steele stamped her foot.

"Ungrateful girl! You are unbelievably lucky to be marrying someone with Lord Steyne's title and fortune. Have you any idea what an honor it will be, to be mistress of his beautiful house in Somerset? And you will have a house in London too, and a house in Bath. The house in The Paragon where Lord Steyne lodges when he is here for the season will no longer be suitable for a married man with a family. No, he will doubtless buy a splendid new town house – maybe in Lansdown Crescent. He is very fond of the views from that part of the city. And you will move from country to city as the seasons dictate, following the *ton* and dancing at the epicentre of fashionable society."

Miss Steele is motivated solely by wealth and position. No wonder she always looks unhappy! And she knows a surprising amount about Lord Steyne and what his properties and preferences are.

"I'm going to lock you in your room now, and 'tis no good calling out for help because there is no one to hear. Unusually, and luckily, the house is empty save us three tonight – apart from two servants, and they won't come to your aid, at least not if they know what is good for them. And the window does not open, so you won't be able to stick your head out and call for help. Now, settle down. Get some rest. You need to look your best for your wedding day, and we have an early start in the morning."

Once on her own, Kitty had a good cry, then walked over to the window. It was as Miss Steele had said – the window was impossible to open – but Kitty could look out across the valley and see the distant blur of the streetlights of Bath. If she'd had her quizzing glass with her, she would've been able to see more of her beloved home city – but wait! Kitty put her hand in her pocket. How fortuitous! The quizzing glass was still there and had not been damaged despite the rough treatment she had suffered when she was hurled into the coach.

Kitty held the glass to one eye and could just make out the Royal Crescent – ah, so near and yet so far, Henry's family home.

And H, where are you, my darling? I pray our love still has a chance.

Henry

"Carter! Carter, wake up!" Henry knelt in the road and gently tapped the side of Carter's face. He had already checked his pulse and found it strong and regular, thank God. His worst fear had not happened – that Carter had been killed. What would he have done without him? It must have been the lack of sleep, but unaccountably, Henry's eyes filled with tears at the thought that the world might be without Carter's powerful presence.

And he still hadn't told Henry his secret!

At least there seemed to be no more ruffians around – once Lord Steyne had made off in his carriage, they had all melted back into the shadows, presumably waiting for the next occasion their lord and master would require their fighting skills.

"A basic error," Carter mumbled.

"What's that?" Henry said.

"We made a stupid mistake," Carter said. "Lord Steyne sent a couple of his men round to the back of the house to make a noise so that we would flee from the front. We were sitting ducks for that wretched man. Maybe we should have gone upstairs – I could have shot him from the window."

"We were never going to win that fight," Henry said. "There were too many of them."

"I suppose so," Carter said. "Oh, my head! We need to get after Kitty."

"That could prove tricky, without knowing which way they have gone. There is no point in us running aimlessly along the road like headless chickens. Besides, that head of yours needs attention. You are in no fit state to do anything. We should go back to the house, patch you up, and plan our next move."

"I am not going to argue with that," Carter said. "Feel a bit woozy, to be honest."

"Can you stand up?" Henry said. "That's it – put your arm over my shoulder."

Henry half-supported, half-dragged Carter back to the house and took him upstairs to his chamber.

"You look terrible!" Henry said. "I am going downstairs to get some water, then I'll clean that head of yours and we can sort out what we do next."

Carter didn't answer, but collapsed onto the bed with a groan. By the time Henry returned with a bowl of water and a cloth, Carter was dozing on the bed. Henry dabbed at the wound on his temple.

"There, that's better. Your color is improving too. Think I'll leave you – you're better off sleeping."

"Want to . . . want to . . ." Carter said.

"You'll be all right."

"Want to come with you," Carter mumbled.

"You need to stay here, to recover. I'm going to look for Kitty."

"But you've had no sleep tonight."

"None of us have. How can I sleep knowing my Kitty must be terrified? Let me go now – I'll be back with Kitty before you know it."

"At least tell me where you're going to look for her," Carter said.

"My instinct is that Lord Steyne wouldn't dare take her back into the city," Henry said.

"Agreed. He'll want to take her somewhere quiet. Maybe up and away from Beechen Cliff – further up to Coombe Down? Question is, what's he planning to do next?"

"That's what I'm going to find out," Henry said. "I think he would have headed east, but not too far from the town, because he would want to be within reach of his men. But in reality, I don't know. Wish me luck! If you could find me hidden as I was in a ditch all those months ago, I'm sure I can find Kitty."

Carter seemed almost to be lapping into semiconsciousness again, but he propped himself up on his elbows to say, "Soon as I can, I will go into Bath and drum up reinforcements. Don't worry, Henry. We'll get her back."

Carter fell back onto his pillow and turned his head from side to side.

"I'm your uncle," he said, "in case you haven't guessed. I have always loved you, Henry, and wanted to protect you – for the sake of your mother, my half-sister."

My uncle! Good Lord! A conversation for another time – I simply can't take it in right now...

Carter's eyes closed and he fell into a deep sleep.

"Best thing for you, my old friend," Henry said as he ran down to the kitchen. "Or should I say, *my uncle?*"

Before he left the house, Henry collected supplies, including his cloak, the heel of a loaf, Carter's pistol, and a knife from the kitchen drawer.

"'Tis a little rusty, but will have to do. Shame I haven't got my sword or my dagger – I wonder which scavenger now possesses them?"

As he crept away from the house, Henry felt as if he were going into battle. He was certainly trying to bring down a dangerous enemy, and one that seemed to have a remarkable amount of foot soldiers at his beck and call. The moon shone ghostly fingers, pointing along the deserted road. Henry wanted to run, to race towards Kitty, but he felt weary to his bones and had to content himself with a brisk walk. His face felt sore from the beating he had received earlier. Putting his fingers to his cheek, he was surprised to find warm blood there. His shoulder wound was playing up too, as it often did when he was exhausted.

When he got down to the main road, he wondered which way to go. The left fork or the right? After a moment's hesitation he decided to take the left fork and make his way to Devonshire Buildings. One of his friends lived there, and although it was a most unseasonable hour for visits, Henry decided to pay a call on George and beg for help.

Walking up Devonshire Buildings, he became a little confused. Which of these terraced houses on the right was it? They all looked very similar, especially at night. Ah! There it was – the white front door. Henry opened the gate and walked through the long front garden and raised his hand to use the brass knocker. But no! This was madness! He should be going to the back door.

Henry walked right to the end of the road, along the top and then down the lane at the back until he found the house. Knocking gently on the back door, he hoped there might be a servant to greet him – but nothing. He knocked a little louder. The whole household must be fast asleep. Henry wished them sweet dreams, but confound it! What was he going to do now?

Henry crossed the alley to the stable behind. Yes, of course. That was what he would do – and George wouldn't mind in the least, because he was such a good friend. Henry gently pushed the bar open.

"Hello, Trigger," he said softly. "Who's a handsome brute?"

George would not mind if Henry borrowed his black bay – would he?

Henry put his hand on Trigger's nose and then ruffled his mane.

"What are you doing?" A man in night clothes stood before Henry with a lantern – and an angry expression. "You're trying to steal my horse!"

"George!" Henry said. "How very pleasant to see you."

George took a step back. "Henry! But, but, you're . . ."

"No," Henry said. "I'm not dead. Know it's a shock, but I'm in trouble and need your help. Please don't ask me any questions because I haven't got time – but I need to borrow Trigger. May I?"

George slapped his own face and pinched himself on the arm. "'Tis no good. You're still there, looking as if you have been in a fight. Obviously no dream. I do not understand any of this but can see you're serious, Henry. Tell me what to do!"

"I'd like you to go to my father's house on Beechen Cliff – you know the one?"

"Yes, indeed."

"My manservant Carter is there. Could you check on him? He's had a bash on the head. Then, perhaps you can help him get some reinforcements? Carter will know what to do. I need to go and look for Kitty."

"Kitty Honeyfield?" George said. "Well, if she's in trouble, why are we standing here talking? Delightful girl! On your way, Henry! Of course you can take my horse. Be off with you. Do you know where you are going?"

"Not really – in fact, not at all," Henry said. "I'm guessing that Lord Steyne will have taken Kitty away from the city."

"Lord Steyne has taken Kitty? 'Pon my soul, that's bad news. Be careful of Steyne. For he is not to be trusted, either with women or with cards. I lost a lot of money to him last year in a game – but only because he cheated."

"Can you prove it?" Henry said.

"Certainly," George said. "If I played against him again, I believe I could unmask him, for all he is a fearsome and merciless opponent. I know how he operates – and I know his weaknesses."

"There may come a time when I ask for your help in proving his deceit," Henry said. "'Tis to do with Kitty's father, Mr. Honeyfield."

"You will have my help whenever you need it," George said. "I promise. And now let me help you with that saddle. I have eyes in my head and can see you have not full use of your shoulder. And, oh Henry, how fine it is to see you alive! I realize I must not delay you, but know this – when all your friends learn of your return from the dead, there will be much rejoicing. You will not have to buy a drink for the next year at least!"

Henry thanked George profusely and set off on Trigger down the lane and thence to the main road where he turned left and started riding up the long hill, climbing higher and higher until he reached the village of Coombe Down. He felt not the cold nor any further discomfort, so focused was he on finding his love.

Kitty! Kitty, my darling! I will go to the ends of the earth to find you!

CHAPTER ELEVEN
Kitty

K ITTY CRAWLED INTO bed convinced she would never be able to settle, but she was so exhausted she fell into a deep sleep almost instantly and was only woken when Miss Steele came into the room at daybreak.

"Time to get up! 'Tis your wedding day, and you need to look your best."

Kitty toyed with the idea of saying she could not possibly look her best after being locked in a freezing cold attic with only a few hours' sleep. Besides, she had a crashing megrim – a direct consequence of the terror of her abduction, and Miss Steele had played a wretched part in that. She might add that if by some misfortune she were to find herself a reluctant bride at the altar today, she would simply say "no" – very loudly – when the vicar asked the all-important question.

But no! She would not say any of that. Kitty did not want to provoke the increasingly volatile Miss Steele.

"If you think you can get out of a marriage," Miss Steele said, "by simply saying 'no' at the altar, then you are more of a simpleton than I had taken you for."

Oh dear! It was unfortunate that Miss Steele knew Kitty as well as she did, for she had an uncanny knack of knowing what Kitty was thinking. Kitty must be on her guard!

"But the bride does have to agree," Kitty said, "doesn't she?"

"A moot point," Miss Steele said, "for if the wedding ceremony has been arranged, it is assumed the bride has agreed. And do not forget your father is favorably inclined towards this marriage. He knows it will save him from ruin. Do want to go against your father's wishes? Disobey him?"

Surely Mr. Honeyfield had not given any meaningful consent to this farce? If Kitty could talk to him.

"And Lord Steyne has sorted out all the legal requirements," Miss Steele said, "for he has obtained a special licence for you to marry – so that you can enjoy the Christmas festivities as a new bride. Is that not thoughtful of him? He has been planning this for ages. 'Tis the best Christmas gift a young lady could receive."

Kitty's resolution not to provoke Miss Steele flew right out of the window like an enraged insect – and buzzed about angrily over Cottage Crescent before darting back into the attic room to deliver its sting.

"I will never marry Lord Steyne," Kitty snarled. "How dare you try to force me into an arrangement I have not agreed to. I will scream when I am in the church! I will rant and shout until all who are there are on my side and I am released."

"Who do you think will be there to hear you scream?" Miss Steele said. "This will not be some society wedding with all your family and friends, but a quiet country event in the small village of Brislington."

Miss Steele paused. Then flushed deeply. Ah! She should not have named the village of Brislington. That had been a mistake.

"There will be no one there who is on your side," Miss Steele continued quickly. "The vicar . . ."

"The vicar will not marry me if I am not willing."

"He will – because he owes his living to Lord Steyne. And the only other persons present will be myself, Lord Steyne, and you – plus the parish clerk and a couple of witnesses chosen by Lord Steyne, I know not the details. You can forget any screaming and ranting – especially when you know what the consequences of your disobedience will be."

"What consequences could there be?" Kitty said. "You have no hold over me, for I would rather be dead than marry Lord Steyne. I care not what you might do to me."

"But you do care about your mother."

"Of course I care about my mama. I miss her dreadfully and think it is terribly wrong that she has been whisked away to a private hospital at such short notice – but surely she will be back soon, for Lord Steyne will not want to pay the fee for my mama to stay there – not when he knows I will not marry him."

Miss Steele gave one of her famous high-pitched whinnies. Her laugh was possibly the most irritating thing about the woman – that, and her tendency to betray a family who had given her a home in Russell Street for many years.

"You are supposed to be a clever girl," Miss Steele said. "You read a lot of books at least – which is not quite the same thing – but you seem to know almost nothing and are entirely lacking in powers of reasoning or deduction."

What exactly could she mean? Trouble, for sure. Miss Steele had an odd glint in her eye. Triumph?

"Your mama has been taken by Doctor Voss – who is actually plain *Mr.* Voss – for as far as I know he has no medical qualifications whatsoever. She has been taken to his hospital – his private asylum."

An asylum! Heavens alive! One heard such tales.

"You do not know where the asylum is," Miss Steele said, "and neither does your father."

'Twas a shame Miss Steele hadn't slipped up again and revealed the name or location – as she had done only minutes before with the wedding venue of Brislington.

"Mrs. Honeyfield will not be returned from the asylum until you have become Lady Steyne."

What an abhorrent thought!

On top of her increasingly painful megrim, Kitty now felt sick. And yet it seemed Kitty would have to marry Lord Steyne if she ever wished to see her mother again. Her mama! The most perfect parent anyone could wish for. When she had been in better health, Mrs. Honeyfield had devoted herself to Kitty, making sure she enjoyed a very happy childhood and was able to grow up with everything she needed, surrounded by love. Now it was time for Kitty to do something for her mama.

"Ah, lost for words, are you?" Miss Steele said. "I know what you feel for your mama. You will not let her stay in an asylum. Have you any idea how they treat women in those places? They are left freezing cold, without enough food – and there are other mortifications in store for the wretched inmates that someone as naïve as you can little imagine."

"You do not need to say anything else," Kitty said. "You may get me ready to go to the church. I will not make it difficult."

"Good! You are seeing reason at last. Get yourself washed quickly. I will get a servant to bring you up something to eat. It will not be what you're used to, mind, just some gruel and tea – but you need to have something in case you faint."

"Thank you," Kitty said automatically.

But inside, she was seething!

"I will be back directly to help you into your dress and do your hair."

Kitty forced both a tear from her eye and the corners of her mouth to turn down. It would not do if Miss Steele suspected in any way that Kitty was hatching a plan.

She will not read my mind this time! I am determined.

Kitty felt strength building inside her. Was this what men felt as they entered battle? Kitty's deep love for H had allowed her to tap into reserves of courage she had not known she possessed. She had become a woman – and was not going to give up her hopes of love easily.

Of course, if the worst came to the worst, Kitty would save her mother from the horrors of the asylum, but there was a long way to go before all hope was dead – and before Kitty might have to give up any chance of married bliss with her H.

Miss Steele swept away with a more than usually supercilious look, and Kitty stared out at the sky streaked with pink and red. It promised to be a stormy day ahead.

Think! I must think! All hope is not lost – there must be something I can do.

A young servant girl came into the room. "Here's your breakfast."

"Thank you. If you could please put the tray on the bed."

The girl set the tray down carefully, then stood in front of Kitty, awkwardly twisting her hands in a none-too-clean apron while fixing her gaze on the floorboards. Then she looked up and opened her mouth as if to speak – but nothing.

Why, the girl was but a child. What was she doing in this place?

"Do not be afraid," Kitty said gently. "If you have something to say to me, please speak."

"'Tisn't right," the girl said at last, "what's going on here."

"I know."

"Have you got anyone?" the girl said. "I'm Martha, by the way. Anyone who might be able to help you? Anyone looking for you?"

Kitty held her breath. Her trust in human nature had been rocked by the wickedness she had encountered recently. What if this young girl, Martha, had been planted by Lord Steyne and Miss Steele to encourage her to defy them, only then to come down more heavily and punish her? Perhaps they would use the laudanum they had threatened her with before, so that she would enter the church in a semi-conscious state and only come to in time to say, "I do."

This was a real fear. And yet Kitty trusted the girl. She still believed in the essential goodness of human nature. Two rotten apples in the barrel of mankind did not mean that everyone would betray her. Did it?

"I have people looking for me," Kitty said. "They are not far – but they do not know where I am. I have an idea, though. The clothes I am wearing – if they were displayed somehow outside once we have all left, like a flag, maybe hanging from a window, why then I do believe if my H was riding past looking for me, he would recognize them."

"H? That is a strange name. But this whole situation is odd – why were you dressed as a boy when you arrived here?"

Kitty smiled wearily. "'Tis a long story. I have not the time to tell you – but one day . . ."

She reached into her pocket. "I can give you something for your trouble. See this? 'Tis a quizzing glass and will help you see objects far away – it magnifies them. Would you like to have it?"

"Yes, please!" Martha's eyes widened. "Thank you, Miss. That would be wonderful. My mama – she cannot see so clearly now on account of many years bent over the needle. Do you think it would help her?"

"I think it would help her a great deal," Kitty said, "and I would very much like her to have it. There! Take it. Hide it in your apron."

"I will do what you ask," Martha said, "but now I must be away down to the kitchen. I will wait for a safe time after you leave before I hang your clothes where they can be seen from the road."

"And if anyone asks," Kitty said, "say I am gone to be wed – against my will – in Brislington. Today!"

A long shot – but perhaps the message would be delivered, God willing.

I trust Martha – and now we have a hope of victory in this terrible battle! Let us hope we win the war.

Henry

Henry did not feel the cold wind as he galloped on and on, trying to find his beloved Kitty.

It is as if I am riding into battle – both exhilarating and terrifying.

There were precious few people out at this hour of the morning. Henry stopped everyone he saw and asked if they had seen or heard anything unusual. A fine carriage speeding along? A young woman's cries of distress?

Everyone was keen to help, but no one had any information. If the shops or taverns had been open, he could have inquired there, but all premises were firmly closed at this hour.

Henry stopped one young woman in the street who was on her way to work in the Coombe Down bakery.

"I feel sorry for you, sir," she said, "but cannot help. A lord has abducted your sweetheart, you say? A lord would be on his way to a big house, and we do not have many big houses up here. There's Prior Park – but that's quite a way off. Always wanted to see Prior Park, I have!"

"The gentleman concerned . . . I mean the *man* concerned does not reside at Prior Park," Henry said. "His estate is further into Somerset, a long way off."

"Do you not think this lord might be on his way to his estate in the country? Would that not be the best place for him to hide out?"

"I do not think he will stray far from Bath," Henry said.

He clung to his belief that Lord Steyne would keep to the relatively local area, as he might have need to call on his men from the city, and not all of them would have horses. Certainly, the ruffians who had attacked Carter and Henry seemed to have nothing but the rags they stood up in – and their fists.

"I wish you luck, sir. Do not like to think of any young lady been taken in by – what did you say his name was?"

"I didn't," Henry, "but since you are interested, I will tell you his name. Lord Steyne."

"I have heard of him!"

"What have you heard?" Henry said, slipping off Trigger.

Whatever the woman was about to say, it surely could not be worse than anything Henry already knew about him – but the information could be useful.

"I have heard he is a rake," the woman said. "He treats women badly – cares not for their feelings."

Then she leaned closer. "'Tis rumoured, sir, that he did get a young woman from Coombe Down with child."

"The villain!"

"Yes, sir," the woman continued, "and he wanted to set her up as one of his mistresses, but her parents would not hear of it. The vicar of our church, he took Lord Steyne to task and made him pay some money to the family so that the girl could keep her child and live with her parents."

"Well, that ended better than for many unfortunates," Henry said. "I am glad she was able to keep her child."

How could men behave like that, thinking they could treat women shamefully with impunity? Thank God for a clergyman with a strong moral sense! Not all of them were this principled, though. Henry had come across some vicars who would do almost anything to get a good living and seemed little suited to looking after the souls of men and women.

"I thank you for your information," Henry said. "Good day!"

As he cantered away on Trigger, Henry could see streaks of rosy-fingered dawn mixed with an angrier red in the sky. The new day was beginning – and he was at a loss where to look next.

He decided to wait a while and plan his next move carefully – and give Trigger a chance to catch his breath too. There was no sense in tiring the horse excessively at this point in the pursuit. Henry sat down by the side of the road and bit into the heel of the loaf he had brought with him, while Trigger nibbled at the dew-drenched grass.

Think Henry, think! Where else is worth exploring?

Henry decided to retrace his steps down the Wells Road in the direction of Beechen Cliff again. Once down on flatter ground, he paused again at the fork where he had gone left but recently. What if he took the right this time? Or should he retrace his steps and return to Coombe Down, then fan out, exploring more lanes and villages? Oh, where would Lord Steyne have taken Kitty?

Trigger pulled at his bridle and neighed.

"Which way do you want to go?" Henry patted the horse's mane. "Lead me where you wish. Ah! The right fork. You want us to travel up there. Another hill! I hope you've got the strength for this, Trigger."

Progress was slow, as both Henry and the horse were getting tired. Henry continued to ask any passer-by for information. There were more people about now as the day had begun in earnest. One kind older lady insisted that Henry accept one of the pasties she had in a basket covered with a cloth.

"Same age as my son, you are," she said. "I know what you young men are like – always hungry."

"I should say no," Henry said, "but I'm ravenous, so thank you very much. Missed my breakfast, I'm afraid."

"Been in a fight, too," the lady said. "You looked in a mirror recently?"

"No, I haven't," Henry said. "No time for vanity, I'm afraid!"

He put his hand on his face and brushed away a few flakes of dried blood.

"Still handsome, though," the lady said. "Were you fighting over a lady? Once my old man fought someone over me. Dead romantic, it was."

"You could describe it as a fight over a lady," Henry said, "although I have to say it did not seem romantic. Not one little bit."

But what came before – oh my! Kitty in her wet shirt pressing up against me! How quickly the mood can change.

Henry gave Trigger at least half of the pasty, and the two of them continued up the hill, revived by the kind gift from the woman.

"Ah," Henry said to the horse. "We're nearly at the Cottage Crescent. I do believe Selina had a school friend who lived here. There's some story about why they moved out – I cannot remember it now. Was it not to their taste? Noisy neighbors? I wonder . . ."

Henry dismounted and walked through the stone gate along the back of the Crescent to the very end house. What was this? A cap lying abandoned on the ground. Was this . . . could it be . . . ye gods! Henry's heart beat wildly as he picked up the cap. This definitely belonged to Kitty. He was on the right track.

Trigger tossed his head as the wind whipped through the trees. And then there was a flapping sound. Egad! Washing? What sort of crescent was this, where someone would hang their clothes out of a window to dry? And in *this* weather? 'Twould never be countenanced in the Royal Crescent – but Cottage Crescent was a very different sort of place. Charming, but much smaller, well away from the city and very much on the wrong side of the river. But wait!

Those clothes! They are the very ones Kitty was wearing.

Henry stared up to the second floor. Kitty's shirt, breeches and jacket were dangling in the wind. Someone had opened the sash windows and shut them over the clothes to hold them fast – and now they were doing a merry dance in the breeze.

Henry wanted to beat on the front door, but needed to exercise caution. Henry had the element of surprise – he should use it to his best advantage.

He went round the far side of the house, tied Trigger up securely and then crept across the grass to the back door. Should he go in? Maybe he should peek through the window.

"Are you H?" a young woman said, opening the door and stepping outside to join Henry in the garden. "Are you H, what's come to save Miss Kitty?"

"I am indeed," Henry said, "and who might you be?"

The girl had used Kitty's pet name for Henry – a good sign, surely?

"Martha. I work here. If you're looking for Lord Steyne and that nasty piece of work, Miss Steele, well, they've taken your Kitty not half an hour since. Right pretty she looked when she left in her best dress and satin slippers."

"I wondered what she would be wearing," Henry said, "because I spotted her clothes from the road."

"That was her idea," Martha said. "She said once they had left for Brislington I was to hang her clothes out of the window as a sign. It was ever so exciting! But quite tricky as well, because the wind kept trying to pull them away from my fingers. I managed in the end to wedge them fast with the sash. Miss Kitty said to show you this." Martha produced the quizzing glass from her pocket. "She said you would recognize it and know I was speaking the truth if she had given me this."

"You did very well," Henry said, "and on another occasion I must thank you properly. But Brislington, you say? What on earth are they going to Brislington for?"

"'Tis Miss Kitty's wedding day," Martha said. "They are to wed in Brislington."

"Like hell they are!" Henry roared. "Is there no end to Lord Steyne's wickedness? I must away and stop this charade before it is too late."

"Miss Kitty told Miss Steele that she will say 'yes' when they want her to," Martha said. "She will say 'I do.' I shouldn't have been listening, but they did not notice I was there."

"Did you hear anything else?" Henry said. "Why would she want to say 'I do?'"

"They have threatened her, sir. Her mother has been taken to an asylum. They have that to hold over her. 'Tisn't right. They are evil people."

"You never spoke a truer word," Henry said. "Now, I think I must be on my . . ."

"Henry! Henry! Are you there?"

By Jove, that was George's voice! Henry untied Trigger quickly and made his way to the road side of the house, hotly pursued by Martha, where he found George, with Carter, Lord Templeton, Mr. Honeyfield, Edmund, and a few other men, all on horseback.

"Henry! Thank God! There you are," George said. "Have you got Kitty?"

"No," Henry said. "I have only just arrived. Kitty is on her way to Brislington. She is being forced to marry Lord Steyne."

"What are we waiting for?" Carter said as he turned his horse back towards the main road. "Come on!"

Henry gave a last wave to Martha, leapt onto his horse, and joined the others as they galloped away to rescue Kitty.

Our own private army – pray God we are not too late.

Kitty

Kitty was flung against the side of the carriage as it travelled at speed, west towards Brislington.

Earlier, in the attic room, she had submitted to being prepared for her wedding day by Miss Steele with no opposition, keeping up the sham of submissive sadness. Miss Steele had first helped Kitty into her undergarments and best dress, then brushed Kitty's hair and arranged it beautifully, carefully placing one of Mrs. Honeyfield's bonnets over her curls. The finishing touches of gloves, shawl, and jewelry were carefully added.

"And now for your satin slippers," Miss Steele had said. "Can you manage? That's it. And here is one of your mama's reticules – see, it matches your dress perfectly."

Ah! So that was why Miss Steele had searched Mrs. Honeyfield's room in a hurry last night. She had not been looking for things to steal, as Kitty had suspected, but for items to add to Kitty's wedding outfit.

But Kitty was not about to trust Miss Steele – for was she not hand in glove with the devil himself, Lord Steyne? None of his wicked plans would have been able to be so successful were it not for Miss Steele's spying and tittle-tattling.

And here Kitty was, in a carriage racing towards her doom,

with only her wits to rely on – and the faint hope that the plan she had tried to put into action with Martha would work. Would Henry and Carter be able to find her before it was too late?

"Try to sit still," Miss Steele said. "You will crumple your dress at a time you need to look your best."

Kitty nodded and lowered her eyes. She had constructed a carapace over her feelings so that Miss Steele could no longer penetrate her mind. But really – look her best? That would be impossible. She might be dressed up in fine clothes, but how could anyone look their best when they felt absolutely terrified – and were to be sacrificed at the altar?

She was about to be married to one of the most revolting men in England – by force. And her mother's safety depended on her compliance.

Kitty touched the lace of her skirt, feeling the silver thread beneath her fingers. Her best dress, the one with the particularly pretty heart-shaped bodice embroidered with flowers, the one she had imagined in her dreams she might wear if she married her H . . .

She shivered and pulled her fancy white and yellow shawl around her. The weather was freezing! If only she had been wearing her red cloak, walking on the Crescent Lawn with her H, how happy and warm she would have been.

Lord Steyne sat opposite Kitty and Miss Steele – and glared horribly. They would soon be passing the turning for Newton Saint Loe on the left. Kitty was going to try her hardest to make sure she knew where she was, in case the opportunity for escape presented itself. She was not over familiar with this area between Bath and Bristol, but she had certainly been to Newton St. Loe with her parents a few years ago, for they had been friendly with the family who lived at Newton Park.

"There is no point looking out of the window like that," Lord Steyne said. "You do not know where I am taking you."

How interesting! So Miss Steele had not admitted to Lord Steyne that she had made a blunder and revealed to Kitty she was to be married in Brislington. Kitty stored this nugget of information away. It might indicate that Miss Steele feared Lord Steyne. What sort of hold did he have over her? Was it purely for money that she was helping him? Or could she have feelings for him? Surely not! The man treated women abominably, and his sneering, contemptuous expression was both repugnant and fixed.

Yet, for all that, he was rich and held a high position in society – thus, to some at least, he was desirable. Poor, silly Miss Steele.

The carriage raced on and on, and the sky outside darkened. Surely there was a storm brewing? Kitty reckoned that at this pace they would be in Brislington before the next hour was up. Should she try to slow the journey? Create a diversion? Revert to her idea of screaming and ranting? But no. All that would mean was a large spoonful of laudanum for her. She must stay alert, she must stay positive – and she must trust that true love would conquer all.

They passed the turning for Saltford on the right, travelling further until they reached the turning for Keynsham. Then Lord Steyne rapped on the roof of the carriage with his stick to indicate a change of direction.

Kitty's heart fluttered like a caged bird. Were they perhaps going to Keynsham? Would she be married in Keynsham? Had Miss Steele mentioned Brislington on purpose, just in case Kitty managed to get a message to Henry and Carter? Was she that devious?

"We've made good time," Lord Steyne said. "We will drop into Keynsham. Horses need water, and I could do with a drink before I shackle myself with the holy bonds of matrimony again. My last try was an unmitigated disaster – wretched girl never produced an heir, and now she's dead – good riddance!"

What a way to speak of his poor dead wife! What she must have suffered. But thank goodness this was merely a quick stop in Keynsham – and it seemed that Brislington was still the intended final destination. Perhaps the slight delay would even give Henry a chance to get there before them?

Kitty bit her lip. She must not be overly optimistic about this. The chance that Henry had managed to see her clothes hanging out of the windows or find her discarded cap on the ground, meet Martha and learn she was to be married in Brislington, was only a remote possibility.

But even a remote possibility was better than the thought of being sacrificed that day to the evil Lord Steyne.

Once they arrived in Keynsham, Lord Steyne ordered the driver to take the carriage into the courtyard at the back of the local tavern, The Condemned Man.

"Get some water for my horses," Lord Steyne ordered a servant who had come out to greet them. "Look sharp! We do not have much time."

The servant scuttled away.

"And in case you had any thoughts of escaping," Lord Steyne said to Kitty, "my driver will sit with you while I go inside. He is under strict instructions not to allow you to leave the carriage for any reason."

"But perhaps some water," Miss Steele said, "for myself and Miss Kitty? And if we should need the ladies' retiring room?"

"You're not getting anything," Lord Steyne said. "'Tis too dangerous for you to be seen inside – and no drink of water means no need for the ladies' retiring room, doesn't it?"

Then with a raucous laugh, he went through the back door of the tavern and reappeared about five minutes later, wiping his foamy mouth on his sleeve and smelling of ale.

As the carriage made its way back to the main road for the last leg of the journey, Lord Steyne let out a long, low burp. There was no indication that he thought he was in the presence of ladies, for no apology followed. The man was disgusting – in both manners and conduct.

And how interesting that he had begun to treat Miss Steele with the same careless disregard as he had treated Kitty since her abduction.

"I don't like the way you're eyeing me, missy," Lord Steyne said to Kitty.

Heavens! The man might be a brute – but he was observant.

"Get those rags out of your reticule again, Miss Steele. We might have to tie this one's hands behind her back again and use the gag. We'll see if it's necessary!"

Miss Steele opened her reticule and brought out the rags. Kitty could see a small bottle in there and a teaspoon.

"Ha!" Lord Steyne said. "See you've spotted the laudanum. Not an empty threat. If we need to pacify you, we will."

"If I am drugged – unconscious even – with laudanum," Kitty said, "I believe the marriage ceremony will not be able to be undertaken."

"Possibly not," Lord Steyne said, "but perhaps thinking of Mrs. Honeyfield will make you behave. You want things to go well for her, don't you?"

"Of course." Kitty lowered her eyes meekly, a shiver going through her spine.

She turned her head to look at Miss Steele, and their eyes met for a split second. What was that? Could Kitty see sympathy in those eyes – after everything Miss Steele had done, was she now having her regrets? Only time would tell!

Hurry, Henry, hurry my love! For I have such desperate need of you.

CHAPTER TWELVE

Henry

HENRY SOON CAUGHT up with the others and galloped alongside Carter at the front of the group of men.

"Thank God you found me," Henry said. "How did you know I would be at the Cottage Crescent?"

"'Twas a lucky break," Carter said. "Thanks for sending your friend George. When he reached me at Beechen Cliff, I was already much recovered and about to make my way into Bath to get reinforcements. We travelled into the city together on foot – running as much as we could."

Carter probably ran all the way – despite his sore head – for he was fighting fit and as brave and determined as any man Henry had ever encountered. George would doubtless have had to exert himself severely to keep up with Henry's manservant – no, to keep up with his *uncle*!

"Everyone was generous with their time and horses," Carter continued, "Mr. Honeyfield and Lord Templeton insisted on joining our army. Brave men, for despite their age, they are as determined to help Kitty as we are."

Henry gave thanks to the Almighty for Carter!

"And as for how we knew about the Cottage Crescent, well, we were lucky," said Carter. "One of the men we talked to had information. He knew Lord Steyne owned a house there."

"How did he know that?" Henry asked.

"He was embarrassed to say at first," Carter said, "but when he understood the gravity of the situation and that it was imperative we must learn all we could about Lord Steyne, he began to be more forthcoming. Said he had actually visited the house once – attended one of Lord Steyne's all-night gambling parties there."

"I have heard about those," Henry said. "I never received an invitation, though, or knew where they were."

"Just as well," Carter said, "for Lord Steyne fleeced all the young men who went there. He plied them with drink and then played them at cards – must have been like stealing from infants."

"We know he cheats at cards," Henry said.

"Definitely," Carter said, "but such behaviour is always notoriously difficult to prove. Anyway, once the young man had been there, he never wanted to go back. What he saw that night truly appalled him. The way women were treated, how much blunt he lost at the cards . . ."

"I know someone who can help us expose the cheating," Henry said. "My friend George – with us today – has been a victim of Lord Steyne's."

"Tell me more!"

"George was always the best of us at cards in my set – he has a real skill. He says he can prove Lord Steyne cheats, if he has the possibility of another game with him. He will need back up, as things could turn nasty – and dangerous."

"It will be my pleasure to arrange such an opportunity," Carter said.

"And we need to find Mrs. Honeyfield, too," Henry said. "She needs releasing from Doctor Voss's asylum."

"Indeed," Carter said. "It must be done swiftly, after we release Kitty."

How wonderful that Carter said *after* we release Kitty, not *if*.

Although I know in my heart that it is by no means certain that we will succeed in this task.

"I am overwhelmed," Henry said, "by the great kindness of all the people here."

He turned his head behind him and scrutinized the faces of the men following – merciful heavens! The men in the pack behind him included friends from childhood and from his university days – and there was a substantial number of his army friends too, as many of them had been granted leave and were visiting Bath for the season.

Henry had never felt such camaraderie in his life! Several of the men smiled broadly – one gave him a thumbs up sign, another waved . . . of course! They were expressing their great joy that he was alive! There would be such a lot of catching up to do after this adventure.

Henry's heart was beating fast, keeping pace with the rhythm of the horses' hooves. Passers-by stared at the strange assembly in amazement, for it was not usual to see a large group of men travelling at such speed.

"We will have to stop at some point," George said, coming up alongside Carter and Henry. "The horses need a drink – and it might be better if we changed horses too, for Trigger in particular is exhausted."

"There is no time to change horses," Carter said. "We need to ride flat out to Brislington. But we will stop for water soon, I promise."

George pulled back to join the other men behind, and Henry and Carter continued to lead the motley army. On and on they went, under a darkling sky. There was a storm brewing, for sure. Hopefully this would not make their task more difficult – but who knew? Weather was important in a battle but did not always have the impact expected.

The official version of the Duke of Wellington's defeat of Napoleon at Waterloo was that Wellington was a superior strategist – and the English soldiers and their allies were more skilled and infinitely braver. However, Henry had heard other theories too, from many experienced soldiers. The weather at the battle had been very unusual for summer – cold, driving rain – and some whispered that these inclement conditions had hampered communications for Napoleon in particular so severely that the weather was a real factor in his defeat.

'Twas strange what you thought about when you were hell-bent in pursuit of a fiend like Lord Steyne! And there was yet another matter that demanded Henry's attention.

"When this is all over," Henry said to Carter, "you will need to explain a certain matter."

"What matter?"

"'Tis no good trying to play games. You know what you said to me at Beechen Cliff – that you are my uncle. You have at last revealed your secret."

Carter flashed a grin. "I thought it was about time you knew. Naturally I intend to discuss the matter with you again when I can, but this cannot be before I have talked to Lady Templeton."

"I understand," Henry said.

And perhaps Lord Templeton, who was at that very moment riding behind Carter, might need to be consulted. Did he know that Carter was his wife's half-brother? Henry bit his lip. There was something he had said once – what was it? Oh yes, when they had been in the parlour at the Royal Crescent and Carter had stood at the side of the room, Lady Templeton had urged him to sit down. Carter had insisted on going down to the kitchen instead, and once he had left the room, Lord Templeton had said,

"He's a treasured servant and saved the life of our dear son, but he isn't part of our family – and never will be."

Lord Templeton must know then, that Carter *was* part of the family. But why would he not want to acknowledge him? Why would he say he wasn't part of the family? Ah! It would make sense if Carter was not of legitimate descent. Yes! Of course! That must be the reason he was not able to be formally introduced as Henry's uncle. And had not Henry's mother once alluded to a baby born out of wedlock, many years ago now? There must be a sad story behind all this – and Henry would make it his business to find out what it was and, if possible, give Carter the family acceptance he so richly deserved.

For if it had not been for Carter, Henry would have perished during the terrible events of last summer – and if it had not been for Carter, 'twas doubtful whether this band of men would have been racing to stop the forced marriage between Kitty and Lord Steyne. The Templetons and Honeyfields owed Carter an enormous debt. There must be a real effort made to repay it.

And what had Lord and Lady Templeton thought when Carter followed Henry to war but did not return? Why, they must have thought Carter had also perished . . . or had Carter not told them where he was going, but had perhaps concocted some tale about having to be away for some time travelling on personal business?

"You're thinking too much," Carter said. "Concentrate on the task in hand!"

"I will try," Henry said. "And we need to work out some sort of plan for when we get to the church in Brislington."

George came up alongside Henry and Carter again. "The horses need water."

Carter nodded his assent, and within minutes they stopped at a cottage by the side of the road to ask for help. A strong country woman brought out bucket after bucket of water – and was then presented with a good deal of money from Lord Templeton and effusive praise from Mr. Honeyfield and Henry.

"I tell you what," Lord Templeton said to the assembled men, "it might be better if those of us more advanced years – by which I mean Mr. Honeyfield and myself – might let you young men gallop on ahead. I am willing to swap my horse with one of you young blades if it would help. He's a fine stallion, and it takes a lot to tire him out."

"Very kind," Carter said. "Henry, you should allow Trigger to have a break, for I know George has been worried about his pride and joy."

George nodded. "Thank you."

"That's settled then," Lord Templeton said. "I will swap my horse for Trigger, and Mr. Honeyfield and myself will follow on, but at a more leisurely pace. The last thing we want to do is slow you down."

This seemed a good plan, for Mr. Honeyfield was looking gray and drawn, clearly suffering from lack of sleep and extreme anxiety. Lord Templeton was sweating profusely, mopping his face with his handkerchief and breathing a little more heavily than usual. Thank the Lord the rest of the crew were younger – many of them had army training – and the horses in the main were fine and strong, in peak condition.

"Have you seen anyone of significance today on this road?" Carter asked the woman who had brought out the buckets of water for the horses. "A fine large carriage with four horses?"

"I ain't seen nothing," the woman said, "for I'm no busybody. Got my work to do – no time to spy on the road."

"Not a question of being a busybody or spy, madam," Lord Templeton. "There is a young woman who has been abducted," – he glanced at the coin purse still in his hand – "and we would all be immensely grateful for any information."

"Well, why didn't you say straight away?" the woman said. "A young woman being abducted – that ain't right. As it happens, I was upstairs doing some household chores earlier – have to keep my own house tidy before I go to clean up at the hospital nearby – and saw out of the window a carriage with an S on the side."

Henry gasped. Lord Steyne's carriage!

"What else did you see?" Lord Templeton asked.

"Was it travelling fast?" Carter said.

"Going like the clappers it was. I remember thinking they must be in a tearing hurry."

"Could you see inside the coach?" Henry asked.

"'Twas too fast to see much, but there was a lady in there, dressed in white and yellow with a bonnet. And two other people."

"We need to go," Carter said. "Quickly!"

Henry took Lord Templeton's stallion, and the younger men in the party set off in the direction of Brislington.

"We will not be far behind," Lord Templeton shouted after them. "Although I might take a small detour, as I have a hunch. . ."

It was good to have had it confirmed that Lord Steyne had indeed passed by – but it made the whole situation more real and raw. Henry urged Lord Templeton's stallion on. Faster! They must go faster!

Kitty, my darling! I am on my way . . . how I wish these words could fly to you and bring you comfort.

Kitty

I must be going mad! For I think I can hear H's voice saying he is on his way. But 'tis only the wind – and my imagination. There is no one near us, and the carriage is slowing down.

"Look lively, girl," Lord Steyne said. "Get out of the carriage! We are here now. St. Luke's, Brislington. Your wedding venue, my dear Miss Honeyfield."

Miss Steele held Kitty's elbow tightly as she descended, and then the driver immediately grabbed her firmly by her other arm. There was to be no escape – at least for now.

The chill wind blew through Kitty's fine muslin dress, and dismal raindrops fell on her bonnet, but she did not care. There was no physical discomfort she would not put up with in order to save her mama. And there was still the hope that Henry would reach her in time, was there not?

"Ah, vicar," Lord Steyne said. "There you are!"

An obsequious robed individual bowed deeply to Lord Steyne.

"This way, if you please, Lord Steyne – and I see this is the blushing bride."

Blushing bride? Victim of a forced marriage, more like! And did the vicar not think it bizarre that the bridegroom had arrived with the bride? The vicar looked depressingly weak – and foolish. Kitty scrutinized the clergyman from underneath her lashes. Sadly, on close inspection, her impression of him was confirmed. He did not look like the sort of person who would care much whether the correct wedding protocol was observed, but seemed totally in thrall to Lord Steyne, bowing and scraping in the most loathsome fashion. How disappointing it was when a man of the cloth was found to be so lacking in human decency and fellow feeling.

The unusual wedding party walked across the wet grass and moss-covered flagstones to the church door. Could Kitty make a run for it? Twist out of Lord Steyne's grip and sprint away through the graveyard? But how far did she think she would get before the driver caught her? And, more to the point, what would be her mama's fate if she refused to enter the church? No, the only option was to keep marching on. And pray for victory.

Once inside the church, there was a small group of people in the front pew on the left – they stood and bowed to Lord Steyne. These must be the parish clerk and the two obligatory witnesses, no doubt all paid handsomely for their services that day.

Lord Steyne walked down the aisle while exchanging words with the vicar, and Kitty was left with Miss Steele and the driver near the baptismal font.

Inside, St. Luke's was of a traditional design, with arches supporting the barrel-shaped roof over the nave. Kitty fixed her eyes on the bright jewel colours in the stained glass windows above the altar. What she wouldn't give to be up there looking down on the scene, instead of living this nightmare.

The rain lashed down outside with an insistent drumbeat, *ta dum, ta dum, ta dum.*

"Like a march to the scaffold," Kitty muttered.

"What was that?" Miss Steele said.

"Nothing!"

"Lord, you are not going to be difficult, are you? I thought we had got all that out of the way. You should know what a lucky young woman you are to be marrying Lord Steyne. Once the ceremony is over, you will not have to worry about money for the rest of your life."

Kitty's eyes flashed with anger. "You know full well why I am agreeing to this travesty of a marriage. I am a hostage for my mother – I am giving my body in exchange for Mama's return to normal life. Is it likely I would betray my own mother?"

"No," Miss Steele said, "for I know how much you love your mama."

"You know? What can you know of love or feelings, you contemptible creature! You have betrayed me and my parents."

Miss Steele flushed beetroot. Could this be shame? Embarrassment? Was it possible Miss Steele was repenting of her part in this sham?

Miss Steele linked her arm firmly through Kitty's. "'Tis too late for regrets," she said. "We must proceed as arranged."

"I will be outside," the driver said. "I need to look at the horses – but don't worry. No one will enter – or leave – without my say so."

"Ready," Lord Steyne called from the top of the aisle. "Proceed!

This was a world away from the idyllic wedding day bursting with love, family, and friends that Kitty had often dreamt of. Where was the romance? The music, happiness, flowers, and bridesmaids? Kitty had always wanted Selina to be her chief bridesmaid.

Oh, where was H?

Hurry my love! There is still time. Are you on your way?

Kitty bit her lip to stop the tears falling as Miss Steele more or less dragged her up the aisle and pushed her towards Lord Steyne before flopping down in the nearest pew.

"Dearly beloved," the vicar intoned.

Beloved? There were only a few people in the whole world Kitty would address as beloved – and none of them were in that church.

"We are gathered here together in the sight of God . . ."

God! Where are you? How can you allow this to be happening to me?

". . . to join together this man and this woman . . ."

Bile rose from Kitty's stomach at the thought of being joined in a physical way to the monster beside her. How would she be able to bear it? But she would have to, if her mama was going to be saved.

". . . an honorable estate . . ."

And now Kitty felt like laughing hysterically.

Where was the honor in what was happening? What a mockery! The giggles rising up from deep inside Kitty threatened to overwhelm her at the thought of the two different uses of the word "estate."

"Are you quite well, Miss Honeyfield?" the vicar inquired.

"Perfectly," Kitty said. "It's just the thought of the 'honorable estate' and Lord Steyne's 'estate' – which Miss Steele thinks it would be an honor to be mistress of. Two kinds of estate – quite different things. Ah! The absurdity! Oh, never mind. You must excuse me."

Kitty bent doubled with the effort of suppressing her unaccountable giggles and started to wheeze. "Cannot . . . help it . . ."

"Do you wish me to proceed?" the vicar asked Lord Steyne.

"Of course, man!" he said. "'Tis merely a young woman's hysteria as she contemplates the joy of her wedding day. Such innocent naïveté! Quite charming. We all know what the female of the species is like – they have a very poor grip on their emotions."

But at least the female of the species has emotions – which you do not! How I hate you, Lord Steyne!

Lord Steyne gripped Kitty's shoulder and hissed in her ear, "This had better not be one of your tricks, missy. Pull yourself together! Think of your mother – that bitch – as I have had to think of her all these years married to your father."

"Trying to . . ."

Kitty's giggles turned into hiccups. Then the giggles transformed from hiccups to a coughing fit, until at last the dam burst and she sobbed piteously, tears streaming down her face.

Kitty wiped her face with the back of her hands until Miss Steele passed her a handkerchief. After a few seconds, Kitty turned to face the vicar. "I am ready. You may proceed."

"I cannot," the vicar said. "I have grave doubts about the wisdom of this match. I cannot believe it would be right to proceed."

Could this be happening? The vicar must have a conscience after all.

The vicar slammed his prayer book shut, whereupon Lord Steyne leant forward and growled something unintelligible in his ear. The vicar frowned – then nodded and opened the book again – and continued the service in a more subdued voice.

". . . therefore is not by any to be enterprised . . . unadvisedly, lightly or wantonly, to satisfy men's carnal lusts and appetites, like brute beasts that have no understanding . . ."

What had Lord Steyne said to intimidate the priest? And was no one listening to the words of the service? What a travesty! Lord Steyne was nothing *but* a brute beast. He considered that his carnal lusts and appetites must be satisfied at all times without any regard to the effect this might have on others.

But why was Lord Steyne so determined to proceed with this marriage? What was it he had just said to Kitty? In between her hysterical giggles and before she moved on to the embarrassing hiccups, coughing fit, and hot, shameful tears? *"Think of your mother – that bitch – as I have had to think of her all these years married to your father."*

There was a clue there. Lord Steyne had called her mama – her darling mama! – a bitch. He must hate her. But how long had he known her? And why did he hate her?

Kitty must think – and quickly! What had Lord Steyne done?

Well, he had encouraged Mr. Honeyfield to gamble. And to make sure Mr. Honeyfield lost heavily and frequently, Lord Steyne had probably cheated in every card game with him until the Honeyfield fortune dwindled alarmingly.

Lord Steyne was therefore responsible for all the measures Mr. Honeyfield had to take to save money – including having to curtail Doctor Jenkins's visits, even though Kitty's mama was in desperate need of proper medical attention.

Then Lord Steyne decided he would take Kitty from her parents, which would be easier now because Mr. Honeyfield needed Kitty to marry someone rich. Mrs. Honeyfield's nerves were in tatters after witnessing her husband on a downward spiral, thus she was less likely to have any real influence over her husband – and Kitty's marriage prospects.

And Lord Steyne had tried to make an end to Henry's life after stumbling across him on the battlefield – because Henry stood in the way of Lord Steyne's desire to marry Kitty.

Kitty had no doubt Lord Steyne intended to treat her as shamefully as he had treated his first wife, whose life had apparently been a misery after her marriage.

But why *did* Lord Steyne hate Kitty's mama? And why would he want to destroy the happiness of the entire Honeyfield family?

Mama has never said she knew Lord Steyne before he took an interest in me. This is in truth a complex mystery, and I am nearly out of time. God help me!

"... therefore, if any man can show any just cause why they may not be lawfully joined together, let him now speak ..."

Henry

The pounding of horses' hooves was followed by a shout of protest from the driver, then the ancient oak door of St. Luke's was flung open, and Henry, Carter, and all the rest of the men ran down the aisle.

". . . or else hereafter forever hold his peace," the vicar said.

"Stop!" Henry shouted. "The marriage cannot go ahead! Miss Honeyfield is being forced to marry this swine against her will."

Carter grabbed Lord Steyne by the arms and pulled him to the side with a great roar of righteous anger. "Monster! Your vile plot has been foiled."

Henry and Kitty flew into each others' arms for a tender embrace.

"My darling!" Henry whispered. "Thank goodness we arrived in time. I dread to think . . ."

"Oh, Henry!" Kitty said. "How I love you!"

"No time for all that," Carter said, holding back the struggling Lord Steyne.

"No need for it," Lord Steyne yelled, "for Miss Honeyfield has agreed to be my wife."

"Only because you put me in an impossible position," Kitty said. "Why, you not only abducted me, but also my mother."

"Mrs. Lydia Honeyfield will be returned when you are my bride." Lord Steyne leered, displaying yellow fangs.

"I do not suppose this marriage you have planned is even legal!" Henry pointed at the clergyman. "Are you a real vicar?"

"Of course I'm a real vicar!"

"And the marriage will be legal," Miss Steele said. "Lord Steyne obtained a special licence some time ago in readiness. There is nothing he would not do for Miss Honeyfield."

"Nothing except treat her with any decency and kindness," Carter said.

"I repeat, Miss Honeyfield has agreed to be my wife," Lord Steyne said. "She has to go through with it. Indeed, she has said she wants to go through with it, so that Mrs. Honeyfield may be cured and returned to her home."

"Why you are doing this?" Kitty said. "Release my mama from the asylum! You have no choice. Not now Henry is here."

"I will not release her!" Lord Steyne said. "Mrs. Honeyfield was taken to hospital by Doctor Voss because she was in severe need of medical attention. I have been kind enough to arrange this – and to pay for the treatment. She will stay there until she is better – and I have married you, Miss Honeyfield."

"There is more to this than meets the eye," Henry said.

"I agree." Kitty stood directly in front of Lord Steyne and glared at him. "What is it you have against my mother? Something from your past – I am sure of it."

Carter tightened his grip on Lord Steyne and hissed, "I am wondering if Mrs Honeyfield rejected you many years ago. Why else would you attempt to destroy the Honeyfields' happiness and that of those close to them? You have been motivated by revenge – and hatred."

"Not true!" Lord Steyne yelled. "I have been motivated by love. 'Twas not my fault that it did not work out in the way I had intended . . ."

"Love?" Kitty said. "You do not know the meaning of the word."

"Ah, but that is where you are wrong," Lord Steyne said. "I will explain. As a young man I saw your mother at a ball in London. She was the most beautiful lady there, and I instantly desired to possess her."

"How dare you disrespect the Honeyfield family," Carter shouted. "I've got a good mind to thrash you."

"No disrespect was intended," Lord Steyne said, "for when I said I wanted to possess her, I meant I wanted to make her Lady Steyne."

"Let the man finish his speech," Henry said. "We all need to remain calm, to get to the truth. Now, pray continue, Lord Steyne. What stopped you courting Mrs. Honeyfield in the proper manner?"

"Mr. Honeyfield sneaked in before me," Lord Steyne whined, "and convinced the beautiful Lydia – that's Mrs. Honeyfield to you! – that she was in love with him, and he with her. Then I heard they had married and moved to Bath."

"Wait!" Henry said. "Did Mrs. Honeyfield even know of your feelings for her?"

Lord Steyne hung his head. "No, she did not. I never even spoke to my Lydia – not once. I was young and shy, and missed my chance. She ruined my life – the bitch!"

By Jove! Lord Steyne was one hellishly disturbed individual. How preposterous to blame someone who never even knew him! And through countless years, his jealousy had festered and resulted in the total havoc of the last six months. A veritable Gordian knot!

"In case you are wondering," Lord Steyne said to Henry, "I did not actively seek you out on the battlefield. I was there with other members of the *ton*. "Twas quite an adventure to see the aftermath of a great battle, and I enjoyed it immensely!"

The man was revolting!

"Anyway, I could not believe my luck when I came across your corpse, or what I thought was your corpse. I was delighted to think that your life was extinct. There would be no rival for Kitty's affections now and I would be free to woo her and make her my wife. This would be the final piece of my plan to rip the heart out of the Honeyfield family."

Henry balled his fists but kept a grip on his emotions. He had seen too much violence at war to know it solved nothing. And he was not going to succumb to aggressive behaviour in peacetime, however tempted he felt.

But oh, the temptation I'm feeling to knock the man's teeth out right now in front of everyone! However, I will be civilized, for only then will this creature give us a truthful account of his misdeeds...

"Imagine my surprise," Lord Steyne said, "when I realized your life was hanging on by a thread – for I saw your eyelashes flutter and your wounded shoulder twitch. I did not reveal to my friends that I had noticed you were alive, nor that I had recognized you, but walked on further with them. After a while, I made an excuse to turn back, saying I had dropped a glove and would catch up with them later."

"Then you dragged me away by my feet," Henry said. "Why didn't you kill me straight away?"

"Because he's a coward!" Kitty said.

"I preferred the thought of a slow death," Lord Steyne said, "and decided to let nature take its course – with a helping hand."

Attempted murder! Lord Steyne had admitted it.

"You must tell them about us, Lord Steyne!" Miss Steele jumped up from the pew. "'Tis time."

"Time for what?" he said. "I will still marry Miss Honeyfield – for otherwise Mrs. Honeyfield will not be returning."

"That's enough!" the vicar said. "I've put up with as much as I can take from you, Lord Steyne. This is wrong. And evil. You have committed dreadful crimes – or tried to. I no longer care what you will do to me. I am leaving!"

The vicar tucked his service book under his arm and ran to the side of the altar, and then escaped out of the back of the church.

George started off in pursuit, but Carter said, "No, leave him be. There is no point in pursuit; he can cause no further harm."

Miss Steele approached Lord Steyne, hands clasped in front as if begging. "You still have me! And things will be better for us now."

"What do you mean?" Henry said.

"Lord Steyne said if I helped him marry Miss Kitty, he would take me as his mistress and set me up in the Cottage Crescent," Miss Steele said. "There, I would live like a lady. He said he loved me, not Miss Kitty, but the world would not understand, and so it would be better if he married her and took me as his mistress."

"You are deluded, madam," Lord Steyne said. "Did you seriously think I meant any of that?"

"I know you meant it!" Miss Steele cried. "I know you love me, and now that it looks as if your marriage to Miss Kitty will not go ahead, the way is clear for you to marry me."

"Love you? Marry you? Are you out of your mind? A lord

does not marry the companion of Miss Kitty Honeyfield."

The blood slowly drained from Miss Steele's face, and she swayed to one side then gently crumpled to the floor.

"She has fainted!" Kitty said, rushing to her side. "Miss Steele!"

There was no end to Kitty's compassion. She could even feel sorry for the woman who had helped to abduct her. Kitty was an outstandingly Christian woman. Why, Henry almost felt sorry for Miss Steele himself. Almost.

Miss Steele lay on the ground now, sobbing.

"Snake! Traitor!" she whimpered. "And I didn't even like that vile over-sized brooch you gave me! Too, too hideous!"

Suddenly, Lord Steyne took the opportunity to wrestle free from Carter's grasp and made off down a side aisle.

"Quick," Carter said. "He mustn't get away – not until we have found out where Mrs. Honeyfield is being held."

"She is here!" Lord Templeton was standing in the doorway with Mr. Honeyfield beside him – and Mrs. Honeyfield.

Every head in the church swivelled round to gaze at the apparition and gasps of astonishment bounced off stone walls and pillars.

Uttering the foulest of curses, Lord Steyne slipped through the rear door before anyone could stop him. He was surprisingly nimble for a man of his age and size.

"Mama!" Kitty ran to her mother and embraced her. "We have all been out of our minds with worry!"

"But how?" Henry said. "How did you find out where the hospital was?"

"'Twas something the woman mentioned when we stopped earlier to let the horses drink," Lord Templeton said. "She said she would be going on later to work in the hospital. Once you and the others had set off again, I asked her which hospital it was. As I had suspected, it was the one run by Doctor Voss and – well, the rest you can guess."

"We were lucky," Mr. Honeyfield said, "for we did not have

to travel far, and I am pleased to say that I found my dear wife in tolerable health. A little confused and anxious, admittedly, but nothing that a good rest and proper medical care will not be able to correct."

"Doctor Voss seemed reluctant to allow his patient to leave," Lord Templeton said, "but I managed to persuade him. In the end, he even lent us his coach and horses so that we could bring Mrs. Honeyfield here comfortably."

Henry grinned. "There is much more to this story than you are telling me. I shall enjoy hearing about it at a later date."

Then he turned and faced everyone. "But now, I would like it to be known that in the early hours of this morning, I asked dear Kitty to be my wife – and she accepted. And what is more, I think we should be married as soon as possible. What say you, Kitty? A Christmas wedding?"

I can scarce believe how things have turned out! Our enemies have been defeated – and now at last I can take my Kitty in my arms without wearing a silly disguise or skulking in the shadows.

CHAPTER THIRTEEN

Kitty

T HE NEXT DAY, Kitty woke in her own bed after an exceptionally long sleep. For a moment, she had almost thought she
was still in that attic room in the Cottage Crescent. Then she
stretched her hands over her head and gave a huge sigh of
satisfaction.

Mrs. Honeyfield put her head round the door of Kitty's
chamber.

"Mama!" Kitty propped herself up on her elbows. "You
should not be out of bed. I should be looking after you."

"I am fine," Mrs. Honeyfield said. "I feel better than I have for
a long, long time and have come to tell you that there is a certain
young man waiting for you downstairs in the parlour; he has
brought a large bouquet of flowers."

Mrs. Honeyfield smiled her sweet smile, and Kitty knew her
mama was on the road to recovery.

"I will go to rest in my room now," Mrs. Honeyfield said, "for
I do feel a little fatigued with all the excitement. Henry has
already spoken to your father in his study about a certain matter –
and he has given his blessing."

Kitty chuckled. "I believe Henry should not have said we
were getting married before he had spoken to Papa."

"The circumstances were exceptional," Mrs. Honeyfield said.

"I think that once in a while, it does us good to break away from convention. Besides, 'tis very romantic, is it not? Such wonderful news, Kitty – I am thrilled for you! Henry is a fine young man, and you both deserve every happiness."

Kitty hurried into her clothes and flew down the stairs to see Henry in the parlour.

"Kitty! How are you this fine morning?" Henry pressed his lips to hers before she could reply and they kissed passionately, clinging to each other like sailors after a shipwreck.

"Henry! I cannot believe all that has happened . . . love truly has conquered all."

"My Kitty!" Henry said, then covered her face with light butterfly kisses.

"I cannot wait to be your wife," Kitty said. "'Tis all I have ever wanted!"

"Yes, about that," Henry said. "I have talked to your father and . . ."

"He has given his consent," Kitty said laughing. "Mama has told me. Papa bitterly regrets allowing that man into our house to woo me and now considers him a blot upon the English landscape."

"As do we all," Henry said. "But we will not talk of Lord Steyne – instead, let us look to the future. I have also talked at length to my own papa, and he has made it possible for me to travel to London and obtain a special licence from the ecclesiastical court. Luckily, the Archbishop of Canterbury happens to be an old schoolfriend of Papa's."

"How convenient!"

"Indeed! For it means we will be able to marry on Christmas Eve, if that date suits?"

"The ideal day!" Kitty said. "And wonderful news! But how long will you be gone for? How long must I face life without you while you are off on your jaunt to London?"

"A week," Henry said, "for I must talk to the army again too. I have finally decided I would like to resign my commission and seek employment elsewhere. But what say you, Kitty? For I will only do this with your blessing."

"I fully support you. You have done your duty to the army – some would say more than your duty."

"Thank you. I have not yet decided what I should do next to earn my living, although, although . . ."

"Go on," Kitty said, "for it sounds as if you have thought of something."

"I have wondered about the law."

"Law?" Kitty said. "Lord! You will have to wear a wig when you are at work. This will suit you well, for I know how much you love dressing up – especially as John Greenwood."

"Yes, a wig! 'Tis very old-fashioned . . . but no need to tease me about dressing up, for that is definitively one of your hobbies too. Darling Kitty, you looked so adorable in your breeches and shirt when you came to me at Beechen Cliff."

Ah! That wonderful time when Kitty had run across Bath to be with her H. And then, in the kitchen, Henry had taken her in his arms, even though she was wet through from the rain. He did not seem to mind she was wearing old clothes from the bottom of her closet at home.

And her hair! What a sight that must have been. H had gently lifted the cap from her head – her dishevelled curls must surely have resembled a badly constructed bird's nest. Shocking! And yet Henry accepted her as she was – more than that, he trembled – with love, Kitty felt sure. For did he not straightaway go down on bended knee and propose marriage?

"Kitty!" Henry said. "I have such fond memories of our time in that kitchen."

Kitty put her arms tightly round Henry. She would never forget H's proposal. It was the most romantic moment of her whole life.

"Darling H," she murmured. "Never in a thousand years would I have imagined a proposal like that – and yet it was totally and utterly perfect."

"I am glad I did not disappoint," Henry said.

Henry will never disappoint me – of that I am certain.

The pair clung to each other wordlessly for some time, before Kitty broke away and said, "Tell me more about wanting to be a lawyer. I promise not to make flippant remarks about wigs or get side-tracked with memories of your proposal. Explain to me, if you can, what is drawing you to this profession."

"My reasoning might sound over-worthy," Henry said. "Pompous, even."

"I am sure it will not. Be honest – tell me what is in your mind and heart."

"Well," Henry said, "our recent experiences have highlighted for me the opposing forces of good and evil – right and wrong."

"We have encountered both in great quantities, that is true."

"And I have been reminded how much we need the law to be strong and fair – we need to encourage men and women to behave. And there needs to be a just system in place – and people to help when things go wrong and crimes are committed."

"Laudable aims," Kitty said. "I agree with you on all points – and would consider it a privilege to support you in your work in whatever way might suit."

"We will make a fine team. For the moment, the law is just an idea, no more, and of course I need to talk to Papa about it – but I believe I could make an impact in that field of work. And that is important to me – to make a difference." Henry wrinkled his nose. "Told you it would sound pompous! Lord! You will think me very dull if I go on like this all the time! Maybe I will not go for law at all but will play my violin round the streets of Bath and beg for farthings to buy my crust."

"Nonsense," Kitty said. "You could never be dull. And I will always be proud of you, Henry, whatever you do."

"Thank you. As I of you. But now I have a question."

Kitty raised an eyebrow.

"Will you be able to live without me for one week while I travel to London to obtain the special licence? What say you,

Kitty?"

"Ah, that will be difficult. I must ask myself whether I am fully up to the task." Kitty tilted her head to one side, then smiled. "As long as you promise to hurry back, I do believe there is a strong possibility I will survive. Now, please sit down. You look as handsome as ever, my darling H – but you also look tired. Did you sleep well last night?"

"I confess that Edmund and I sat up longer than we should have – there was much to talk about. And I was a little anxious about asking your father for your hand, and thus spent a restless night."

"Never mind. Coffee will revive you! The maid will be bringing a tray very soon."

"Then we had better make the most of the time we have before she comes in. Come, sit next to me on the sofa, Kitty."

Kitty felt suddenly shy as she sat down next to Henry, their thighs touching. Was this man really to be her husband and partner in life? What would marriage be like?

Henry's fingers crept towards Kitty's, then they clasped palms and gazed into each other's eyes.

"I think about you all the time," Henry said softly.

"Me too!" Kitty said.

Everything would be perfect! Henry's rugged hand felt right in hers, his pulse strong and reliable. He would protect her in life, as she would him. They would make their pairing work – for the rest of their lives.

Kitty stood up, then sat down again on Henry's lap, as she had in the Templetons' withdrawing room so recently. He put his arms around her waist, and she laced her fingers through the curls at the back of his head and pulled him gently towards her.

Kissing felt different when one was engaged. 'Twas more like the overture to something special – and deeper. Every nerve in Kitty's lips tingled as she felt Henry's warmth and excitement. She moaned softly, enjoying the intimacy – and the thought of what was yet to come when they were married.

Presently, she pulled away from Henry and sat beside him.

"The maid will be bringing the coffee in soon," she said, "and it would not do . . ."

"Of course," Henry said. "I understand."

And sure enough, three seconds later there was a faint cough followed by a discreet knock at the door, and a maid brought in a silver tray of refreshments together with a cheery expression of approval.

When they were alone again, Henry said, "I have to ask – do you know what will happen to Miss Steele?

"Well, Papa said last night that he felt a little sorry for her. I think we all do."

"You are too good, Kitty," Henry said. "The woman is a menace. If it had not been for her . . ."

"I know how much she helped Lord Steyne – oh, sorry! We said we would not mention his name! But he did deceive her terribly, and she has worked for our family for many years."

"Please tell me she is not still here," Henry said.

"Ah, no," Kitty said. "We all agreed she had to go."

"She will not join Lord Steyne, though?" Henry said.

"No," Kitty said. "She has most definitely seen through him, and last time they were together he was far from friendly."

"Indeed!"

Kitty sighed. "Although there will never be a return to Russell Street for Miss Steele, I am pleased Papa made sure she had somewhere to go and gave her money for the journey – for what would happen to her otherwise, if she was alone and without any means whatsoever?"

"Indeed. 'Tis hard for a woman. You are right to be concerned for her welfare, despite what she has done to your family. So where will she go?"

"To her married sister in Bristol. Miss Steele will join her household to help with the children. She said her sister had been writing to her for some time offering her a home. Perhaps she sensed Miss Steele had got caught up in a difficult situation and was not very happy? We will never know."

"'Tis a good result – and more than she deserves," Henry said. "But Lord Steyne needs to be dealt with. I wanted to chase after him when he ran from the church, but he was away in his carriage with his driver before anyone quite realized what was happening."

"But he did not actually manage to force me to marry him," Kitty said. "Thank goodness you all arrived in time to stop him! He did not, in the end, commit the crime of forced marriage."

"True," Henry said, "although is not abduction a crime?"

Kitty tensed. Her abduction was proving hard to forget. And Henry was right – abduction *was* a crime, and a heinous one, at that. But it happened relatively often, and it seemed the present-day world did not care enough to punish this sort of transgression with a custodial sentence. Especially if it resulted in marriage, which abduction often did. A desperately sad, unwilling marriage, where women suffered greatly. Thank the Lord Kitty had been spared that!

"Attempted murder is definitely a crime," Kitty said. "Lord Steyne did his best to do away with you. If it had not been for Carter, Lord Steyne would have been the direct cause of your death."

"True, but exceptionally hard to prove," Henry said, "especially for one such as Lord Steyne who probably has half the judges up and down the land in his pocket. No, we have to get justice in a different way."

"How?"

"Well, we know Lord Steyne is a cheat at cards and has defrauded many people, including . . ." Henry coughed.

"You can say it," Kitty said. "I know my father has been weak."

"He was taken in, and tricked in the vilest way possible, as were many, many others. However, George and Carter are hatching a plan to expose Lord Steyne as a scoundrel."

"That sounds excellent," Kitty said, "for I would not like

anyone else to fall victim to his tricks."

"If he can be discredited," Henry said, "he will have everyone in the *ton* shunning him; this will be the worst punishment of all for a man to whom his status and position in society is everything."

"Agreed, for he is a man of vanity and worldliness. God willing, his disgrace will mean no lady in England will ever again be encouraged by her family to consider him a worthy matrimonial prospect. Although I fear for the less well-born young women he may exploit in the future."

"Dear Kitty, we cannot solve all the world's ills, although I am determined to do my best to help those less fortunate members of society."

"I understand more now your desire to enter the law," Kitty said. "I myself wish to help the less fortunate, particularly women who have fallen upon hard times through no fault of their own. Dear Henry – together we might be able to start some reforms. We could try to right some injustices."

"A noble aim!"

"Now," Kitty said, "let us turn to lighter subjects."

"Yes, for our conversation is getting ponderous again, and today is a day for much rejoicing. What about this? A play on words for you. Lord Steyne has a high regard for himself, but he is nothing but a stain on society. Kitty! Stain! Lord Steyne? Why are you not amused?"

"I did understand your very feeble joke," Kitty said with a grin, "but thought I would not dignify it by laughing."

"At least we can tease and joke now. There were a few times when I feared the worst. We have been lucky, Kitty dearest."

"In truth, we have! And I will always be grateful to Carter, for you have told me how much he helped you."

"Ah!" Henry said. "Carter! There is much I have to tell you about that man – but it will have to wait until I return from London."

"Intriguing! I will see if I can try and work out what it is before you get back. Perchance he is a highway man in his spare time? Or harbours a desire to run away and join the circus?"

I expect Selina will be glad to explain the mystery to me regarding Carter while my H is away.

"By the way," Henry said, "my mama would like you to accompany her to the opticians in Milsom Street soon, to have an eye test. She is determined you shall have spectacles to use when you read music – and at other times too."

"Very kind of her," Kitty said. "She has already given me the quizzing glass."

"Yes, and you gave it to Martha. Mama says she will also arrange for you to be measured for a quizzing glass made to your exact requirements while you are at the optician."

"How very kind! And you have reminded me about Martha. I think we should offer her alternative employment. She deserves better than the Cottage Crescent."

"'Tis already in hand," Henry said. "As soon as Mama heard about Martha, she wanted to offer her a job at our home. She will arrange it all."

Kitty squeezed Henry's arm gently. She was marrying into such a thoughtful family.

"And of course, Selina says that you can expect to be meeting up with her constantly for the entire week of my absence," Henry said. "You will not be lonely – not for one second."

"Dear Selina," Kitty said. "I cannot wait until she is my sister."

"You two will have a rare time when I am gone," Henry said. "I believe I will hear the giggles from London. Please be careful, though, that she does not lead you astray."

"Lead me astray?"

"I still remember, when you were all but six years old, how my dear sister encouraged you to jump over the edge of the ha-ha at the edge of the Crescent Lawn and you sprained your ankle. You should have said you did not feel confident enough to jump."

Kitty smiled. "I had my reasons for risking my ankle. How was I to know it would go disastrously wrong?"

"Reasons? And what pray, were they?"

"You will be big-headed if I tell you."

"You must tell! Please? I cannot leave without knowing."

"Why, you are very persistent, Henry! But can you not guess?"

"No! Otherwise I would not be asking."

"'Tis simple," Kitty said, "I wanted to impress you. Yes! Even at the age of six, I admired you and wanted you to like me."

Henry threw back his head and chortled. "Excellent! The beginning of a lengthy and successful campaign. You have a lot in common with the Duke of Wellington, I do believe, for he had to wage his campaign over many years before he finally defeated Napoleon. I certainly like you now, Kitty, and admire you immensely. And love you – very, very deeply . . . come here again, my dearest, sweetest . . ."

How intoxicating to be kissed by my soul mate! And I can feel his desire rising, with such promise of what is to come . . .

Henry groaned and buried his face in Kitty's neck. "I am afraid I must be on my way soon, for Carter and I leave this evening, and there is much to do."

"You have not had your coffee yet," Kitty said. "Let me pour it for you."

She carefully lifted the coffee pot decorated with gold swirls and swags of multi-coloured flowers. This was part of a much-loved set of bone china Kitty's parents had been given as a wedding present. 'Twas reserved for special occasions – and important guests, like a future son-in-law.

Kitty poured the fragrant coffee into a delicate matching cup, added cream and sugar, and passed the saucer to her beloved H. Not a drop was split, despite her body trembling with emotion.

"I could get used to this," Henry said, "having you wait on me hand and foot."

"Is that what you think marriage is about?"

"No," Henry said. "It is about all sorts of other things – loving you forever and being one with you. Then, hopefully we will be blessed . . ."

". . . with children! How I look forward to being a mother."

And I look forward to being one with my H, to joining with my husband, and loving him forever.

Henry

Henry's week in London went smoothly. He managed to obtain a special licence so that he and Kitty could be married on Christmas Eve, and he resolved matters with the army authorities, resigning his commission. They thanked him warmly for his service and Henry went on his way with a light heart, feeling more at peace than he had for a long time.

He would never again take his good fortune for granted. There were not many people who could say they had returned from the dead – why, it was almost like being born again, to a new life full of promise and opportunity. Henry would be able to turn his attention to a fresh purpose and career now – with Kitty walking alongside him on life's journey.

One evening shortly after Henry's return to Bath, he attended a ball in the Upper Rooms with Kitty.

Carter and George had done as they had promised and set up a card game with Lord Steyne. He was keeping a very low profile, but they had eventually tracked him down at his lodgings in The Paragon where he had gone to ground to lick his wounds. George issued the invitation without mentioning the Templetons – and Lord Steyne swallowed the bait. He had seemed keen to re-enter society, doubtless thinking the *ton* would have forgiven him his peccadillos by now.

After Kitty and Henry had enjoyed a dance together at the ball, Henry led her to the Octagon card room next to the ballroom, and they stood in the shadows watching George and two other gentlemen playing cards with Lord Steyne. The men were hunched over one of the small wooden tables, glasses of wine resting on the green baize next to ivory counters. Carter was standing with his back to the wall not far from Henry.

It was not long before Lord Steyne gave a cry of triumph.

"I have won! Victory is mine!"

Then George stood up and shouted, "This man is a card shark! Look! Come here everyone! I can prove it."

Carter ran over and secured Lord Steyne's hands behind his back.

"I am getting quite fond of doing this," Carter muttered. "Hold still, man, damn your eyes!"

After a dramatic pause, George leaned forward and whipped three crucial cards out of Lord Steyne's jacket pocket.

"Ladies and gentlemen!" George said. "The missing cards! Moreover, Lord Steyne has been using other fraudulent and perfidious techniques that have long been outlawed amongst respectable gentlemen . . . why, he even started the game dishonourably by dealing the cards improperly, giving himself more than his opponents, and he does not limit himself to cards, but cheats at the dice too. What I could tell you about the way he plays Hazard . . . "

Cries of outrage erupted from all over the Octagon.

"Shocking!"

"Should be horsewhipped! The rogue!"

"Double-crossing rapscallion!"

"Slubberdegullion!"

And there was Selina, in the shadows on the other side of the Octagon. She was staring at George with open admiration. Henry's sister, showing partiality for a young gentleman? This had never happened before. Ah, would it not be sweet if George and Selina . . . but no time to consider that now.

Lord Steyne started to protest his innocence, causing Carter to put his hand over his mouth.

"Each point I am making is backed up by solid evidence," George said, leaning back on his heels as he continued to outline the illegal playing style of the disgraced lord.

"George seems to be having the time of his life," Henry whispered to Kitty. "Seems to think he is a barrister at the high court! But do you understand what he is saying?"

"Not at all," Kitty said. "For I have never played card games like this – only childish games years ago."

"Not over fond of cards myself," Henry said, "therefore I have somewhat lost the thread of what George is saying. But I know it must be true, for look! Everyone is smiling and cheering. There must be many men in this room who have been caught out by Lord Steyne. Now they can all demand their money back. He will be obliged to pay – this is good news for your dear papa."

"And Lord Steyne is permanently disgraced," Kitty said. "I suppose I ought to be angry that the *ton* readily lose their good opinion of a man because he cheats at cards – whereas if a man cheats a woman, they tend to turn a blind eye."

"'Tis not fair nor just," Henry said. "But the *ton* are not always principled, are they? Their approval or otherwise is not a good indication of the absolute right or wrong of a situation."

"True," Kitty said, linking her arm through Henry's. "Let us leave and go back to the ballroom. We will dance – for I do not want Lord Steyne to see us."

"Hopefully we will never see him again," Henry said. "The *ton* have shown their disapproval, and he will not be welcome in Bath. He might have to go and live abroad now, on the Continent – preferably somewhere over-hot and stifling."

"I wish he would go and live in that horrid ditch that he dragged you to," Kitty said. "I will be first in line to cover him with branches and throw some mud on his head."

"The punishment should fit the crime," Henry said. "'Tis exactly what he deserves."

"And did you notice when he started shouting, he opened his mouth so wide you could see some of his back teeth are black with rot?"

"Horrific! Too much sugar! But he is rich," Henry said. "He

will be able to purchase himself a set of Waterloo teeth. There are many fine sets available…"

"Not funny!" Kitty said. "Especially when you think what nearly happened to you. Come on. Let's dance."

Within minutes, Kitty and Henry were back in the ballroom and found their places at the end of the set. It would be some time before it was their turn to dance – the ideal opportunity to catch up.

"How is your mama?" Henry asked.

"She gets better every day," Kitty said. "We suspect her frail state was exacerbated greatly by Miss Steele's inexpertly made narcotic potions. Do you remember I overheard Lord Steyne and Miss Steele talking about 'quantities?' They must have been referring to making up the draughts used to drug poor Mama and make her more pliable. Now she is being treated properly again, under the care of Doctor Jenkins, she is making great strides forward. I must remember to thank your parents for their great generosity in funding Doctor Jenkins's visits."

"We will soon be family," Henry said, "and my parents will not see your parents in any hardship, rest assured."

"Thank you," Kitty said, "and there is good news too about Doctor Voss's establishment, where my mama was taken. Doctor Jenkins is a very influential figure in the world of medicine, and he has managed things in such a way that Doctor Voss, or should I say *Mr.* Voss, has been dismissed for running a very poor and irregular hospital. Another doctor recommended by Doctor Jenkins has taken over, thank the Lord. No longer will the patients be treated badly, but they will have the chance to be cured and sent back to their families. Is that not good news?"

"Certainly is. Ah! At last! Our chance to dance!" Henry's feet flew across the floor. "I say! This rhythm is extremely captivating!"

There was precious little time for conversation until the dance came to a conclusion and Kitty and Henry faced each other again, laughing and somewhat out of breath after their exertions.

"The musicians are playing well this evening," Kitty said. "I once heard a very special violinist here. He is not in the band tonight. I wonder where he might be."

"A mystery!" Henry said. "And I will have you know, when you were dancing with other men and I was John Greenwood playing up there in the musicians' gallery, I was vastly jealous."

"You had no need to be jealous," Kitty said. "You are the only man I care for, but I did enjoy seeing you up in the gallery wearing that ridiculous hat – and you were the only person in the whole room to wear a full-face mask."

"Do not forget that John Greenwood is very shy and self-conscious about his appearance."

Then Henry smiled, for a very amusing idea had popped into his head. The flautist and the pianist. Ah, yes! What if . . .

"Would you excuse me, Kitty dear?" Henry said. "I need to disappear for ten minutes for I have something to fix for our wedding. You will be pleased – but 'tis a surprise."

"Of course I excuse you," Kitty said. "I will go and sit over there with Selina and Edmund. I have much to talk to Selina about."

"I cannot believe that is true," Henry said, "for she has told me that all the time I was away, you both chattered non-stop."

"There is always something new," Kitty said.

"I will have to take your word for it," Henry said. "But what young ladies find to constantly prattle on about, I do not know."

"What a tease you are, Henry! No doubt you think we only talk about young men such as yourself, or perhaps dresses and fashion. But there is much more that we dissect and analyse. For instance, I know about Carter now – I mean, that he is your uncle."

"I am glad Selina told you," Henry said. "My parents have known for some time, of course, but they had not thought it right to tell us. And Carter never said a word until recently. It explains so much."

"When my mama was ill," Kitty said, "in particular when

Miss Steele was drugging her with strange potions, she told me that Lady Templeton had an older half-sibling – but she knew no more than that."

"Apparently Mama spent many years looking for her half-brother," Henry said, "and when she found him as a grown man, she wanted him to live with her and Papa, openly as her acknowledged relative. Carter would not – he said it would bring a shadow across the family – so Mama persuaded him to become my manservant to keep him close."

"Will he still be your manservant?" Kitty said.

"It will possibly seem like that, for appearances' sake. But Carter is determined to carry on certain other – more secret – work. I will tell you more of that another time – not while we are in public. And I will have to swear you to secrecy."

"You can rely on my discretion," Kitty said. "Always."

"I know," Henry said. "'Tis another of the many reasons I love you. Now, I am off to organize the surprise I talked of."

He ran up the stairs two at a time to the musicians' gallery. Dear Kitty. He loved to see her excited and full of chatter. She had suffered greatly during her ordeal with the dastardly Lord Steyne. At least now the man had been discredited in front of society and they should have no further trouble from him.

"Hello!" Henry said to the musicians.

The pianist and flautist were on the point of launching into another piece with their usual violinist, the young man who was courting Lady Templeton's abigail.

"Members of the public are not allowed up here," the flautist said.

"Unless they are particularly attractive young women," the pianist said, "which obviously you are not."

"I won't take up much of your time," Henry said. "I merely came to ask if you're free on Christmas Eve. Are you available for work?"

"Well," the flautist said, "I prefer to relax on Christmas Eve. However, I wouldn't say no if the money was right."

"Yes," the pianist said. "Our availability entirely depends on how much you're going to offer us."

"A goodly sum, do not worry," Henry said, "and 'tis very local. A house in the Royal Crescent – and a Christmas wedding."

"Wait a minute," the flautist said. "I've seen you before!"

"Doubtless you have seen me dancing downstairs with all the other young men," Henry said.

"It's more than that," the pianist said. "I recognize you too. Your voice."

"Imagine me wearing a full-face mask," Henry said.

"John Greenwood!" the flautist said. "Is it really you?"

"In a manner of speaking – although my real name is Henry Templeton. I am looking for musicians to play at my wedding reception and would be honoured if you would agree to perform."

"Henry Templeton!" the pianist said. "Bless my soul! Why, you are the talk of the city."

"Yes, indeed," the flautist said, "for you came back from Waterloo after all thought you had been lost in battle. And to think – you are our own John Greenwood."

Henry finalized the arrangements with the musicians before going downstairs again. What a pleasant surprise Kitty would have on their wedding day when she saw who was playing in the band at the reception.

"Is everything sorted out to your satisfaction?" Kitty asked as Henry joined her, Edmund, and Selina at their table.

"Absolutely," Henry said.

"Where are you to live when you are married?" Selina asked. "I don't suppose you have even thought about it, for all has been such a whirlwind."

"We could live with my parents," Kitty said.

"Or mine," Henry said. "At least at the beginning, until we find a place of our own."

"If I tell you something," Edmund said, "would you promise to act in a particularly surprised manner when Papa mentions it?"

"Of course," Henry said.

Edmund grinned. "Remember the day Kitty came over for tea and you played pianoforte duets with her? When Papa wanted to ask my advice about something?"

"Ah, then. Yes, I remember Papa dragged you away, saying he had to consult you about something."

That was shortly before I kissed my darling Kitty for the first time . . .

"Well," Edmund said, "obviously the whole family were keen to get out of that room to leave you two alone. It was somewhat of an excuse from Papa – but he did also genuinely want to discuss something with me. You see, he has bought Number 2 the Royal Crescent, next door to us, because he thought it would encourage me to get married, give me a place of my own in Bath to live – and bring up a family. I have no intention whatsoever of getting married any time soon, as you know, for I am having far too much of a good time."

"You mean you haven't met anyone silly enough to say 'yes' to you yet," Selina said.

"Edmund, you have not met the right young lady yet," Kitty said. "You must be patient."

"Ladies, I thank you for your opinions," Edmund said. "Anyway, Papa has bought the house – but I have told him I do not require or need it. And now I happen to know he intends to give Number 2 Royal Crescent to a certain pair of lovebirds as a wedding present."

"'Tis exceedingly generous of him," Henry said. "I cannot think what I have done to deserve it."

"You came back from the dead," Edmund said. "'Twas truly appalling when we thought you had died – and by some miracle you are here again. And the icing on the cake, the one thing that has us all jumping for joy, is to know you and Kitty are to be married."

"Thank you," Henry said gruffly.

Dash it all, he felt like blubbing like a baby. Everything was catching up with him at last. But it was wonderful to be back, and to be able to be seen openly with all his friends and family – and to be about to marry the beautiful, the wonderful Kitty.

I cannot wait to be joined to my darling love, for us to possess each other fully and completely.

Kitty

After a flurry of preparations, with both the Templeton and Honeyfield households in a frenzy of excitement, Kitty and Henry's wedding day dawned.

Although Kitty had dreamt of getting married in her best muslin dress, she could no longer bear to look at the garment, associated as it was with the despicable Lord Steyne. The dress had been shoved to the back of her closet in disgrace. She would take it out again one day and think about the daring rescue effected by Henry and the others – but the rest of the events, in particular what might have been, would not be dwelt upon.

Thus it was that when she walked up the aisle on the arm of her proud father, she wore a shimmering new dress created by the most fashionable modiste in Bath, another generous gift from the Templetons. The gorgeous satin and lace confection with exquisite beaded embroidery was everything that a young woman might desire.

And yet, although Kitty was grateful for this beautiful gown, she knew she would have been just as happy to wed her H in the breeches, shirt, and jacket she had worn when he had proposed in the kitchen of the house at Beechen Cliff. For if her adventures had taught her anything, they had shown her what qualities to admire in life – loyalty, sacrifice, and love.

For true love conquers all! And here I am walking up the aisle to my beloved H.

And Henry! Never had he looked more dashing or debonair.

Ah! His sweet, kind face as he said his vows in the service – was there ever a more pleasing sight? And his courage and valour – what a man. A real hero.

Kitty knew it was unlikely that she and Henry would ever again have to face the terrible struggles they had endured over the last six months, but if misfortune *did* come their way in the future, she was sure that together, they would be able to face it.

The collective sigh from the congregation when Henry and Kitty were finally pronounced man and wife was beyond heartwarming. A soldier had returned from the dead and was marrying his sweetheart – a young woman who had waited for him long after all hope had been extinguished. 'Twas as if a towering, flaming beacon of sensibility had flared up in the church.

Kitty turned to see married couples looking at each other – she could hear their sighs of contentment. And the unmarried! Why, their eyes were darting round the congregation – with eager hope? George was gazing at Selina . . . how very interesting.

As the happy couple walked down the aisle arm in arm, their bridesmaid Selina following, Kitty nodded and smiled to her friends and family. Her parents had strange expressions – were they laughing or crying? Perhaps 'twas a touch of both.

And there Carter was, looking uncharacteristically smart – and a little awkward – in his new double-breasted tailcoat. How wonderful that he would still be Henry's manservant – at least as far as the world was concerned. Once the front door of Number 2 Royal Crescent was closed to visitors, he would take his role as Henry's proud uncle and be a true part of their family.

With the Templetons only next door at Number 1 and Kitty's parents but a stone's throw away in Russell Street, the couple would not want for company. And in time, with God's blessing, if children arrived, many dear family would be nearby to help and enjoy the widening circle of Templetons.

Will it not be wonderful when the children arrive? Will we not have fun playing with them? It will be as if Henry and I are children again and can continue to enjoy the fun and friendship.

"Take my arm, Mrs. Templeton," Henry said as they went up the flight of steps into Number 1 for their wedding reception.

"I wondered who you were talking to for a moment," Kitty said, "then I remembered my new name."

The house was ablaze with roaring log fires. The ladies would have to be careful not to stand too close in case their fine muslins and silks caught fire, for there was already a vast throng of guests packing all the downstairs rooms. Fireplaces, windowsills, and tables were decorated with armfuls of trailing ivy and scarlet berry-studded holly, all brought in by the servants from the nearby woods and fields and artfully arranged by Lady Templeton. Dried orange slices hung from festive green boughs, filling the air with their distinctive spicy cinnamon and citrus scent. And everywhere, the bright blaze of candles and the babble of excitable chatter. The *ton* were out in force!

"The house has never looked more celebratory," Henry said. "Mama has pulled out all the stops to combine Christmas with our wedding."

"'Tis almost too overwhelming," Kitty said. "I cannot take it all in."

"Do not worry, Kitty dearest," Henry said. "This will be but for a few hours – and then you and I will go next door to our house and . . ."

Kitty blushed. Her mother, Mrs. Honeyfield, had made several oblique references in the past weeks to what Kitty must be prepared for in marriage. She had repeated her thoughts that some women endured their marital duties – but some enjoyed them.

As before, Kitty hoped very much she would enjoy joining with Henry. Then she blushed more deeply, becoming almost puce as she flooded with feeling. She already knew she would enjoy being married, for had not everything to do with the kissing between her and H been leading up to this?

"I know what you're thinking," Henry said. "You were imagining what we must both endure tonight."

He wiped his brow melodramatically and Kitty giggled, for she had shared Mrs. Honeyfield's theories of endurance versus enjoyment with Henry only a few days before. He had found the concept very funny – and talking about it between the two of them had led directly to much exploratory kissing. This had convinced both of them that they would fall firmly into the enjoyment category.

"What are you two laughing about?" Selina said. "Come on, you must circulate! Time enough for you to whisper sweet nothings to one another later. Now you need to chat to your guests. There are some here who have not seen you for a long time, Henry – they are still in shock that you are alive!"

"And have any of these guests caught your eye, Selina?" Henry said. "Although I've only been married for an hour or so, I can thoroughly recommend it. Surely it is your turn to choose a partner? Let me look around the rooms for you and see who might suit."

"Muttonhead!" Selina said, swatting Henry on his shoulder.

"Ouch! I am still tender there from being shot, I will have you know!"

"Then Kitty will have to be very careful with you this evening when you retire," Selina said, before giggling like a mad thing and moving swiftly away.

"I have no idea why you chose Selina as a bridesmaid," Henry said to Kitty. "She's very badly behaved. 'Tis certainly time she got married – but I can't for the life of me think of anyone who is strong-minded enough to take her on. Unless . . . well, George would be a fine match. Perhaps I should have a word with them both? Throw them together?"

"I too think they would suit," Kitty said, "but remember, Henry, it is up to Selina who she chooses. It should not be decided by her brother."

"I stand corrected," Henry said. "We will see what transpires . . . but possibly a helping hand could be in order?"

"A gentle nudge would not go amiss," Kitty said, "nor an opportunity to allow them to see each other again."

"Shall we invite them both to dine with Mr. and Mrs. Templeton at Number 2 in the new year?" Henry suggested.

Kitty nodded. "A fine idea."

"Ah, good! The music has started up," Henry said. "What an excellent band. Aren't they playing well?"

Kitty whipped out her new quizzing glass and had a good look at the musicians.

"There are more people in the band than I thought there would be . . . oh, Henry! I can't believe it! You didn't?"

"I did," Henry said. "I asked the flautist and the pianist from the Upper Rooms to join the musicians here today. See how the flautist is winking at us? And now the pianist is waving."

"He needs to concentrate on the music."

"Yes, indeed," Henry said. "He played a wrong note in that chord, and I am not sure I shall pay him after this."

"You weren't tempted to join them today?"

"To be honest, yes. I thought it would be highly amusing to dress up in my John Greenwood outfit again, full-face mask included – but then I remembered."

"Remembered what?" Kitty said.

"I remembered that I'm a married man and must behave responsibly at all times."

"Sounds a little tedious," Kitty said. "Almost middle-aged."

Henry took her in his arms. "I can promise you one thing, Mrs. Templeton. Our marriage might be many things – but 'twill not be tedious. One day it will be middle-aged, and one day, God willing, we will be together in our old age. And that is what I look forward to most of all, to living my whole life with you, my darling Kitty. To growing old together."

"Give it a rest, you two," Edmund said, walking past, "for you are not standing under the mistletoe now. No need for kissing! Grub's up, by the way. Cook's surpassed herself, and there is an unbelievable spread in the dining room. The table's positively groaning under the weight of myriad delicious-looking dishes; roast beef, venison, goose, chestnuts, mince pies, plum pudding, jellies, trifles, syllabub, almond biscuits, fruit, wedding cake . . . the most wonderful collection of Christmas foods, served a day early as a wedding breakfast. We will be eating the leftovers for weeks."

"They say music is the food of love," Henry said, "so what better treat than to enjoy a fine feast while listening to beautiful music with my lovely wife beside me. Lead the way, if you please, Mrs. Templeton!"

MUCH LATER, KITTY and Henry were together alone at last, in their new home of Number 2 the Royal Crescent.

"I still cannot believe how kind your parents were to give us this house and all the beautiful furniture," Kitty said.

"'Twas very thoughtful of them," Henry said. "Why, there is even a fine Pleyel pianoforte in the withdrawing room. And I absolutely promise it will never be necessary to fill in any windows in our home to avoid the window tax, especially in your bedchamber. Your days will be filled with light – forever. No more daylight robbery!"

"I do love the daylight for reading," Kitty said, "and for gazing at you, dear Henry."

Henry took her into his arms and, despite herself, Kitty trembled, feeling a little nervous.

"There is no need to be anxious," Henry said softly. "We'll work this out together. Marriage is new for both of us."

"Shall we try the pianoforte first?" Kitty said.

"A very good idea. Mozart?"

"Yes, the Mozart duet in D major," Kitty said. "Our favorite."

"And you can wear your new spectacles to see the music," Henry said. "You look so adorable in them."

As the two of them nestled together on the duet stool, playing the familiar harmonies and phrases, Kitty felt contentment creeping over her – and trust.

When they had finished the piece, she turned to Henry and ran her finger gently down his cheek.

"Ready," she said. "Shall we try a different kind of duet?"

"My darling," Henry said.

His mouth descended upon hers. Then he gently lifted Kitty into his arms and carried her to the bedchamber.

"Shall we make sweet music?" he murmured.

EPILOGUE

O N THE FOLLOWING morning, Christmas Day, Kitty and Henry walked hand in hand across the Crescent Lawn, stopping at the ha-ha to look out over the Crescent Fields and the valley beyond, right up to Beechen Cliff. They were now truly man and wife.

As soft snowflakes began to fall, Kitty pulled her red cloak more closely around her. She felt happy, she felt warm – and full of love for her wonderful husband.

"Our music last night was indeed sweet," she said.

"The most beautiful melody I have ever heard," Henry replied, "and I think it is time, Mrs. Templeton, for an encore."

The End

About the Author

Jenny grew up in Bath, in the west of England, and spent much of her childhood exploring this beautiful city and wondering about the kind of people who lived there centuries ago. She was an avid reader from an early age, inheriting the love of a good story from her Irish grandmother.

After studying music at college, teaching in secondary schools for a number of years, and starting a family, Jenny finally found the time to pursue her dream of writing.

She now lives in London with her husband, writes short stories for UK women's magazines, and has had a number of romantic comedy novels published.

Website – jennyworstall.wordpress.com
Facebook – facebook.com/jennyworstall
Twitter – x.com/JennyWorstall
Amazon – amazon.co.uk/stores/Jenny-Worstall/author/B007IVNY1G
Instagram – instagram.com/jennyworstall